Fae Bound

Fae Bound

BERRING COLLEGE
BOOK THREE

KAYLA BROOKS

A Note About Content

Dear reader,

Please note that this is a book written for adults and contains themes, events, and language that are not appropriate for everyone. If you would like a comprehensive list of these elements, please go to https://kaylabrooksauthor.com/content-warnings for more information. I want my readers to have their best possible reading experience, so if any of these elements will cause you pain or distress, please feel free to skip reading this book. I promise, I won't be offended. I want you to read something that you'll enjoy! If you read this book and feel there is something I should have mentioned in the content list, please let me know so I can add it! I don't want anyone to be caught by surprise, especially by something that might be triggering or painful. My email address is kayla@kaylabrooksauthor.com and I promise, I will always want to hear if there's something I can do to improve your reading experience.

Sincerely,

Kayla Brooks

CHAPTER 1

Taylor

I listen in our dark house for any signs of stirring. I'm torn between wanting silence and the chance to leave without notice, and sounds that would mean my choice is made for me.

A rustling from the living room tells me it's the latter.

"Taylor? Is that you?"

"Yeah, Mom. It's just me."

The deep shadows of early morning meet with the darkness of the closed-up living room. No one other than a vampire would be able to make their way through the room without tripping.

Actually, it's so familiar at this point that I don't think I would need my vampire eyes to know exactly where she is.

Huddled on the couch, clutching an unnecessary blanket around her shoulders, and staring at the chronically darkened window.

I have a pang of anger, wishing she were still asleep so I could go without saying goodbye, followed by a pang of guilt for wishing I could go without saying goodbye.

"I was going to get on the road before the sun," I whisper

to her. This isn't a house where anyone speaks above a whisper. Not in the nineteen years since my birth, at least. I'll never know what things were like before I destroyed her life and she fell into this perpetual mourning.

"You have to go?"

I have to go the same way I have to drink blood. Maybe worse. I could survive a long time without blood, but this house has been killing me for nineteen years now.

"Yeah, Mom. I have to go. I promised my roommates that I'd get the keys and everything sorted out, remember?"

She grunts a response. It's probably the most acknowledgment I'll ever get.

"You need me to do anything before I go?" I hope not, but chances are good she won't move from this spot in the next week until I come back to check on her.

"Is the fridge stocked?"

I nod, though she's not even looking at me. We've had this conversation enough times that we don't have to hear or see each other's response to know what comes next.

"There's plenty of blood to last the week," I promise her. "I checked last night."

"Well, you'd better go, then." A twist of her lips turns her face ugly for a moment. "Your roommates will be waiting for you."

Yep. Same old conversation we've had over and over again already. I give a defeated nod and turn to go. "I'll be back in a week."

She grunts again, the only indication that she's still alive at all.

CHAPTER 2

Bee

"Hey, Gloria, do you have—Oh my god! Again?" I shield my eyes from the tangle of naked limbs on the bed in front of me. You would think, after growing up with a pack of wolf shifters, then spending the summer with a family of wolf shifters, I would have learned to knock before entering a room. Of course, this particular room is supposedly my own bedroom for the summer. Foolish me, thinking it might be safe from the never-ending wolf sexcapades I've been treated to for several months now.

"Sorry, Bee!" Gloria calls, at least sounding somewhat embarrassed, though I can also practically hear laughter bubbling under the surface. My rat of a roommate isn't actually sorry at all, is she?

"You know, I could have sworn there were other rooms in this house," I tell her, still covering my eyes until I know for sure it's safe to look. "Like, don't you have your own bedroom somewhere around here?"

Her family's farm was designed to house a small pack, so a shortage of bedrooms is not the issue here.

My adoptive brother, owner of half of the naked body

parts I just saw, decides to join the conversation. "We were packing and talking about what we're going to miss when we go back to Berring, and I pointed out that there are still a few rooms we haven't . . . um . . . christened? And then, of course, we had to fix that, so . . ."

"So you decided to fuck in my bed? You realize that I don't even fuck in my bed, right?"

My cheeks are hot enough that I'm surprised the whole room hasn't caught fire.

"Hey." Gloria pulls my hand from my eyes and searches my gaze with genuine concern. "I'm really sorry. I know the hormone excuse officially got old two months ago. I swear, we'll try to do better."

I spare a glare for Grey before turning back to Gloria. "It's fine," I assure her. "It's really fine. It's not like I was going to sleep in here again, and I am happy for you. Just . . . can you please promise me to keep it in your own room at the new house?"

Gloria nods solemnly. "We will keep the sex out of your room in the new place. And I'm sorry. Let me make it up to you by carrying your stuff out to the truck?"

I give her a narrow-eyed look, trying to make her believe I might not forgive her, but Gloria was my first college friend, and Grey has been my friend since before I can remember. Of course I have to forgive them.

"Well, I suppose if you insist on carrying my luggage, I won't stop you."

She grins and wraps me in a hug before skipping out of the room. Grey stands there awkwardly for another moment, scratching the back of his neck and looking at a spot on the floor to my right. "I'm sorry too, Bee," he mumbles. "I kind of lost my head this summer, didn't I? I guess I'm just not used to having this kind of freedom."

I suppose I could comfort him with a sisterly hug, but the

guy was just having sex in my bed. My hand darts out as if it has a mind of its own, and my fingers clamp down on his nipple and twist.

"Fuck, Bee! I thought we were past the purple nurple stage of our relationship!" Grey glares at me and rubs his chest.

"Oh, quit acting like such a delicate flower. Any damage I caused has already healed, and we both know it." I turn and am about to leave the room when I think better of it and turn back to look at Grey.

"You know what? I think there's a way for you to make this"—I indicate the rumpled bedding—"up to me."

Grey looks genuinely pleased and hopeful, like the sweet summer child he is.

"Really? How?"

"I get to go out whenever I want without any kind of check-in or approval from you. And no following me and trying to do the sneaky bodyguard thing either. You know I'll catch you, and then I'll have to think of creative ways to make you pay."

His face darkens almost to an eggplant-purple color.

"Bee, be reasonable. I'm just trying to keep you safe. You need to let someone watch your back."

"Grey, if you never let anything happen to me, nothing will ever happen to me. And the whole reason I came to college was so something could happen to me."

Literally, anything, I silently beg the universe. I'm about to start my sophomore year of college, and I'm still a virgin who's never even had an orgasm. For the love of everything good in this universe, could I please have *something* happen to me this year?

"Did you just quote a movie at me?" Grey asks in a very suspicious voice.

"If you don't know, why should I tell you?" I shrug and head outside to supervise Gloria's packing adventure.

CHAPTER 3

Bee

Any goodwill garnered from Grey and Gloria apologizing earlier has officially evaporated. I'm not exactly sure when it happened, but at some point in our four-hour drive to college, the three of us had forgotten that we actually love each other. Not that I'm pointing fingers or anything, but I think it had something to do with my brother's decision to eat an entire package of cheese sticks when he knows that he can't digest cheese properly.

If I never smell Grey again in this life, it will be too soon.

Actually, I may just kill Grey so I don't have to smell him again.

"I still don't understand why it had to be him," Grey grumbles from the back seat, where we banished him two hours ago.

Gloria slides a slitted look to me. Good. She's not ready to forgive him for his transgressions either.

"Well, considering *you're* not even going to be allowed in the house, and we do need *someone* with supernatural strength to help us move in, I'd say it's pretty bold of you to ask a question like that," Gloria tells him through clenched teeth. Her hands tighten on the steering wheel, and I wonder if she's entertaining the same type of neck-wringing fantasies as I am.

"Come on, Gloria," he whines. "You can't still be mad at me! It wasn't that bad!"

She uses a finger to roll all of the windows up at once, proving that it actually still is that bad.

Grey flops back in defeat, and Gloria—just in the nick of time before I start feeling queasy again—rolls the windows back down.

"Okay," he admits. "I should have known the cheese was a bad idea. I'm sorry. Now, can you please tell me why living with a vampire is better than living with me?"

"Because the two of you have no self-control and will flunk out of college if you're living in the same house?" I volunteer.

"How about, because Taylor is actually civilized and has promised to help with the cleaning?" Gloria adds.

"But—" Grey tries to interrupt, but Gloria cuts him off.

"Besides, Bee and I are both trying to expand our horizons. Living with you expands zero horizons for either of us."

"But—"

"And you need to work on living your own life and making your own friends," I tell him. Preferably, he'll make friends that keep him out of my hair, I add silently to myself.

"But, not only is he a vampire. He's . . ."

"Tall?"

"Good-looking?"

"Surprisingly smart?"

"Delightfully competent?"

Grey glowers as Gloria and I ping back and forth with each other.

"Fine," he finally concedes. "I get that he's not all bad. But he is such a vampire. Like, how did you find the absolute unit of being a vampire, and why doesn't it bother you more that he's a vampire?"

I roll my eyes heavenward. Of course he'll never understand. He's spent his entire life knowing exactly who he is and where he fits in. Me? I've never fit in. Maybe I would have fit in if I'd grown up with other humans. Or even vampires. But I grew up with shifters, and every single day of my life has held some reminder of how I'm not one of them.

They've never tried to exclude me.

No, that's a lie. Some of them have tried to exclude me.

But the wolves claiming to be my family—my adoptive parents and brother and some others—have never tried to exclude me.

It just . . . happened.

I was never invited to heat parties because I never went into heat. I was never put forward as a potential mate because, as I said, no heat. It's amazing how many guys in the wolf community have no interest whatsoever in someone they can't be mated to. And then there's the fact that the pack leader, my adoptive father, has had me watched by a pack of guards since before I could walk.

No, my golden brother, heir to the kingdom, does not understand what it's like to be an outsider and to seek out other outsiders.

Gloria shatters my dark train of thought. "You aren't going to say anything to Taylor, are you?"

Grey huffs again. "If you say I can't, I won't. Doesn't mean I won't think whatever I'm going to think."

"Taylor helped a lot last year," Gloria reminds him with an admonishing look in the rearview mirror. "And it would be pretty shitty to turn back and act all racist after he helped us out so much."

Apparently, the seat beside Grey is extremely interesting. "I suppose so," he mutters.

I swear he's regressed over the summer. He spent all last year living with vampires and working with them to bring down the nasty frat boy who tried to rape Gloria, but after a summer on the farm, he's acting like the worst kind of bigot. Worse than our dad, honestly. I vow to slap some sense into him as soon as we get out of the car.

CHAPTER 4

Taylor

The house isn't big—thank fuck because I wouldn't be able to afford it—or fancy—again, thank fuck—but it is on a tree-lined street in a friendly neighborhood of almost entirely college kids.

And my mom isn't here, which is probably its biggest selling point for me.

As I pull up to the curb, the morning light isn't so bad that I'll have to worry too much about it. I check that my cap is shading my whole face before I get out of my car, but I won't be in any real trouble unless it takes more than an hour to get the keys.

A middle-aged man—human, I can tell immediately by scent—hops out to the curb from a small car parked nearby.

"You Taylor?" He squints up at me suspiciously. I can't take offense. It's the response I've learned to expect ever since I grew to head and shoulders above most people. Everyone's seen me as a threat since eighth grade, unless they already saw me as a threat because of my species.

Whatever. It is what it is.

I roll my shoulders, trying to remind myself that he won't

feel any less threatened if I hunch, but I'll feel better if I stand up straight.

"Yeah. Taylor Faulkner." I stick out my hand. "Are you Mr. Hunt?"

He ignores my hand but nods a confirmation. If anything, the suspicion on his face grows.

"What about the other roommates? Are they also . . ." He doesn't finish the question, maybe realizing in time that it's illegal to base housing decisions on species.

"You said I could get the keys today?" I try to force the change of subject on him before things can derail any further.

He gives another grudging nod. "I suppose I did say that." He holds up a key chain with three gleaming keys on it. "Remember, any noise complaints, trouble with the law, or failure to keep up with the lawn, and I'll have you out of here so fast you won't know what happened. You understand?"

"Yes, sir." Sometimes, it's best to just let people have their crazy. This isn't the type of guy who might change his mind about me. I might need to ask one of my roommates to deal with him in the future, though. The thought gives me a sick feeling, but I'll have to deal with it later.

The house is, thankfully, exactly as advertised. My new landlord grumbles to make sure my roommates check the lease agreement and don't "step a single toe out of line, you hear me?"

"Yes, Mr. Hunt," I manage to say in my most diffident voice. My people-pleasing voice. My "I get why you hate me, but I promise you don't have to be afraid" voice.

Not that it has ever actually helped with a single person when trying to figure out legal shit or anything like that. Everyone sees "big, dumb vampire," and they never see anything else.

I choose my room as soon as my landlord is gone. The small one with the tiniest of windows. It's a basement apartment that just happens to not actually be in a basement. My roommates would hate it, so obviously, I should be the one to take it. I've already moved my three bags of stuff inside long before the time my roommates said they would be here.

My roommates roll up in the late afternoon, about an hour after we'd planned, but it will make it easier to help them move. The sun is barely past the point where it can be seriously dangerous to me. I still grab a wide-brimmed hat before going out to meet them. I won't be useful to anyone if I let the sun drain me before we're done moving.

"Thank god you're here!" Bee flings herself at me as soon as she's out of the car and glares over her shoulder at her brother. "Grey is not welcome inside the house for the time being, so we're counting on your help with the heavy lifting."

Grey, aka Jimmy, aka Bee's adoptive brother and apparently some kind of big deal in the shifter world, glowers at us. Or maybe just at me. How am I supposed to know what he's thinking? I ignore him, though, because there's so much to unpack here. Like, first off, the fact that Bee has her arms wrapped around me like she's a damsel in distress and I'm the brave knight who's come to rescue her. And she smells really good. And the heat of her skin is like a taste of heaven everywhere it brushes me. And I somehow don't think she's going to appreciate my help nearly as much once she realizes the effect she's having on me.

I try to casually shift my hips so I won't accidentally poke her. "Um, why isn't Grey welcome inside the house?" That seems like a safe enough topic.

She lets go of me and opens the back of their truck to start unloading it. "I'll spare you the details and just say that he thought eating a bunch of cheese at the beginning of our trip was a great idea. It wasn't a great idea." She spares another glare for the man in question before grabbing a backpack from the top of the giant pile of stuff that's been jigsawed together to fit into the truck bed.

Grey huffs and starts pulling things from the back and setting them out neatly on the pavement. "Am I ever going to live this down?"

"No," Bee says at the same moment Gloria says, "Doesn't seem likely." The girls share a look, then burst out laughing.

This I remember from last year. The spontaneous giggle fits. The constant ribbing. I was surprised when the girls asked me to be their third roommate. Pleased, too, of course. What guy wouldn't enjoy finding out that the women in his life see him as a kind of protector? But I'm still not one hundred percent sure why they asked me and not, well, Grey. Gloria and Grey have been inseparable for months now, and Bee and Grey are family in everything except blood. Why wouldn't they ask him?

And I'm pretty sure, based on his continuing dark looks in my direction, that he's asking the same question.

Oh well. Having a house to share with the girls is going to solve so many of my problems. Like how I could never have paid for a house if I were living on my own, and how I would have died trying to do another year of living with Mom and driving the hour to and from school each day. Whatever Grey's issues are, they're nothing compared to what I'm escaping, so he can scowl at me all he wants to.

"I already got set up in that third bedroom," I say, slinging a duffle bag over each shoulder. Sweet mother of god, how are these things so heavy? Which of my roommates has apparently packed a bunch of bricks for college? "Which room should I take these bags to?"

"Um." Gloria squints at the bags I'm carrying from behind the giant box in her own arms. "I honestly have no idea. Just dump them in the living room, and we'll sort them out later, I guess."

Bee gives her a pointed look. "And by 'sort them out later,' you do mean sort them out before letting your hormones get the better of you again, right?"

I'm not one hundred percent sure what she's alluding to, but I can guess the gist of it. Gloria has the decency to look embarrassed. "I promised we'd do better, didn't I?"

Yep. Suspicions confirmed. The horny wolves have been doing horny wolf things.

Which is fine.

I'm not judging.

Wolves are allowed to do whatever the fuck they want and fuck however much they want, and it has nothing to do with me.

I suppose it might have something to do with me when I'm sharing a wall with the horny wolves in question.

I make a mental note to buy some earplugs as soon as I get the chance.

A weird thought pops into my head. This will be the first time in my life I'm sharing a house with anyone living. And that includes the literal definition, since neither Mom nor I is technically alive, but also a more metaphysical definition. Mom hasn't lived any kind of a life since I was born. I don't even really know what it will be like to share a space with people who eat and fuck and speak above a whisper and leave the living room couch on occasion. Last year, I spent some time crashing in Grey's dorm along with a lot of other people, but I did my best to stay out of the way whenever possible. And it's not the same, anyway, because it's not like my name was on a lease agreement with theirs or anything.

My heart is doing the vampiric version of pounding—a slow, almost painful squeeze in my chest every few seconds— by the time I set the duffle bags on the couch and head back to the car for more. What is this feeling? Nerves? Excitement?

And why do I feel like I might puke just from the thought of sharing space with two other people?

Two living people, I remind myself. Two living people who don't know what it's like to be raised on vampire charity in a mostly human town.

Before I can embarrass myself by having a full-blown, all-systems-down panic attack, I sneak back into my room and lock my door.

Just in time. Just in time. Just in time.

The words chase each other through my head, taking form from my own mocking voice.

Big Baby Taylor made it just in time.

I press back against the door and let it support me as I slide down to the floor. Wrapping my arms around my shins, I let myself rock, the same way I did on my first day of school so many years ago.

Is Baby Taytay gonna cry?

No. No. No. Get your shit together.

I squeeze my fists as tight as I can. Count to ten. Release. Count to ten.

The self-soothing mechanism I taught myself to replace the breathing exercises suggested for humans finally takes effect after four rounds. I do another three rounds of it just to be sure I'm in control again before I go out to continue helping my roommates move.

CHAPTER 5

Bee

Taylor disappears as soon as the truck is emptied. It was nice of him to help at all, especially considering the death glares Grey kept sending him.

"So, I was thinking, now that you're moved in . . ." I overhear Grey saying to Gloria.

"Nope!" I shut him down before he can work his magical wolf pheromones on her. "We need to finish getting the house set up, and you need to get moved into your own house. No christening of the new house until tomorrow."

Grey turns to Gloria with a pleading look, but she stays strong.

"Bee is right. We have roommate stuff to deal with. No boyfriends."

He pulls her to him by her belt loops and nuzzles at her neck.

Barf.

Gloria laughs at whatever he whispers in her ear, then pushes him away and shoos him out the door.

"Sorry about that," she says to me once the door is closed

with Grey on the other side. "I swear, I haven't forgotten that whole 'trying to do better' promise we made you earlier. And you're right. We should focus on getting the house set up tonight. Maybe you can see if Taylor is up for roommate bonding while we get organized?"

Taylor answers quickly when I knock, swinging the door open and leaning confidently against the doorway.

He's the picture of cool and calm, except for the bruise-like circles under his eyes.

"What's up?" he asks, eyes flicking out toward the living room. Probably checking if Grey is still out there.

"We thought maybe we could do some roommate bondage—I mean bonding—now that it's just the three of us here." God, just kill me now. Why must I always be so fucking awkward?

A smile twitches at the corner of his mouth, though. "So, is one of us going to get all tied up or what?"

I hide my face in my hands. "Can we please just forget that slip and move on?"

"What slip?"

I peek between my fingers to see him giving me a bland smile. An "I've already forgotten" smile. An "anything you say, boss" smile.

I let my hands drop and try to ignore the fire in my cheeks.

"Um. We thought maybe we could work on decorating the living room together, since it's our shared space, you know. We wanted to make sure you feel comfortable out there too."

An unreadable look ripples across his face before he's back to that bland smile.

"Sure," he says in a voice that sounds a little pinched and a little higher than usual. "I'd love to help with it."

I let out my excitement in a squeal and give him a hug, but hurry to let go when his muscles tense at my touch. Right. I noticed before and then forgot. Taylor doesn't seem to like being touched. Wolves tend to be extremely touchy-feely. They communicate half of what they need to say through touch and body language. I shouldn't assume vampires are at all the same, though. I shouldn't assume anything, I remind myself.

CHAPTER 6

Taylor

Bee really needs to stop touching me.

She's way too pretty, and I'm not sure I have the kind of self-control necessary to keep resisting . . . well, all of the things I need to resist if I'm going to keep living peacefully in this house.

I try to make myself small as I come down the hallway. In my house—my other house, the one I grew up in—the living room is Mom's space. I should only enter if I'm bringing her blood to drink or passing through as quietly as possible. No reason to believe this house will be any different.

I'm greeted with matching wide smiles and excited "heys" from my roommates when I come in. I almost check behind me to see who they're actually greeting before I realize it really is me that they're—for unknown reasons—so happy to see.

Gloria and Bee are like a matched set because they are so completely opposite each other. Like two puzzle pieces. Or those salt and pepper shakers that are carved to fit together on the table.

Gloria has dark hair and broad shoulders and looks like she'd be more at home wearing a dirndl and carrying milk pails over the Alps or something. She stands almost a head taller than delicate, blonde Bee, who always seems to float rather than walk.

Not that I've been watching her like that since last fall or anything. No. I have not—not even remotely—been sneaking peaks at Bee since the first time I met her. That would have been inappropriate, given the circumstances we met under then and the fact that she's my roommate now.

That's my story, and I'm sticking to it.

Besides, even if I had noticed the way Bee moves, or dresses, or lightens every room she enters, I know she's too good for me. I am agonizingly aware of how much I could never offer her. Money, obviously. I mean, I have none. But also standing in either of our communities, or a happy, normal life, or any kind of family.

No. I realized last fall, approximately ten seconds after meeting her, that Bee isn't for me. But at least I can be something to her. I'm pretty sure it's Grey who insists she needs someone protecting her, not Bee, but I don't mind acting as protector. I love the idea that I can help her like that. And Gloria too, of course. But Bee is the one whose image and voice and walk are seared into my brain.

Bee is the one who waves me over with a genuine grin.

"I was thinking we could set up a kind of reading nook here," she tells me. "Put a comfy chair in this corner, some bookshelves behind it, maybe add some fairy lights and a side table? But if it sounds too girly for you, you have to let me know."

I stare at the corner in question. Too girly? No. The perfect amount of girly. I can picture her curled up in an armchair and reading, surrounded by a halo of tiny, sparkling lights. I have to clear my throat before I can speak.

"No. I mean, it sounds nice. It sounds really nice, actually. It's just—"

"Bee will buy the stuff," Gloria cuts in as if reading my mind. Which maybe makes the whole situation even more humiliating.

"Oh, right. Um . . ." I feel my vampire equivalent of a furious blush, my cheeks heavy with the slow-moving blood near the surface of my skin. "You should definitely get what makes you happy, then." And, just like that, I sense this common area turning into another room that I won't feel welcome in. Not by anyone's intention; I just know I'll never feel comfortable sitting in chairs that my roommates chose and paid for without any help from me. Bee will snuggle in and get comfortable in her reading nook, and I'll do my best to stay out of her way. I'll stay small and in my room and make sure there's no reason for them to regret asking me to move in.

Bee claps her hands and bounces in excitement, oblivious to my distress. "I'm so excited to get everything all set up and looking nice!"

Gloria—always the more practical of the two—gives her a tired smile. "How about we chill on the couch that's already here and watch a movie or something for the time being? Shopping can wait until tomorrow."

I could kiss her for that suggestion. No way am I up for shopping today.

Bee looks at me questioningly. "Okay," she agrees. "Movie tonight. Shopping tomorrow."

Some of my anxiety dissipates as we watch something silly that I don't have to pay much attention to. Gloria snacks on some kind of dried meat throughout, while Bee serves herself something colorful from the freezer. I leave my blood bags in my own fridge in my bedroom. Neither of my roommates would want to see me feeding on human blood, I'm sure.

The next morning, I wake up with a ball of nerves tumbling around in my head, though.

What if they've changed their minds and don't want me

around after all? What if they decide they don't want a vampire in their house and kick me out so Grey can move in? What-if after what-if rears its head and stomps through my thoughts while I sit in the living room and wait for my room-mates to wake up and come out.

Part of me—a large and shameful part of me—seriously considers staying in my room so they can go out without me and I don't have to risk their rejection.

Better to face rejection now than later, though, when it would be even harder to figure out new living arrangements.

"Oh, good!" Gloria beams at me as she emerges from her room, looking ready for heavy labor in jeans and a flannel shirt. "It looks like you're ready to go. Grey should be here any minute with the truck, and Bee is . . . well, it takes her a bit longer to get ready than the rest of us, but she should be out here soon."

Totally worth the wait, I think, when she does come out with her hair arranged in shining, golden curls and her face made up to look glowing and shining and somehow natural all at the same time. And she's got a lightweight dress that skims over her curves and makes my mouth water with wanting her.

No. Bad. Off-limits.

I force my attention away from her to find Grey giving me a death glare from across the room.

Shopping with Bee turns out to be . . . is *harrowing* the right word? Yes. It's a harrowing experience.

I knew going in that Bee has money. It's not like she hides the fact. Most of what we moved in yesterday belongs to her.

But knowing it and experiencing it firsthand are two different things.

It's one step away from a classic movie shopping montage where Marilyn Monroe sits back and watches a stream of models come out and twirl in a variety of outfits for her. It's that, except with couches and armchairs and dining tables.

Okay, maybe I'm exaggerating slightly. I'm not exaggerating that much, though. I have to curl my toes in my shoes to keep from panicking and calling the whole thing to a stop every time her credit card leaves her purse—which happens a lot and without a second thought. She's not worried for a second about that payment going through.

Me? I've never even had a credit card. I've had the poor vampire kid's free blood card—BAP, for the Blood Assistance Program. I've had the yearly debit card they gave me for new clothes before school starts. I learned exactly how many shirts and pants I could buy so I wouldn't have to do laundry twice a week and the kids at school wouldn't realize I was rotating the same three outfits over and over. Funnily enough, they always figured it out anyway. There was no escaping that milestone each year, when someone would announce, "Isn't that the same shirt you were wearing yesterday?" to the entire locker room, and from that moment on, I would be Stinky Laundry Boy until the end of the school year. It never mattered that the clothes were clean. It mattered that they were cheap, and worn, and ill-fitting. It mattered that I was different, and poor, and an easy target.

"Come sit in this one!" Bee's squeal breaks into my reminiscing—thank fuck, because I'm on the verge of spiraling big-time—but it takes me a moment to figure out she's talking to me.

When I give her a blank stare, she takes me by the elbow and steers me over to the chair she was just standing by.

"Sit! Let me know!"

"Let you know what?"

She rolls her eyes in a good-natured way. "If it's comfortable for you! You're so much bigger than Gloria or me, so you need to test the chairs to make sure they work for you."

"Oh, no. I don't think we need . . ."

"Just sit, or we'll be here forever," Gloria insists. "Believe me, once Bee gets started, there's no stopping her."

I sit on the very edge of the chair. I'm too big. I know it. I'm more than halfway convinced that I'm too big for anything in this store, and they're just waiting to see if I'll leave on my own or if they'll have to kick me out.

The least I can do is try not to break the furniture by sitting down too hard.

"Oh, come on," Bee whines. "You have to get in there and try to get comfy. How else will you know if it will work for us?"

How else will I know if this chair was built to hold my weight? That's what I'm worried about.

"What if it breaks, though?" I mumble toward Bee's feet.

"Then we definitely don't want to buy it, if it's going to break just from sitting on it."

She says it like it's so easy and obvious. If it breaks, I don't want it. If I don't want it, I walk away.

"Won't someone be mad?" I glance around to see where all of the salespeople are.

Bee lifts her chin, every inch the self-assured princess. "Yes. Me. I'll be mad if the furniture here is flimsy enough to break in the store."

Accepting my defeat, I lean back in the chair.

If I thought furniture shopping was it, I was sadly mistaken. As soon as we get the new things unloaded in the house, Grey says he told his roommates, Jeff and Gabe, we would meet up with them on campus for—drumroll—even more shopping.

"Let's walk in," Bee suggests, and I shuffle my feet and look at my toes.

Gloria agrees. "Yes! It's such a nice day."

Then they both remember who I am and turn to me with embarrassed looks.

"Oh, shit," Bee says. "I wasn't thinking that through, was I? The sun is still too high for you."

"He doesn't have to walk with us," Grey grumbles, earning a death glare from his girlfriend. "I just mean that we could walk, and you could meet us at the bookstore," Grey amends, at least talking to me instead of about me this time.

I shrug uncomfortably. I don't want to be where I'm not wanted. "There are tunnels so I can get to campus during the day. It's not a big deal."

Bee and Gloria come to stand on either side of me and take me by the elbows.

"Come on," Gloria says.

Bee says, "You'll have to lead the way through these tunnels."

The tunnels are almost empty as I lead my friends through to the Berring College Student Union exit, but that doesn't mean there are no potential dangers down here. Case in point, I'm currently leading three living people through tunnels that were built to allow vampires free passage during the day to anywhere in the city. And, yes, I know that not all vampires are vicious killers. I'm not a vicious killer. But it only takes one. The girls will be safe as long as I'm here with them. I just need to remind them to not come down here without me.

We're met on the other side by a grinning Jeff and Gabe. Jeff was the first friend I made in college, and I feel a pang of guilt when I realize I didn't do much to keep in touch over the summer. He smiles and pulls me into a crushing hug despite that. The guy is amazing at making me feel like I'm actually wanted. Gabe gives me more of a bro hug, which is fine, since that's all we've ever been. Jeff basically adopted both of us in our first class together as freshmen, then kept us around while we dealt with all of the drama. I like Gabe just fine, but he doesn't bring people together the way Jeff does, and I'm not equipped to be the social butterfly like that at all. I can barely act normal and friendly toward my room-mates, even though they've been nothing but kind and welcoming to me. I'm not sure I was born with that part. Whatever part allows people to open up to each other and attach themselves.

"Okay, listen up." Jeff claps to get our attention after he's sufficiently greeted everyone. "Our game plan goes: bookstore, then coffee and bagels, then back to the girls' place for an after-noon of video games. Who's with me?"

We all murmur varying levels of assent. Grey is making it obvious that he'd prefer an afternoon alone in the house with his girlfriend, but Gloria readjusts his attitude with a sharp elbow to the ribs. I'm not particularly excited about coffee I can't afford and bagels I can't eat, but the fact that Jeff seems to genuinely want me along has the usual effect. I agree to everything without argument.

We've had just enough time to disperse around the book-store—me looking for the cheapest used books available, Gloria loading Grey's arms with thick textbooks, and Jeff and Gabe wandering through tables of Berring-branded tchotchkes—when I hear a triumphant whoop from across the bookstore, where Jeff is pumping his fists in the air. I look a little more carefully and realize there's something clutched in his hands.

"Any ideas?" Bee looks at me expectantly.

"Not even the faintest clue," I admit.

We go over to investigate and find him sorting through a shelf of mugs.

"Do you think you're more of an 'I bleed maroon' guy or a 'vampires do it in the dark' guy?" he asks me, holding up two mugs for my inspection.

"Um . . ." Is neither an option? I keep that thought to myself. Jeff means well. "I guess the maroon one?"

He shoves it into my hands and turns back to the display.

"Now, for Bee, I'm having a little more trouble. How about 'wolf snuggler'?"

Bee makes a face, and Jeff puts the mug back without argument.

"'I came to college and all I got was this stupid mug'?" Jeff holds up the mug in question, and Bee rolls her eyes and puts it back on the shelf.

"Don't take this the wrong way, Jeff. You know I love you, but, well, I like nice things. These mugs are not nice; they're tacky."

"And funny!" he argues.

She rocks her head side to side to show that she's not particularly convinced about that.

"But," Jeff keeps arguing his case, even though Bee has obviously made up her mind, "wouldn't it be fun if our whole friend group had matching mugs? Even though we're not sharing a house, we would share this!"

Giving a put-upon sigh, Bee takes another look at the mugs.

"I suppose you already have mugs picked out for Grey and Gloria?"

Jeff holds up two mugs with a sheepish grin. One has a wolf mid-shift and says "No pants? No problem!" Definitely the mug for Grey. I'm pretty sure everyone who visited their dorm last year got an eyeful at some point. The other just has illustrated wolves all over it in a variety of silly poses. Damn. That actually is a pretty good mug for Gloria.

"Fine. This one will be mine." Bee grabs a maroon mug with gold letters that say "It takes all kinds" on one side and "Berring College" on the other.

"Yes!" Jeff shouts so that I worry about getting kicked out and does a little happy dance, his hands even more full of mugs than before. "Our little family of mugs is complete!"

I try to stealthily slide mine back onto the shelf—it's not

that I don't appreciate what he's trying to do; I just don't have the money for frivolous spending right now—but of course, Jeff catches what I'm doing.

"No! You have to!" Jeff gives the mug a pointed look, then looks back at me. "Please?"

It's going to break the guy's heart if I flat out refuse, but I really can't blow ten bucks on a mug I don't need.

Bee snatches the mug before I have to come up with an answer. "This one is on me. If I'm going to start an ugly mug collection, I might as well go all in, right?"

I try to project my thanks to her without saying anything out loud, but she prances away like she didn't just save me from an awkward situation. I'll have to think of a way to thank her later.

"Happy unbirthdays!" Jeff shouts at Gloria and Grey when we catch up to them.

Gloria raises a skeptical eyebrow. "Is that actually a thing? Because it sure sounds like something you made up to justify . . . buying mugs?"

"Not just any mugs! These are matching friend mugs!"

I have a theory that Jeff has more exclamation points available to him than the rest of us. I'm not complaining. It's just something I've noticed after knowing him for a year. He gets excited about things that other people don't, and he shares that excitement more than other people do. If not for him getting excited about things in our freshman classes last year, I'm not sure I would have any friends now as a sophomore.

And now I realize that the conversation has gone on without me while I was reminiscing.

"Sorry, what was that?"

Grey doesn't look too annoyed at having to repeat himself, thankfully. "I asked if you'd heard from Devon and Marcus yet?"

"Oh. No, I think they're both still living at the frat house."

And that is the last place I want to be. Being around one vampire—myself—is enough for me most of the time. Being stuck in a house full of them, and most of those vampires being the worst kind of rich, entitled assholes ever? Sounds like hell on Earth. I'll pass, thanks. But Devon and Marcus are both good guys. "As far as I know, they're still, you know, fighting the good fight and trying to clean up the fraternity. But I'm not exactly invited, you know?"

My friends are all giving me the same quizzical look.

"What?" I shrug uncomfortably under their scrutiny.

It's Bee who says what they're all obviously thinking. "But I guess I kind of thought all vampires stuck together. You don't want to join the fraternity at all?"

"And deal with more people like Vincent Davenport?" Or my mother? Or even worse, my father? I suppress a shudder. "I'm sure the guys are doing their best, but it will be a long time before I trust anyone in that house." And even if I were dying to join, no way they'd let in a broke no-name like me. Devon is a stretch for those guys, since he's a made vampire instead of a born one, but Marcus's pedigree makes up for it. I don't have a powerful boyfriend to help open those doors for me. But it's not like my living friends know about any of that stuff. In their minds, all vampires are essentially created equal.

"Huh," Bee murmurs. "I never thought about it."

Thankfully, they drop the subject, going on to talk about what mugs Jeff picked out for Devon and Marcus and debating how well the gifts will go over.

CHAPTER 7

Bee

"What do you want to drink?" I wave the box of tea in one hand and the bag of coffee beans in the other. "It doesn't have to be one of these," I add. "It's just that I only have two hands, so I can't show any of the other options. There's also some beer and wine, I think." I hope I'm not promising something that isn't there, but we'll figure something out either way.

Devon grabs the coffee from my hand before anyone else answers. "I'll get started making this."

Marcus, his ridiculously besotted boyfriend, gives a fond headshake. "I'll take coffee too," he says.

I turn to Taylor, who looks uncomfortable at even this small amount of attention on him.

"Um. I'll take whatever everyone else is having."

"I'll probably have tea," I say, "and it's no problem to heat some more water. But I'll try to not take it personally if you choose coffee instead. Or, you know, whatever you actually want to drink."

Is it my imagination, or did the corners of his mouth just hitch up in a smile for the barest of moments?

"I wouldn't want you to take it personally," he tells me with a mock serious expression.

Jeff, always with the most perfect timing, jumps in then. "I'd love tea. But coffee is fine. As long as I get to drink it from my new favorite mug."

I raise a skeptical eyebrow at the row of supremely tacky mugs lined up on our counter. "Really? This is your favorite mug?"

He snatches the mug in question and cradles it to his chest like a baby. "What's wrong with my mug?"

Gloria saves me from having to answer by bringing him in for a side hug. "There's nothing wrong with it. Really. Whatever makes you happy. But . . . bite me? Really?"

Jeff holds the gold-and-maroon mug up with a ridiculous, dreamy, lovey look on his face. "A guy can hope, you know?"

Grey swoops in to hug him from the other side. "Just to be clear, when you talk about biting, you are talking about the girl who's barely spoken to you in a whole year, and everything she's said to you was mean?"

Jeff sighs out her name. "Lacey."

Poor Jeff. He's got no chance with the ice princess vampire who was my RA last year, but he's been carrying a torch for her since the freshman meeting where she called him out and embarrassed him in front of everyone. There really is no accounting for taste, I guess. If Jeff has started actually hoping a vampire will bite him, though, maybe we need to keep a closer eye on him.

Taylor taps Jeff's mug in the center, where an illustrated mouth has a trail of blood dripping from it. "You have to admit, this is kind of messed up. I can't believe they're selling something like this here."

Jeff shrugs apologetically. "If it makes you feel any better, I don't actually want Lacey to, like, drink from me or anything.

It's more about the excitement of knowing she could, you know?"

Taylor puts his hands up in defeat. "I guess. If you say so. I won't claim to understand."

I glance over at Devon, who's still at the coffeepot, and notice Marcus has wrapped his arms around him from behind. Maybe this isn't the type of conversation we should be having around the guy who was turned into a vampire against his will less than two years ago. Judging by the look on Devon's face, this is a little too close to home for him, and Jeff, as usual, is completely oblivious to his misstep.

"Okay," I break in with a bid to change the subject. "Coffee is brewing. I'll heat water for anyone who wants tea, and you're welcome to dig through the refrigerator if you want something else. Video games in the living room in five minutes?"

Devon visibly relaxes. "Yeah. Video games in five."

Taylor takes his cue and sets Jeff's tasteless mug on the counter before steering him out of the kitchen.

The next time I see either of my roommates without a crowd around us is hours later, after everyone else has gone home. Grey tried to convince Gloria to let him stay the night, but she just gave him a raised eyebrow and told him she had work to finish. I'm proud of her. If Grey had his way, they would probably both drop out of school tomorrow so they could spend all day, every day in bed together. She's too smart for that, though, and the premed biology degree she's working on is going to be too much work to let Grey have his way all the time.

Taylor is washing everyone's mugs in the sink while Gloria cleans up the detritus of snacks and junk food left behind by all of our human and shifter guests in the living room. I settle in next to Taylor at the sink and start drying mugs as he finishes rinsing them.

"Thanks for getting Jeff out of here earlier," I tell him. "He's a good guy, you know? Just oblivious."

Taylor chuckles. "Oh, I know. For all Jeff's strengths in welcoming people in and making friends, he has equal weaknesses in saying exactly the wrong thing at the wrong time. Devon knows that too. He won't hold it against Jeff."

I huff out my own laugh. "Yeah. I guess after being roommates for a year, Devon knows how to deal with Jeff's shit."

"And he's got Marcus to defend him."

"That he does. They seem to be doing well. I'm glad they found each other."

We continue washing and drying in companionable silence, and I think about how Gloria and Grey, then Devon and Marcus, seemed dragged toward each other last year like they were magnetically charged. I wonder what that feels like. I've never felt anything like that. Though now that I'm thinking about it like that, I'm sure Grey never felt anything like that until he met Gloria. He was always the typical horny wolf shifter who never felt a serious connection with any of his hookups. As far as I can tell from Gloria, she was pretty much the same before she fell for Grey. I don't know Devon and Marcus as well, but I get the sense from both of them that they never fell for anyone like that until they met each other. As much as I might want that for myself, I'm starting to think I need to readjust my hopes. The longer I go without feeling anything like that, the more I think I'm just not built that way. Maybe, instead of holding out hope for some deep connection or whirlwind romance or true love, I should just focus on something I can actually control. I should focus on finding adventures and experiencing new things. Bungee jumping, maybe, or skydiving. Grey will never allow it, but I just won't tell him. I hum as I clean and think of every kind of adventure possible. Maybe I could learn to ride a motorcycle or a horse. There are horses on Gloria's family's farm, but they all work on the farm as much as any of her family does. And I could go to a dive bar and play pool with some sketchy people there. There was a pool table in our dorm last year, but I never tried playing. There were a lot of things I wanted to do last year that just never happened. This is going to be my year, I decide. This is the year I break out and have every bucket list life experience I can think of.

CHAPTER 8

Bee

It had to happen sooner or later. As it turns out, the sooner, rather than later, happens on our second night in the house.

Grey turns up while we're still putting the finishing touches on the living room with all its beautiful new furniture.

Yes, I may have gone a little crazy with the shopping, but there's a reason my parents gave me a credit card when I went to college, and I don't see why I shouldn't use it.

Of course, as soon as Grey shows up, Gloria lets him in with an apologetic look at Taylor and me, and the two wolves disappear into her room.

If only they were inaudible as well as invisible right now.

A particularly loud moan makes it impossible to hear the movie we put on. Taylor doesn't say anything at all, but his eyes bug out as he tries to control his distress.

I snicker, partly at the absurdity of the situation, and partly at the look of horror etched on Taylor's face.

"Sorry," I say. "I guess I've gotten used to this. They were like this all. Summer. Long."

Taylor turns slowly to me, that same look frozen on his face. "I think I had an idea what it would be like, but the reality is . . . a lot more," he admits.

I shrug. "I wish I could say it'll get better, but they've been going at it like bunnies since last year, and they're showing no signs of letting up."

Another feminine-sounding moan fills the air, and Taylor's eyes get giant for a moment before he shuts them tight and buries his head in his hands.

"This is gonna kill me," I think I hear him mutter. Or maybe he didn't actually say it out loud, but I'm hearing his thoughts mirrored in my own brain.

Brilliance strikes me then.

"Let's get out of here." I grab his hand without thinking about how he doesn't seem to like being touched and feel a zap of static between our fingers that I try to ignore. "Come on. Right now. Let's just go."

Taylor looks like he's on the verge of arguing when another moan erupts from Gloria's room.

"Yeah," he agrees. "Please."

We're out the front door without actually agreeing on a destination.

"Is there a movie you wanted to see, or . . ."

Taylor avoids my eyes. I'm pretty sure it's the money thing that's holding him back, since he's seemed increasingly uncomfortable every time I've offered to pay for something.

"There's a diner nearby," I mention. "Obviously, I know you wouldn't eat any—"

"No," he cuts in. "It's perfect. Let's go."

The diner is close enough to walk, and Taylor seems happy enough to let me lead. He doesn't say a word the entire time, though.

I get it. We're new at this whole roommates thing. He doesn't want to . . . actually? No. I don't get it.

"Okay." I turn to him before we reach the branch where we need to turn for the diner. "What is it? Why won't you talk to me? I thought, after everything last year, we were kind of friends. Or at least kind of friendly. But now we're roommates, and you've barely said five words to me in two days. Did I do something wrong?"

Taylor gapes at me like he's at a complete loss. Like he doesn't speak the same language as me and can't figure out how to let me know.

"Wrong?" he finally asks, sounding strangled.

"Yeah. There's definitely something wrong, and if I did something to cause it, you should let me know now so I don't keep doing it."

He stares at me some more.

I give up and start walking again. "And now I've done it again, haven't I? I know I come on too strong with the shopping and the clothing obsession and the talking way too much and trying to win everyone over with gifts and clothes and . . . Maybe I come across as a shallow, self-centered, brainless bimbo whose only skill is spending money, but I swear there's more to me than that. If you would just open up a little for me, I could show you."

"But you don't," Talor says, easily catching up to me with his long-legged strides.

"What?" I have to stop again and look at him to try and read his face.

He looks down at the ground and toes a pebble in front of his foot. "You don't come across as any of those things," he tells either me or the pebble in front of him.

"But . . ." I reel, searching for a way this makes sense. "But you hardly talk to me. And you seem so uncomfortable every time I touch you. And you looked like you wished you could die instead of going shopping with me."

He murmurs something my weak human ears can't pick up.

"Huh?" Usually I'm a little more eloquent than this, but my brain is too busy scrambling for an explanation right now to put any effort into conversation.

"It's not that I don't like you or that I hate shopping with you or that I don't like when you touch me," he says, loud enough for me to hear this time. He peeks at me from beneath his eyelashes before looking straight back at the pebble again. "You and I come from completely different worlds, Bee. And you weren't meant to be so close to my world. I'm trying to keep you safe from it."

And I'm pretty sure that's the stupidest thing I've ever heard in my life. I climbed into a truck filled with manure and ran away from home when I was seventeen. I managed to get a job and could have lived a happy life on my own with almost no money and no friends to help me, if my mom hadn't convinced me to come home. I don't need him to keep me safe any more than I need my brother or my parents to.

I kick him in the shin and start walking again. It takes him less than two full strides to catch up to me again, but at least the lingering sound of his shout of surprise warms my heart a little.

"I'm not joking, Bee. You have no idea what my life is like —what I'm like—and you shouldn't trust me like you do. You have no reason to feel safe out here alone with me, but you're just walking with me like you've never heard of vampires before, and you have no idea what I could do to you. Why aren't you afraid of me? Or at least suspicious of me. I mean, you grew up with Grey, didn't you?"

I keep walking, but I give his words some serious thought.

"Yes, I grew up with Grey, but that doesn't mean I have to believe the same wrong thing he believes. Just because someone has the physical ability to hurt me doesn't mean I should stay away from them or be afraid of them. Don't you get that? If I was afraid of everyone who can hurt me, I'd literally be afraid of everyone. I grew up surrounded by wolves who were stronger than me before they hit puberty. Should I have been afraid of them?"

Taylor won't meet my eyes. "No, of course not," he concedes. "But you didn't grow up around vampires, and I know you don't want to admit it, but it's different. Believe me, I want you to be able to trust me, but when it comes down to it, I'm just another monster like the rest of them."

I sneak a look at him and am shocked into silence by the earnestness on his face. I was on the verge of making the same argument to him that finally worked with Grey. *If you never let anything happen to me, nothing will ever happen to me.* But Taylor is wearing his hurt and fear right on his face for me to see. He really believes that he's a threat to me that I should be worried about. It isn't just run-of-the-mill protectiveness rolling off him. He's truly afraid of what he might do to me.

"Hey." I catch his arm and feel another zap of electricity. "You've never shown me a reason to fear you, even given the fact that you're bigger and stronger than me, and you've given me plenty of reasons to trust you, even if you don't trust yourself. You're stuck with me, end of story."

His deep brown, almost black eyes finally meet mine. More than anything, he looks sad.

"I'll try to remember that," he says, and then we're at the diner, and he's opening the door for me like this is a date. Boy takes out girl. Boy treats girl to food. Girl kisses boy in return.

But none of those things are accurate. This is the story of the boy and the girl saving each other from their embarrassingly sex-crazed roommates. This is the story of the boy and the girl becoming friends. Hopefully, this is the story of the girl finding someone to go on adventures with and the girl making new friends she never would have met back home.

Maybe I'm paranoid. Maybe I have more attention for our surroundings because I'm not eating anything. Maybe my senses are heightened because I'm already worried about being so close to Bee after our earlier conversation.

Whatever the case, I'm certain that guy in the corner booth is watching us. He came in a few minutes after Bee and me, and he hasn't touched the plate of food the server sat in front of him. It's not like I've been able to catch him looking at us or anything, but I swear I keep feeling a prickle on the back of my neck. He may not be looking at us, but he's definitely paying more attention than he should.

And I can't make sense of him either. He doesn't have the musky scent of a shifter, but he's warmer than a vampire, with an audible heartbeat that I can hear all the way from where I'm sitting. But he doesn't smell . . . this is terrible, but he doesn't smell like food the way humans do. What the fuck is he? And what does he want with us?

"Do you think it's safe to go back to the house yet?" I ask, hoping we can get away from this guy.

Bee rolls her eyes and takes a bite of lemon meringue pie. My mouth waters as she licks the last traces from her fork. "With those two? You'll learn soon enough that it's never safe. Seriously, I thought they might calm down by the end of the summer, but they keep going at it like their lives depend on it." She waves her fork in the air for punctuation. "I foresee many late-night diner visits for us, my friend."

I can't help but smile. "It's been that bad, huh?"

"I was really hoping that having you living with us would, I don't know, have a cooling effect or something, but that was wishful thinking, I guess."

"Well, I'm truly sorry that my presence hasn't stopped my roommate from getting laid." My lip twitches, and I can feel a laugh bubbling beneath the surface, but I manage to keep it under control.

Bee, on the other hand, bursts out laughing and doesn't hold back. Her hand thumps the table. Tears stream down her face. I finally give in and join her.

I imagined a lot of possible ways for this living arrangement to go, but laughing until I cried with one roommate while we've been kicked out of the house so we don't have to hear our other roommate having sex was beyond my imagination.

Our watcher is still there when we leave, and his table still has the same full plates the server dropped off before. The skin between my shoulder blades crawls as I'm walking out, and it takes all of my determination not to spin around to see if the guy is staring at us.

Whether he's actually staring or not, he's definitely watching. I have no idea if he's watching me or Bee, though.

I can't think of any reason for someone to watch me, but I decide to keep an eye out just in case. If he doesn't realize I've noticed him, he'll slip up and show what he's up to eventually.

Bee giggles and leans on me as we walk the dark path

home. It wasn't dark when we left, but now it's dark and ominous and every kind of creepy.

I don't want to worry Bee when it's probably just my anxiety-riddled brain at work, so I keep my worries to myself.

Do I hear footsteps behind us?

I slip my arm around Bee's shoulders. If someone attacks, I'm picking her up and running as fast as I can. If I can at least get us closer to the house before I have to face a fight, maybe there's a chance to get Bee to safety so I can face the danger without worry.

"I guess you're comfortable touching me now?" she asks in a sleepy, giggly voice that would be adorable if I weren't so preoccupied with worry right now.

"Touching?" I say before realizing what she's talking about. "Oh. Yeah. I guess, now that I've watched you eat your weight in pie, we really are friends, right?"

She lets out a whoop. "Yes! I knew I could wear you down! It was only a matter of time!"

I squeeze her a little tighter to my side, wishing she would be quieter so I can hear whether someone is following us. Also wishing she would keep going because her enthusiasm is contagious.

"Yeah," I tell her. "That's exactly what happened. You wore me down."

Bee adds a little jump to her cheer this time, and feeling that movement—all that life and energy—right next to me, and the way she's touching me without worrying about my size or my teeth or my diet of human blood, makes me melt a little bit more.

"Maybe . . ." I hesitate to put the rest of my thought into words, in case I can't pull it back in time, but Bee leans into me with anticipation. "Maybe we can do this again sometime? I mean, you don't have to, but I didn't mind spending time with you."

Bee's nose wrinkles when she grins. I file this information away for future use. I have no idea what future use it could have, but I lock it in a safe spot in my memories anyway.

"Well, I'm glad, because I didn't mind spending time with you either," she says. "And it doesn't have to be food all the time, you know. We could do activities that you can actually partake in too? Like movies or . . . arcades? Arcades are places that people go, right?"

I don't want to ruin our moment by pointing out that I'm never going to have money for movies or arcades. I'd rather go to a restaurant and watch her eat and have an excuse for not participating, but I learned a long time ago that people who grew up with money never understand what it's like for people like me.

"Yeah," I tell her. "I've heard that arcades are places that people go." And suddenly, my imagination takes over, and I can see her with the flashing lights of a video game playing across her face or smiling that everything smile in a movie theater. And now all I want in the world is to be there to see it. Even better if I can be the one who actually gives her that happiness instead of just observing it. I mentally rearrange my budget and try to figure out where I can stretch it or do without something entirely. "Maybe next time our roommate is preoccupied, we can go out and explore together."

Am I imagining things, or is she leaning closer in toward me? Is her heartbeat always this fast, or has its normally quick flutter increased in the past few seconds?

Am I leaning down closer to her? Bad idea! Warning bells ring in my head, and I step back with a jolt and usher her into our—thankfully—quiet house.

CHAPTER 10

Bee

I have no idea what's going on between Taylor and me. For example, was Taylor about to kiss me? No clue. And why do I keep feeling electrical shocks every time I touch him? Is this . . . I'm not even sure. Is this what other people are talking about when they talk about attraction? I have no idea how to tell whether I'm feeling actual vibes or just imagining things.

Damn Gloria and Grey and their disgustingly mated bliss! If not for the fact that I'm one million percent sure of what I would walk in on, I would be marching into Gloria's room right now to bombard her with questions.

But, best-case scenario, she and Grey are asleep right now. Almost definitely naked. Possibly in wolf form, I suppose, but that would still mean they were technically naked. In a less ideal possible scenario, they're mid-fuck and just being quiet about it. I've seen enough of that already, thank you very much.

I press my face deep into my pillow and silently scream out my frustration so no one with superior hearing comes running to check on me.

Am I actually feeling something from Taylor, or is it all in my head? How do people ever figure this shit out?

I need to come at this from a rational standpoint. Flipping over, I stare up at my ceiling with its rickety ceiling fan.

First, whether I was feeling any kind of vibes from Taylor or not, I need to figure out how I feel about him.

He is, objectively, attractive. He's big and tall and broody in an interesting way. His face is symmetrical, and his body is well-formed.

And none of that has been enough to capture my interest in the past.

He's also a genuinely nice guy, as I learned last year when he helped deal with our corrupt vampire issue, and as I learned again tonight when he agreed to hang out and watch while I ate an inhuman amount of pie. He never complained or hinted that he had better things to do or reminded me that he can't eat the same food as me.

But I've known other nice guys before, and I've never had my heart kick up to hummingbird warp speed around any of them. Ever. That giddy feeling when I thought maybe we were leaning toward each other and maybe he was looking at my lips and maybe I was about to have my first kiss? I've never in my life felt anything quite like that.

Okay, so maybe there's something there.

Trying to recapture that heart-racing feeling, I trail my fingers down my stomach, feather touches that I think, maybe, just maybe, will do the trick this time.

But it's like trying to tickle myself. My body responds with boredom and annoyance and frustration. Just like every other time.

Balling my fist, I punch the mattress beside me in frustration. You would think, growing up in a wolf pack, that I would have learned something about masturbation. I mean, wolves do it. All. The. Time. Female shifters make a big deal about gifting sex toys to each other when they have their first heat. The pack is a very fucking sex-positive place. So how am I still defective like this? How is it so hard to even get slightly turned on when I've grown up with everyone telling me how great sex is?

But, I remind myself, tonight, I definitely felt something with Taylor. More than I've felt before. Maybe even half of what other people have described to me about this stuff. Fluttering heartbeat? Check. Possible tightening of my stomach muscles? Check. Warmth in the lower regions? Maybe check? I guess I didn't quite get a chance to reach that point.

Anyway, whatever is going on here, it has to be worth exploring, right? If the mere possibility of a kiss can make me all heart-racy like this, what might an actual kiss do?

CHAPTER 11

Taylor

Maybe Bee notices that it's a little overly convenient how I'm ready to leave exactly when she is, but she doesn't say anything, just smiles and asks if I want to take the tunnels. If she weren't way too good for me, I would be trying to figure out how to make her fall in love with me.

She deserves to fall in love with someone who can actually give her what she needs, though, so I shove my feelings down deep and settle into my role as friend and protector. Hopefully, I'm good enough for that.

"I've decided I need to have an adventure," Bee blurts out about three steps down the tunnel that will take us to campus.

"A . . . what?"

"An adventure. I realized recently that I haven't had enough of them."

I spare a sidelong glance at her. "All of that stuff last year with having to look over our shoulders and wonder if powerful vampires were coming after us . . . that wasn't exciting enough?"

She gives a dismissive hand wave. "It's not about excitement. It's about living life. Having experiences. You know? Hiding from Vincent wasn't an experience. It was just . . ."

"Terrifying?"

"I was thinking more obnoxious than terrifying."

"You realize that makes you a little terrifying, right?"

Bee snorts out a laugh. "Whatever. You know I'm right. That stuff last year wasn't fun, and it got in the way of the things you're supposed to do freshman year."

Her laughter is infectious. And it feels good to let loose a little bit. "Okay. Let's just say, for the sake of argument, that I get where you're coming from. What are the adventures you think you missed out on?"

She shrugs. "All the crazy freshman stuff. Get blackout drunk. Go streaking. Lose my virginity."

I trip over my own toes but manage to stay upright.

"Oh. Right. All of those things."

"But I didn't do any of that last year, so now I have to catch up."

All possible words stick in my throat as my brain gets stuck on that other thing she said.

"How about you?" she continues, oblivious to the fact that she's turned me momentarily inside out. "Is there anything you wanted to do last year that you need to catch up on now?"

"I . . . um . . ." Brilliant. Just look at my intelligent brain forming all sorts of coherent thoughts and then communicating them. "I'm sorry. Did you just say something about your virginity?" Oh, damn. That was supposed to stay as an inside thought, but I just blurted it out loud, didn't I?

"Yeah. Is that, like, too embarrassing to admit? Maybe I should have kept it to myself, but everyone else I know lost theirs a long time ago, and now I'm the lonely weirdo. But if I could have done it last year, that would have been fine, you know? Plenty of freshmen are still virgins. Probably. But I'm not a freshman anymore, so now it feels weird and sad. Shit. I'm babbling now. Please tell me you won't start thinking of me as the sad weirdo now that you know."

I gape at her, still trying to catch up with everything she just said. "I don't think you're a sad weirdo," I finally manage.

"Okay." Bee takes a slow, deep breath, and I try very hard not to hear her heart pulsing and her blood swishing through her veins. I try even harder to not notice her scent of warm skin and hot blood and a hint of something citrusy and floral. Or the lift of her chest with each deep inhale. "If you say I'm not sad or weird, I will take your word for it. But I still feel like it would have been better to get that out of the way last year so I could move on to other things this year."

"But . . . that isn't something you want to rush or do with the wrong person."

She makes a rude sound at that. "Honestly, I'm not convinced about that. I mean, as long as I'm not in danger, I'm pretty sure that sex is sex. It doesn't matter who it's with. I'm not expecting to fall in love with him. I just want to know what it's all about so I can stop feeling left out."

I'm at a loss for words. I shake my head to try and get my thoughts going again. "Okay. So, if I allow that your premise is sound—which I'm not saying, but for the sake of argument—how are you making sure you're not in danger? I mean, Gloria didn't think she was in danger from Vincent, and when she found out, it was almost too late. And I don't know the details of what happened with Devon, but I know he didn't think he was in danger from the person who turned him into a vampire. You have to admit that there are a lot of dangerous people that you would never guess were dangerous until you were already in danger." I seem to have gone from completely tongue-tied to being unable to stop the flow of words pouring out. "I don't like the thought of you ending up in a dangerous situation just because you wanted to check some milestone off your list. There's no way to make sure someone is safe."

"Ugh," she groans. "You're worse than Grey."

"I'll make sure to let him know that next time he's giving me the stink eye and implying I might be one of the monsters you need protection from."

"For the love of everything you hold dear, please don't tell him I said that. He'll be insufferable if he catches any whiff of someone else agreeing with this ridiculous bodyguard routine."

"Okay, I won't tell him, but Bee, I'm serious about this. Don't go off on your own without anyone to watch your back, okay? I won't tell Grey that I'm watching out for you, but you need to let *someone* watch out for you."

She rolls her eyes at me like a teenager. "You're going to be watching out for me while I go out looking for hookups."

I swallow past the uncomfortable lump in my throat. "Alright. If that's how it has to be. And you'd better believe I will be right there to get you away if I think a situation feels off."

"My hero," she says drily.

"Damn right," I confirm as I lead her up the steps to the liberal arts building, where she has her first class of the day.

Before we get through the door, two bodies pounce on us. Gabe is lucky I can smell that he's human before I start throwing punches. I'm still on high alert when he lets go of me and gives me a light punch on the shoulder.

"Dude, I can't believe I got you like that," he says with a grin. "Aren't you supposed to be able to hear an attacker coming ahead of time?"

I level a glare at him, then at Jeff, who has an arm thrown casually over Bee's shoulders.

"My hearing is good, but it's not like your footsteps sound any different from everyone else walking to class," I point out.

Jeff shakes his head like he's disappointed in me. "You gotta be on guard. Grey keeps complaining to us about how he wishes he could be there to keep his little sister safe. You, my friend, are her best line of defense."

Now it's Bee's turn to glare. "Grey is going to be at our place plenty, and I promise you, he's not going to be watching me while he's there because he's too busy doing something else."

Instead of being intimidated by her glare, Jeff cracks up.

"Fuck, but that is the absolute truth. That boy cannot seem to control himself."

Bee turns and starts walking toward her class. "What about the rest of you? Are there girlfriends or boyfriends in the picture that are going to keep you busy this semester?"

Before Jeff can get his dreamy look and start talking about how much he wants Lacey to bite him, Gabe interjects. "*Some of us*"—he gives Jeff a pointed look—"are keeping our options open. Grey can afford to get distracted because he knows Gloria will help pull him out of whatever hole he digs himself into. Me? I will only be doing casual, no strings, until I graduate. Probably forever, but my mom doesn't like when I say that." He looks Bee over appreciatively. "Now, if you know of someone who's interested in something casual . . ."

My hand is starting to curl into a fist when Bee bursts out laughing. "Oh, wow. Thank you. I needed that compliment today," she says through her laughter. "I know you're not actually interested, but it's nice of you to pretend. Anyway, I'd better get to class."

She practically skips into the lecture hall with a smile and a wave over her shoulder.

Gabe turns to me with a questioning look. "Am I the crazy one here? Bee is, objectively, very attractive. Why would she think I'm pretending?"

I have to calm the protectiveness raging through my veins

before I can answer. "Maybe because you've never come on to her before? I don't know."

I'm definitely not telling him about the virginity thing. First, I don't want to betray her confidence. Second, I'll probably lose my shit if Gabe starts seriously going after her. I don't think Gabe is the type of guy who specifically goes after virgins or anything like that—we wouldn't be friends if I got that impression from him—but the thought of Gabe hooking up with Bee, the thought of Gabe being Bee's first, somehow has my shoulders so tense I can barely move.

Jeff looks back and forth between the two of us thoughtfully.

"What?" we both ask at once.

"Nothing." He shrugs. "I'm just going to be really upset if some sort of rivalry over a girl messes up our friendship."

He walks away, and Gabe and I share a look before hurrying to follow him.

"What are you talking about?" Gabe asks. "I was just stating a fact. I find Bee attractive. Most people who like women probably find Bee attractive."

I manage to stop my growl before it comes out.

"Yes, most people probably do find Bee attractive." Jeff slides a look at me. "Taylor? Do you find Bee attractive?"

"It wouldn't matter if I did," I say, and yes, maybe it does come out as a growl. There are some things I can't control.

"And why not?"

I look between my two friends. My two human friends. My two friends who aren't dirt-poor and only able to go to school because of a full-ride scholarship and a patchwork of charity programs.

"Isn't it obvious?"

They both shake their heads, but Jeff is giving me a knowing kind of look that probably means he's about to say something that most people would never say out loud, and the corner of Gabe's lip is twitching like he's on the verge of smiling over some secret I'm not in on.

"She's my roommate. I can't let myself think about her like that."

Jeff grins in triumph. "You are so into her! Just admit it!"

"No. Not only is she my roommate, she's . . ."

"She's what?" Gabe says.

Too good for me, I want to say, but even saying that much would be admitting to something I can't allow myself.

"Can we just drop this? Please? Even if I was admitting any kind of attraction—which I'm not—there's nothing I could do about it because we all know someone like her is not meant for someone like me. End of story."

"Fine." Jeff throws his hands up. "We can drop it. For now. Mostly because I need to get to class. But we will be revisiting this."

CHAPTER 12

Bee

So, maybe I could have been a bit smoother about admitting to the whole virginity thing. I guess Taylor reacted as well as I could have hoped. Maybe I had some idea that he wouldn't be completely boorish about it, but instead, I got the same hypocritical fucking lecture I've gotten my whole damn life. Wait until you're ready. Wait until it's with someone special. But also, there's probably something wrong with you because you haven't been ready yet, and there's probably more wrong with you because you haven't found someone special yet.

Give me a goddamn, motherfucking break. Do these people not realize how they keep trapping me in this awkward in-between space that I can't get out of?

Whatever.

I grind my teeth through an entire history lecture and retain absolutely nothing from it. But who cares, anyway? It's not like anything will happen to me if I flunk out. Aside from having to go back home. But I knew I would have to go home eventually anyway.

I'm in an absolutely foul mood by the time I finish the

ninety-minute lecture on . . . something about serfs? I need something to snap me out of it, so I head down to the coffee kiosk that's always set up near the front entrance.

"I don't even care, just make sure it has caffeine and whipped cream on top," I tell the guy at the register and hand over my credit card without looking at the cost that flashes across the screen. A lot of people would be jealous of my life. I realize that. I've lived the kind of life where I don't have to look at prices before handing over a credit card. But it's also the kind of life where I could never get lost in a public place because every single adult in my vicinity knew who I belonged with. I understand how that's a dream for a lot of people. But what outsiders don't understand is that while I never got lost, I never explored either. And while it's nice to buy things without worrying if I can cover the costs, it's not nice to get halfway through high school and realize most of your friends only hang out with you because they're hoping you'll pay for their shit. And here's the thing. Of course I paid for their shit. Partly because why not, and partly because I was afraid of what would happen if I didn't. I'm pretty sure I wouldn't have any friends anymore, that's what would happen.

I take a deep pull on the sugared monstrosity in my cup and start to feel myself relax from it. So far in my life, there is nothing that can't be at least helped by sugar. I'm not saying we can create a utopia by baking cakes, but I do think it's worth considering. Maybe the world could take it in shifts to bake pastries for each other and—

"Hey."

I scream at the top of my lungs, spin in a circle, and throw my cup at my assailant.

Er. Roommate. Taylor is standing there, hands held out like he doesn't know what to do with them, with coffee ice cream drink covering his hair and whipped cream dripping down his face.

"Shit. I can't believe I just did that."

The stunned look on his face tells me he can't believe I just did that either.

"Um. Don't worry about it. I guess I learned my lesson to announce my approach from a distance from now on."

I bury my face in my hands and groan. "I'm never going to live this down, am I?"

"With me or with everyone else?" he asks, seemingly perfectly calm and collected now that his initial shock has passed.

"Yes? Both?" I ask him from behind my hand. Yeah, there's no part of this that I'll be able to put away and forget about.

"Well, I, for one, am comforted to know that you can fight back in case of sneak attacks. We might want to work on finding a more effective weapon for you, but at least we know you can aim a projectile coffee from a few feet away."

"If I help you get cleaned up, will you stop teasing me about this?"

The jerk actually grins. "Not a chance. Besides, unless you were planning to lick this off me, the best method is probably for me to do it myself."

And why am I now imagining licking coffee off him?

"Right." I give myself a shake. *Pull yourself together, Bee.* "I am really sorry about that. If there's any way I can make it up to you . . ."

"Like what?"

He looks genuinely curious, which I guess means I have to come up with an idea or two. "Oh, I don't know. I mean, you're probably not interested in getting an extra sugary coffee drink to go with the one you're currently wearing, right?"

"I'm afraid not. But maybe I'll think of something later, and then it will be payback time." He grins and rubs his hands together in an over-the-top, goofy way that I would have never imagined he was capable of. I mean, Taylor doesn't do "goofy." Ever, at least as far as I've seen. Sometimes funny, but never goofy. Never over-the-top. But right now, he's rubbing his hands together like a cartoon villain.

"So, you're saying I should watch my back?"

He nods solemnly. "You should definitely watch your back," he agrees.

CHAPTER 13

Taylor

The way I see it, being covered in sugary drink is a more than fair price to pay if it means a pretty girl is going to lick it off me. Unfortunately, Bee doesn't seem too interested in exploring that option. I try and fail to not check out her ass as she walks away before I go in search of a place where I can clean up.

Then stop dead in my tracks. The stranger I was sure was watching us in the diner the other night is lounging on a bench less than ten feet from me. Not looking at me and not looking in the same direction that Bee just went, but still giving me a prickly feeling all the way up and down my arms.

Maybe it's nothing. Maybe it's a coincidence. Berring isn't so big that you can't randomly cross paths with the same person even though you don't have any classes in common. But I'm getting that same feeling from him now as in the diner. This is a guy who's pretending to have business here. Everyone else—students, professors, coffee kiosk workers—all have some obvious purpose for being here. He's just sitting, head tilted back and noticeably not looking at anything in particular. And not smelling like a vampire or a human or a shifter, which has alarm bells clanging big-time in my head.

Ignoring the ice cream dripping down my cheek, I walk closer to the bench as casually as I can. If he's here following me, he already knows I'm here, but if he's here for some other reason, maybe hasn't even noted my existence, I want to take this chance to learn more about him.

He's got a heartbeat, I can tell by about five feet away, even in the between-classes crowd that's milling around, but it's faster than most of the humans around us. His body temperature, on the other hand, seems to be lower than normal. Shifters run so hot I can usually feel the heat pouring off them. With humans, it's more a case of their body heat tripping my predatory vampire senses into high alert. This guy is cold, though. Like room temperature. Like me. I can't figure it out. Whatever he is, I've never encountered it before.

He stands suddenly, turns to look me directly in the eye, then gives me a smirk before walking away.

Well, I guess that answers my question about whether he noticed me or not.

Feeling defeated and also kind of gross, I head back home to shower and change into some clean clothes. There's nothing I can do about a stranger who seems to coincidentally turn up around either Bee or me, but I'll be on the lookout for him going forward.

CHAPTER 14

Bee

What with the drink-throwing incident and then needing to get another drink for myself, I'm almost late when I slide into one of the last open seats in my next class.

Chemistry lecture. Oh, happy days.

I try to readjust my attitude before class starts, but the drone of Professor Biles's voice quickly has me descending back to the depths of boredom.

"Remind me again why I chose chemistry?" a guy I hadn't noticed sitting beside me before mutters.

I glance around, trying to figure out who he's talking to. Based on the fact that he's looking straight at me with a mischievous grin, I conclude he's talking to me.

"Um, why *did* you choose chemistry?" I whisper.

He slouches in his seat with a sigh. "I don't know. I guess I thought it would be easier than biology? How about you?"

I shrug. "Same, I suppose. I took physics last year, and I still needed some science credits but somehow ended up in the most painfully dull class I've taken in my life."

The girl in front of me turns in her seat to give me a

quelling look, but it's not like Professor Biles can hear me when I'm back here in the thirty-somethingth row. And she knows I haven't said anything that isn't true.

My neighbor ignores her too, leaning closer to continue our conversation. "Not a science major, I take it?"

"No way. I'm undecided, but science is definitely not going to be it when I do declare a major." Not for the first time, I have a pang of jealousy of Gloria discovering her calling to become a doctor last year. I've never felt a calling to do anything other than find a little bit of freedom and enjoy my life.

He reaches over for a fist bump. "Right on. I'm the exact same," he says.

"Which lab are you in? I'm in the Wednesday 3:00, but I've never seen you before."

"Tuesday 3:00. And I don't know about yours, but my chemistry lab is at least as boring as the lecture. The TA who runs it is Katrina. I'm convinced she would prefer it if she only had to deal with chemicals instead of students. What about yours?"

"Same, except he's not Katrina; he's Zach, and I sometimes daydream about making it more interesting by mixing random things together to see if they explode."

My neighbor grins and sticks his hand out. "I'm Ceallach. You?"

"Bee." I shake his hand, giddy over meeting my first new friend of this school year.

We sit in silence for a bit more of this painfully boring lecture before Ceallach turns to me again. "You know, there's a trick to this, if you're interested. It takes some practice, though."

"A trick to what?"

He draws a circle in the air that takes in the entire lecture hall. "This. Classes. School. Boring lectures."

"What, like a study hack or something?" I can hear the skepticism in my own voice. I've never been particularly bad at academics, but I've also never found a shortcut that works the way it's supposed to.

Ceallach rolls his eyes at me. "Sure. Call it a study hack. I think of it more as a sixth sense. The same way you can see the emotions on someone's face, with enough practice, you can hear the thoughts in a person's head. Sense the correct answers on a test."

I raise my eyebrows and give a slow nod. "Riiiiight. So I could use my sixth sense to know what the answers are without studying. I see." I turn back toward Professor Biles, annoyed at being caught up in Ceallach's little joke.

"Fine. You don't believe me. Or maybe you think I'm crazy. I'll prove it."

I side-eye him. Of course I don't believe him.

Ceallach closes his eyes and takes a slow breath, then starts whispering so only I can hear. It takes me a moment to figure out what he's saying, but then I recognize that Professor Biles is saying the exact same words, just with a half-second lag.

"How did you . . ." I look back and forth between Ceallach and the professor to confirm that I really am hearing the exact same lecture from both of them. "Okay, I can admit that's a neat trick, and I have no idea how you did it."

With a devious grin, Ceallach stops lecturing and turns back to me. "Easy. You reach out with your mind and sense the other minds around you. You've never even tried?"

I chuckle, still halfway convinced he's playing a trick I just haven't figured out. "Why would I have tried something like that?"

His smile slips a little. "Because it's one of the fae gifts?" he says uncertainly, eliciting a snort from me.

"Well then, if it's a fae gift, I guess I'll get right on it."

Ceallach's smile drops the rest of the way from his face. "You . . . you really don't know?"

Annoyed again, I try to focus on the lecture, but of course, my brain can't settle on chemistry when the person next to me is apparently seriously trying to tell me about fairy mind powers.

At least Ceallach seems just as annoyed. He leans in close to me to try and get my attention. I do my best to ignore him.

"Okay, Bee. I can accept that you didn't know before, but now you're going to start recognizing your gifts for what they are, and you're going to start practicing with them, and eventually, you'll be ready to ask some questions. I'll be around when you're ready."

Then he sits back and doesn't speak for the rest of the lecture, which is probably best, because I can't hear anything over the cacophony in my head.

CHAPTER 15

Taylor

When I get home, I waste all afternoon searching for what type of person has a fast heartbeat, low body temperature, and doesn't smell like food to a vampire. And I come up with absolutely nothing. I allow myself a moment of self-pity and bang my head against the desk a few times.

Usually, I'm really good at shit like this. Computers make sense to me, and understanding computer searches is just a learned skill, honed after years and years of needing to look everything up myself. But I'm coming up with absolutely nothing with even a vague basis in reality. There's one nut job I keep coming across who seems to have dedicated their life to screaming into the void of the internet about their conspiracy theories about the fair folk and how they walk among us. That's an interesting rabbit hole I keep getting sucked into, but none of it is remotely real. Finally, I shut down my computer and lie down on the sofa, secretly hoping that somewhere, if the fairies really do exist, one of them is just as frustrated with trying to figure out what I am.

Somehow, I doubt it.

I'm startled out of my stupor by the front door banging open and two intertwined bodies practically falling through it. I figure out that it's Gloria and Grey immediately, but they don't notice me.

"Eh-herm." I try to be both loud enough to draw attention and quiet enough to not embarrass anyone.

"Oh. Shit. Sorry." To her credit, Gloria does look genuinely sorry. "We shouldn't have assumed the house was empty."

I stand up. "No worries. I've got studying I can do at the library. You two . . . have fun." I'm not sure if I feel embarrassed because I feel like a voyeur or if this is just plain old jealousy crawling up my spine. "I'll get out of your way."

"No! I mean, you really don't have to do that for us." Gloria gives Grey a stern look. "We can control ourselves."

I stuff my laptop in my bag and start backing toward the door. "It's really not a problem." Then, before I have to continue the awkward conversation, I flee.

The sun is low enough that I can walk aboveground, which is nice. I can almost tell myself it was my idea to go for an evening stroll, and it feels like a sign when I cross paths with Bee a few blocks from our house.

"You don't want to go home right now," I warn her.

"Why would—oh my god, the wolves are at it again, aren't they?"

I give a sheepish smile. "They didn't expect me to be home, so I caught half the show before they were even through the door."

Bee presses her palms against her eyes and groans. "What is wrong with them? I swear, it's getting worse. It's like they have absolutely no self-control around each other."

"I don't know. I mean, yes, it crosses all sorts of boundaries that I never even knew I had, but it's also . . . sweet . . .

how they found each other and care so much about each other."

Bee responds with a glare. "I thought it was sweet until the third time I walked in on them. Now, I'm feeling very, very salty."

I smother my laugh so she doesn't direct her ire at me. "So, what should we do? Diner again? I was heading to the library, but I don't really have anything I need to study."

She gives me a calculating look that has all of my alarm systems jangling.

"If Grey is going to make living in my own house uncomfortable," she finally says, "I'm going to give him a taste of the potential consequences." With that ominous pronouncement, she starts walking in a new direction.

I have to jog to keep up with her. "Bee? Um, it's not that I'm trying to stop you from doing . . . whatever you have in mind right now, but is it possible that it would be a better idea to get something to eat first and then see how you feel?"

Bee spares a withering look over her shoulder but doesn't slow. "I'll eat later. Right now, I'm going to go out and live a little bit. Now, are you coming with me, or do I have to go without you?"

"You know I'm going to come with you," I mumble, doubling my stride to catch up with her. "Can you at least tell me where we're going?"

She grins. Not a happy, not-a-care-in-the-world grin. No. This is a cold baring of the teeth that has me questioning if she really is as human as she claims. This is a calculated smile to terrify any enemies in the vicinity.

"I'm going to get a tattoo."

I trip and almost fall flat on my face before coming to my senses and racing to catch up to her again. "Did you just say you're getting a tattoo?"

"I sure did." Her grin doesn't falter.

"Bee, come on. You can't just get a tattoo on a whim because your roommate brings her boyfriend home."

One of her eyebrows twitches, reminding me somehow of a grenade pin being pulled. I flinch before I catch myself.

"Maybe you can't," she says in a cheerful voice.

"But . . . aren't tattoos forbidden or something in your community?"

She shrugs. "Forbidden isn't the right word, and the shifter community is separate from me. Shifters generally don't do any kind of body modification because they would immediately heal as soon as they shifted, so there's no point. For a shifter to actually keep a tattoo or a piercing or anything like that, they would have to keep from shifting until it healed naturally on their human form. And, yes, shifters do tend to be judgmental about body modification for that reason. Which is exactly why Grey is going to lose his shit when he realizes that I've done it."

"Okay, but that doesn't make this any better, does it? You shouldn't have something permanent done to your body out of spite."

"It's not spite. It's . . . actually living for once. Everything I've done in my whole life has been approved of by my shifter family. But I'm not a shifter, and I need to live for myself. Now, are you with me or against me?"

I can feel my arguments draining away. "I'm with you. I am. I just . . . need to make sure you're not going to regret this, okay?"

Bee slows, then stops to look at me. "I'm not going to regret this, I promise."

"And how do I know that you're not just saying that?"

She squints at me like she's trying to see into my soul, then huffs a laugh and shakes her head at a joke I'm not in on.

"Taylor, of course I'm just saying what you want to hear, but I've had a weird fucking day, and I can't go back to my own house, and all I want to do right now is get a tattoo. Are you in, or are you out?"

"You're going to get a tattoo whether I agree to come with you or not, aren't you?"

She gives me a humorless smile. "One hundred percent."

I take a moment to calculate the potential costs and benefits of throwing her over my shoulder and carrying her home. Cost: she would never forgive me. Benefit: Grey would appreciate it. Cost: she will definitely just go without me.

"If there is anything off about this place," I tell her, "or if anything doesn't feel right, we leave immediately and find a different shop."

She smiles—a real smile this time—and starts walking again.

I trail after her, praying she really knows what she's doing. "So, what are you thinking of getting? And why? Because it can't just be a potato or something like that."

Her eye roll is eloquent.

"I'm serious! You should go in with a plan, right? Or else you're more likely to get something you regret."

"Don't you trust me to come up with something better than a potato, at least?"

"Sure. So what have you come up with that's better than a potato?"

She huffs and walks a little faster.

"Wait a second." The truth breaks over me like icy water. "You haven't thought of anything, have you?"

"Well . . . no. But whatever I think of when I get there will be better than a potato."

I let out a long sigh. Just because vampires don't need to breathe doesn't mean we don't have the instinct to take the occasional deep, calming breath. I find myself needing to take a lot of calming breaths around Bee.

"Let's start with a different question. Do you know where you're going to get it?"

"Someplace Grey will see it but that's easy to cover up when I go back to live with the pack."

That makes me blink a few times. "You really want to piss Grey off that badly?"

"Yes," she answers without hesitation.

In, two three four. Out, two three four. I'm not sure if my calming breaths have the same effect that a human would get, but I have to do something.

"Come on, Bee. I get that you two are family and that family is complicated, but he is going to murder me painfully when he realizes I helped you with this."

She slows a little bit and looks sidelong at me. "Okay, fine. I'll get it where he won't see, and it will be our secret, and it will be enough for me to know that I did it. But only because I don't want to give him any reason to hate you."

At least there's that.

She stops in front of a run-down cinder-block storefront with a blinking "TATTOO" sign in the window. The window and door are covered by thick metal bars on the outside and heavy black curtains on the inside.

It might be the most disreputable building I've ever stood in front of. Which is saying a lot for a kid who grew up as poor as I did.

"Last chance to back out," I tell her.

She opens the door and walks in like a queen visiting her subjects. No chance of talking sense into her now, so I follow her through.

CHAPTER 16

Bee

Does Taylor maybe, possibly have the tiniest point about how I should have made a plan before going in? Fine. Maybe. Just a small, tiny, minuscule point. But I could have thought and planned forever and never managed to find a tattoo worth getting. Best just to take the leap. Something will seem right in the moment. Hopefully.

The dinginess of the building's exterior did give me pause, but the interior is sparkling clean and well-lit. My worries instantly ease. Whoever is in charge of this place understands the importance of cleanliness in a tattoo shop. That seems like a good sign, at least.

A tall, beautiful woman with black hair and lipstick comes in from the back of the shop and stops mid-greeting, eyes darting between me and Taylor.

Maybe she's not used to having humans come in. Or maybe it's my fluttery pastel dress that's caught her off guard.

Whatever. I've taken the leap. Now I have to follow it through.

"I'm here for a tattoo."

"Right. Sure." She visibly works to collect herself. "We do

tattoos here. But . . ." Her eyes flick nervously to Taylor as she trails off.

"But what?"

Taylor clears his throat. "I think she's worried I'm forcing you to be here."

I turn to look at him, then back at her. "What do you mean? Why would anyone be forcing someone to get a tattoo?"

Now, Taylor is looking embarrassed. "It's not supposed to happen, but it does. There are some vampires who will . . . claim . . . humans."

"Claim them as what?"

He shrugs uncomfortably. "As property, I guess you would say. Or as blood slaves? For easy feeding. I hadn't thought about how it might look with the two of us coming in together."

I have to actually close my eyes to process this. "Hold up. You're saying that there are vampires out there who basically keep humans as pets—no, not pets, farm animals—and they might tattoo their human farm animals the same way we might brand cattle?" How have I never heard of anything like this before? I want to dissolve right here and seep into the linoleum from embarrassment at the way this woman is looking at me.

"For the record," she says, "we don't do that stuff here. Strictly aboveboard. But we do have to report any suspicious client activities."

"Like vampires and humans coming in together?"

"Like vampires and humans coming in together," she confirms. "The licensing bureau would be all over us if we let something like that happen."

I blink at her a few times, realize I'm staring, and force myself to look at Taylor instead.

"Well, what do we do now?"

He shrugs. "I guess that depends on how serious you are about this. I mean, Grey and I will probably both sleep better if you don't go through with it. Or, if it would help, I could stay out here. They probably have a back entrance they can sneak you out of if they decide I'm a danger to you."

A couple of things become suddenly, blindingly clear to me. First, this woman is legitimately worried about the danger Taylor presents to me. Second, Taylor has been confronted his whole life with people who see him as only a danger.

I face the woman and put on my best "mature adult who can make her own decisions" face.

"This guy is my roommate. He's not forcing me into anything, and if I need to sign something saying that, I will, but I'd like him to come with me. I trust him."

"You're sure?"

"Very sure," I promise.

She sighs and motions us through the door she first came through.

The room is just as spotlessly clean as the entrance was, which I think is another good sign. It seems a little presumptuous to make myself comfortable on the fancy-looking massage table in the middle of the room, so I opt to stand and take in the artwork covering the walls, a mix of finished tattoos and illustrations on paper. I'm about to ask if I can choose any of these pieces of art or if I have to come up with my own tattoo idea on the spot when one of the illustrations stops me in my tracks. Purple flowers, wilting, but instead of the petals falling, they turn into butterflies and fly away across the page. I'm not sure why, but it calls to me in a way none of the others do.

I can't look away, even to talk to the woman who led us back here.

"Can I get this? Is that allowed?" I ask without turning my head.

Taylor steps up beside me on the left, and the woman stands to my right.

"I can't think why not," she says. "I just drew it as practice, you know. It doesn't have any deep meaning for me as an artist, in case that's what you're hoping."

I smile. "I guess that means you drew it for me without realizing it."

CHAPTER 17

Taylor

"**D**oes it hurt?"

"No." Bee hastily lowers her hand and gives me a guilty look.

"Itch?"

"No."

I raise an eyebrow at her, hoping to coax out more than one syllable. One-syllable communication is usually my thing, not hers. It feels weird to have her so in her head like this.

"It's just new, okay? I'm still getting used to it."

I give a congenial hum. Yes, part of me is freaking out about the verified fact that Grey is going to blame me for this and come after me as soon as he finds out I'm the one who enabled it. Part of me is downright giddy that Bee invited me along. Not only did she let me tag along to the tattoo shop, but she also brought me in and let me be in the room while she was getting it done. Those are not the actions of a person who brings you with them out of a sense of obligation. Whatever else I might be to this girl, I'm someone she trusts. Maybe even cares about. So I'm letting my guard down. Maybe even teasing her a little bit. And I don't think she minds.

"Okay, I'm freaking the fuck out," she concedes, scratching at her abdomen, then wincing when she remembers that won't make her tattoo magically disappear. "Gloria will be fine. She'll probably even understand why I did it. But Grey is going to lose his shit, and then he might tell his parents, who will lose their shit times two, and then they're going to drag me back home and have a security detail on my ass for the rest of my life. What was I thinking? How could you have let me do this? Aren't you supposed to be the voice of reason in our current living arrangement?"

I pull her to a stop and make her face me. "Bee. Bethany. I would middle-name you, but I don't know it. I need you to calm down. In just the past day, I've seen you get a tattoo, and I've heard you cuss more times than the entire rest of the time I've known you, and you've told me more about your sex life than I ever expected to know. I'd like to think we're becoming friends, which means you can talk to me. Please, can you calm down for me right now and tell me what the actual issue is?"

She gapes at me with wild eyes, staring around us without actually seeing anything.

"I got a tattoo today."

"Yes, you did."

She gulps. "And I paid for it with my credit card."

I nod. These are known facts.

"My parents are going to see this on the credit card statement. My dad, I mean . . ." She shakes her head to clear it before answering. "My dad is going to see this on my credit card statement."

Bee covers her mouth, but it doesn't stop the rattling sob from escaping.

"Okay, believe me when I tell you I understand about unsupportive families," I try to comfort her, "but that doesn't mean we curl into the fetal position and pretend nothing is happening."

"No, it's not that." She shakes her head again. "Or it's not only that. I mean, he is supportive. They are supportive. Just in their own way, which doesn't happen to be very understanding of me stepping outside of the very pretty vase on the nice tall shelf they've put me in, and if they think I've gotten out of hand, they'll have Grey drag me back home, and I'll never experience anything again in my life. How could I be so stupid? What was I thinking, putting it on the credit card when I know they're going to see the statement at the end of the month—and that's if they don't check it before then?"

Giving her a little shake, I look her straight in the eyes. "Bee. Breathe. In. Good. Now, out." She follows my instructions, and her heartbeat almost immediately begins to slow. "Good. Let's do another one. In. Hold it. Okay, now, let it out. A couple things. Grey isn't going to take you back home, because that was part of the agreement I remember him making last year with his father or pack leader or whoever he talked to. Isn't that right? I remember you sending him back to negotiate because you weren't willing to go back, so he's not going to try to take you back now. Besides that, I'm also not going to let anyone take you where you don't want to go. I may not have any powerful family members to ask for help, but if it really comes down to it, I can find a basement to hide you in until any danger has passed. Do you trust me?"

She gives a dazed nod.

"Good." It feels better than it should, this level of trust. I'm not sure I deserve it, but I'll try to live up to it. "So, what you said about the vase. Is that why you chose that tattoo?"

Bee absently rubs her fingertips across her abdomen again. "Yeah. I guess that's why it kind of spoke to me. I probably should have planned something beforehand, but I didn't, and then that picture seemed too perfect to ignore. Like it was meant for me or something."

"Okay then. It was meant to be. No one can argue with

that." And I mean that completely, and I'll defend it even if—when—Grey tries to kill me for my part in this.

I hate to leave Bee when she's still freaking out about the tattoo, but my phone buzzes with a message that I can't ignore.

Mom: I ran out of blood.

How? It's supposed to be delivered twice a week. Unless something happened to require extra blood for her to heal, like going outside at midday, which she has never done in nineteen years as far as I know, the Blood Assistance Program should be delivering an ample supply for her.

I give Bee an apologetic look.

"I will be back, but I'm going to have to run home and deal with something tonight," I say.

She looks curious but doesn't ask any follow-up questions, which I'm thankful for. At least she seems calmer than before. I don't know what I'll do when there's an emergency with my mom and my roommates at the same time, but I don't have to face that issue today.

Mom is sitting in her usual place—her nest in the living room—when I come in.

Instead of greeting me, she gives me a confused look. She's burrowed into a pile of at least three blankets with her feet tucked up on the armchair, so she looks more like a heap of blankets with a head perched on top than a woman.

I hold out a blood bag for her, and she stares at it in blank confusion before looking up at me.

"What's that?" Her voice is dull. The only emotion I can detect from her is a hint of suspicion.

"You told me you ran out of blood, so I brought you some blood," I explain.

She looks at the blood bag again, eyes narrowing. "How do I know it's safe?"

I drop my hand with a sigh. She's cycled through this stage of her mental illness more than ten times since I've been old enough to be her main caregiver.

Well, old enough is a relative thing. I've been taking care of her since I was seven. That's when I was old enough to realize someone needed to take care of her. Since then, she's gone through one of these low periods at least once a year.

I check in the fridge beside her chair to find that, yes, it is completely empty.

"What happened to the blood, Mom?" I ask.

A shifty look from her, but no answer.

"Mom? Did someone deliver your blood this week?"

"It wasn't safe. I could tell without even opening the bags they weren't safe, so I threw them away."

I drop into the other armchair with a thud, too tired to stay standing and also deal with this. "You threw away all of the blood bags? The entire delivery?"

"Didn't you hear me?" Anger tinges her voice. "They were all bad."

"Okay," I placate her. "If you say they were bad, I guess they were bad."

It would be nice if she could take care of herself well enough to call the BAP and ask for a replacement delivery, but that's never been within her abilities.

Opening the nozzle on the bag in my hand, I hold it out to her again. "Here, you should try feeding. This is the blood I brought from school. It's safe. I know because I had a bag right before I got here."

She thinks about it for a long moment, staring at the bag like she might be able to see the poison or bacteria or whatever it is she's afraid of this time. When I'm about to give up and drink it myself, she leans forward and lets me bring the nozzle to her lips. Once she starts, vampire instincts take over, and she frees her hands from the blanket pile to hold the bag herself. I hurry to pull out another blood bag from my backpack, which she takes and finishes even faster than the first. Glad I came prepared, I hand her a third bag as soon as the second is done. If she's able to drink three in a row this quickly, it probably means she's gone a couple of days without feeding. Which means I need to call the BAP for her and have them make sure she isn't just tossing the blood in the trash as soon as it's delivered. And if they can't make sure she's feeding, I guess I'll be coming home more often. Being back here for an extra night makes me want to grind my teeth to dust. The thought of having to be back here full-time . . . no, I'm not even willing to think about that. I have to find a better solution.

CHAPTER 18

Bee

Ceallach finds me before class this time, while I'm sitting in the student union and trying to enjoy my drink in peace before the torture that is chem lecture.

"Well? Have you been practicing?" he asks without preamble as he drops into the seat beside me.

"Practicing what?" I'm sure that doesn't come out as casually as I'd like, but come on. Last time I saw him, he was talking about superpowers and mind reading. How am I supposed to react?

He smiles indulgently. "You know what. Your fae gifts. If you don't practice, you'll never get control of them."

"Look, I don't know what you're talking about. I don't know anything about fae gifts or fae anything. I'm human, so even if I did believe whatever fairy tales you're trying to tell me, I wouldn't have a place in them."

Ceallach looks annoyed at that but doesn't give up. "Bee, I don't know who told you that you're human. Probably the same person who's been hiding you from us for almost twenty years. Don't you want to know the truth of who you are?"

"Fairies. Aren't. Real," I say. And if someone has been lying to me about being human my whole life, I'm pretty sure I know who it is, and I'm not ready to face that. My parents have been difficult and overprotective and oblivious to every problem I encountered growing up, but I've never thought they were liars.

Ceallach grabs my wrist, and heat flows into my arm at the touch. Not the comfortable heat of skin-to-skin contact, though. I feel like my skin is burning where his fingers are pressing into it.

"Ouch! What the—"

"I'm sorry, but I need to make you see," he says, and the world around us drops away.

Instead of the coffee shop, there are suddenly towering trees all around me and grass underfoot. The chair I was sitting on is a moss-covered rock now.

And Ceallach has changed too. Instead of nondescript jeans and a solid-colored top, he's dressed in what looks like a combination of linen, grass, and flowers. His skin has an iridescent quality, like an oil slick leaving trails of rainbow as he moves.

Oh. And he has wings. Translucent, sparkling, dragonfly wings that stretch out several feet on either side.

I have enough time to swallow, take a breath, and mentally deny everything I'm seeing, and then the world I know reemerges around me.

Coffee shop. Chairs. College students. Everything back to normal, except me, sitting there with my mouth hanging open.

Ceallach lets go of me and sits back with a smug smile.

"We didn't really go," I hear him through a haze and a buzzing in my ears. "That was just a bit of a glamour to show you what's possible. So, now that you believe me, let's start practicing."

My throat is coated in rust when I try to speak. "What . . . How . . ."

He huffs out an annoyed breath. "Bee, you're half fae, which means that you were born with certain gifts. The fact that someone hid that from you—hid *us* from you—doesn't change what you are. Let me help you. Let me teach you."

Too many thoughts are crashing together right now for me to make sense of any of them. There's the thought about the impossible thing I just saw, and the thought about how accepting any part of this story means accepting that my life has been built on lies, and the thought that I don't know this man, and I don't know how he's tricking me, but it has to be a trick because his explanation is impossible.

I jerk up out of my chair, only remembering to grab my bag by instinct. "I have to go," I tell him, or maybe myself. "I have classes. And . . ." I try to think through the hum of conflicting thoughts. "I just have to go."

"I'll be here when you're ready for my help," he calls after me. "It would be best if we didn't wait too long, though, because Grandmother is impatient to meet you."

CHAPTER 19

Bee

I t takes a full day and one long, sleepless night before I've wrangled my thoughts into an explanation that involves some kind of hypnosis combined with too much caffeine in my drink. I manage to get through my classes, but I haven't retained anything. Right now, I'm running on adrenaline and lack of sleep.

"Hey, what are your plans for the rest of the day?" I ask Taylor, partly because I want to know and partly because I'm desperate to get away from my own drama.

He looks at me askance. "Please don't tell me you've got another bucket list item to cross off. Wasn't the tattoo enough for, like, a week at least?"

Well, no, because now I'm still buzzing a bit from . . . whatever it was that happened with Ceallach. I don't really want to deal with that right now, so I'm looking for anything that will keep my mind off fairies and lying parents and hallucinations.

"Nope. There are too many things I need to cross off the list. I need to get to work if I'm going to do everything I want to."

A surprisingly high-pitched whine for such a large man escapes his throat.

"Bee, your brother is already going to kill me when he finds out about the tattoo. If you really need to do something rebellious right now, how about going to bed and taking a very rebellious nap. Or reorganize your closet. Nothing says big changes like closet reorganization."

"My closet is exactly as organized as I need it to be, and there is no possible way I could sleep right now. This is for your own good too, you know."

Taylor is a very quiet guy, but he can be extremely expressive. Right now, the tilt of his head and the quirk of his eyebrows are radiating skepticism.

"It's true! Don't think for a second that I haven't noticed how you stay holed up in your room most of the time. You need to get out and live a little."

"One, I'm a vampire. By many definitions, I'm not alive anyway." He ticks off one finger. "Two, I realize this doesn't make a difference in everyone's world, but it is a weekday, and I've got an early class tomorrow, and assignments, and studying. Three, I can't afford to go out anywhere, and don't you dare offer to pay my way because that's not how friendships work."

I glare at the three fingers he's still holding up, then hold up my own first finger. "One, I don't care about any technical definitions of being alive or not. You're my friend, and I want to see you living your life. Two, you're right. It doesn't matter that it's a weekday or that you have an early class. As long as you can stay awake enough to fake your way through tomorrow, you'll survive having one late night. Three, we can find something to do that doesn't cost money." I can see he's about to argue, so I hold up a fourth finger and wave my hand in his face. "Four, aren't you worried about me going somewhere without you and getting hurt while you were busy doing something else?"

I can almost see steam coming out of his ears. "That's not fair."

"Who said anything about fair? I learned to fight dirty a long time ago."

Taylor visibly slumps, and I feel bad for him. But not bad enough to overcome this buzzing need to move and do and act that's taken over my body.

"What do you have in mind?"

"The time has come," I tell him with a grin, "for me to lose my virginity."

CHAPTER 20

Bee

I t takes a few hours to convince Taylor that this is a good idea, then dress him in something acceptable for a party—it turns out, the man literally owns less than ten shirts—then dress myself in something acceptable for a party. Okay, that last one was the real culprit, but it's not easy to choose an outfit to lose your virginity in. Especially when your whole wardrobe is "cute good girl" when what you want to project is "sexy and confident." I settled on a dress with a sweetheart neckline that makes my chest look curvier than it is and a strawberry print. It's still more cutesy than I'd like, but at least it's not pastel like so many of my other dresses.

Taylor tugs at the hem of his shirt, and I smack his hand to make him stop.

"You look fine," I say. "Actually, you look great."

"I look like I'm wearing a shirt that's too small for me," he argues.

"It's not too small. It's just more fitted than you're used to."

And Grey is, admittedly, quite a bit smaller than Taylor. None of Taylor's shirts look like something you would wear to go out, though, and Grey's been keeping a few outfits at our house so he doesn't have to pack when he stays over. He'll never even know I borrowed his shirt for Taylor.

"Bee, are you really sure about this?"

I smile brightly. "Of course. Grey won't mind you wearing his shirt. He's got plenty."

Taylor scowls. "First, I don't think that's true at all. Second, that's not what I was asking, and you know it."

I'm spared having to answer by a shout to our left.

"What a small world!" Gabe jogs toward us with a grin on his face. "I take it you two needed a break from the grind of classes and homework?"

"More like we needed a break from oversexed wolf shifters," Taylor volunteers.

"That was going to be my next guess," Gabe laughs.

"And what about you?" I ask. "The horny wolves must be making things awkward at your house as much as ours."

He makes a put-upon face and sighs heavily. "When it's not Grey and Gloria, it's Jeff."

"What, still with the Lacey obsession?"

"It's either moaning about Lacey, or asking me to be his wingman, or trying to set me up with people. The man does not understand that not all of us are ready to settle down and start a family."

Taylor blinks a few times. "Wow. Yeah, I could see why you would need to get away for a bit."

"And I got lucky and ran into you two! What are the odds?"

"I don't know, but we'll count ourselves lucky," I say. "So, should we actually go in or just stand out here in front of the door?"

Gabe grins. "After you."

I'm hit with a bout of nerves as soon as the noise and the press of bodies at the party hit me. "I think I need a drink," I announce, and the guys help me navigate through the crowd to a cooler full of a sweet-smelling, purple drink.

Gabe dips a plastic cup in and hands it over to me before getting his own. He offers one to Taylor, who makes a comically horrified face at the very idea.

"So, aside from escaping from our roommates, what are we planning tonight?" Gabe has to shout to be heard.

"Well, I don't know about you two, but I'm looking for a hookup."

Gabe's eyebrows shoot up, and he gives Taylor some kind of significant look that I can't read before he turns back to me.

"Okay then. Let's find someone for you."

Poor Taylor has the same sour expression on his face that Grey gets every time he senses I'm going to ask for something he doesn't want to give me. At least Taylor is keeping his mouth shut about it. If I told Grey I wanted to find a hookup at a party, he would lose his shit and lock me in my room. Which is why I'm living with Taylor now instead of Grey.

"How about him?" I point to a somewhat rat-faced guy standing by the wall. I don't find him particularly attractive, but I at least don't find him intimidating.

Taylor's eyes bug out, and I can see a muscle working in his jaw, but he doesn't say anything.

"What about him?" Gabe asks, taking a sip of his drink.

"Do you think he would sleep with me?"

Gabe turns to me with an arched eyebrow. "You meant to ask that the other way around, right? Because you are so far out of his league, I would be surprised if you were willing to slum it like that for a night."

Oh. That wasn't where I expected him to go with that.

"Okay then. Not him. How about that guy by the keg?"

Swinging around to look, Gabe gives him a slow appraisal. This guy looks less like a rat, which is probably good, but he looks entirely douchey, which might hinder my enjoyment if I have a quick hookup with him.

"Taylor," Gabe murmurs, "wasn't that the asshole in our history class last year?"

Taylor's head jerks in surprise. "Oh shit. That's the 'are you aware' guy from our history class."

I look back and forth between my two friends. "I give up. What's an 'are you aware' guy?"

Gabe shakes his head and laughs. "He would constantly correct the professor during class, and he was wrong most of the time, but he couldn't just state his wrong opinion like a normal person. He had to preface every statement with 'are you aware,' and then he would spew the most unhinged conspiracy theory and refuse to listen when the professor let him know he was wrong."

Then Taylor jumps in. "Are you aware that there was a plot uncovered in 1923 to replace all of the royal families with bear shifters? Are you aware that the real reason the vampires lost the Civil War was that their president was on a ship that was secretly sunk without anyone knowing about it? Are you aware that World War II was actually funded entirely by soy farmers who wanted to create scarcity, thus driving up the prices of their crops?"

I narrow my eyes at him. "You had to have made all of those up. No one would ever believe any of that."

Taylor stares me down. "Maybe I made one of them up. But two are actual quotes that I remember him saying. And I'm not telling you which one is made up."

"Okay," I agree. "Definitely not that guy. So, who would you suggest?"

Taylor and Gabe seem to take their task seriously, scanning the crowded room together without speaking.

Taylor speaks first. "Okay, I want it on the record that I

hate this plan. But if I have to choose someone, it has to be him." He jabs his finger toward the living room window.

The guy standing there is human, if I had to guess. He's handsome enough, I suppose. At least, his features are symmetrical and proportionate. He's taller than me, I can tell from here, but most people are. It's not like his height would be a deal breaker either way.

"Okay. That guy," I agree. No time like the present, I think, throwing back the rest of my drink and walking over to him.

His face lights up when he notices me. That's a good sign, right?

"Hey, can I get you a—"

I cut him off with an impatient wave of my hand. "You don't need to get me anything. You want to come back to my place?"

He chokes on air and starts gasping for breath and coughing.

After taking what feels like an age to get his coughing fit under control, he repeats, "What do you mean, come back to my place?"

I'm not sure how I thought this would go, but explaining this to him wasn't what I expected.

"I mean . . . my place has a room . . . that we could go into . . . to be alone?"

"Oh. Right. I would definitely like to go someplace to be alone with you."

"Okay then. Sounds good." Things are looking up again. I love it when I make quick progress like this.

He glances around the room. "You know, we don't actually have to go someplace else. Why don't we find a private place right here?"

On one hand, this appeals to my sense of urgency. On the other hand, my own room is my comfort zone. Shouldn't my first time be somewhere I'm familiar with? But, on the other other hand, there's a chance Grey is back at the house. That decides it.

"Lead the way," I tell him.

He takes my hand and tugs me around a corner and through a side door I hadn't noticed before.

"What is this place?" I'm completely distracted by our change of scenery. We're hemmed in on all sides by high walls covered in climbing vines that muffle the noise from the party. No lights from the house bleed out, so this tiny garden is lit exclusively by the moon and stars. If it weren't a clear night, I wouldn't be able to see at all.

"Pretty great, isn't it?" the guy—maybe I should have asked for a name before following him out here—asks breathlessly.

"Yeah, but how do you even know about this place?"

He smiles down at me. "I've been to a few parties at this house. But you are by far the most beautiful girl I've seen at one of these parties. I can hardly believe someone like you would . . . Actually, I'm not going to finish that thought. I'm just going to count myself lucky to be here with you."

Right. Reality smashes through the calm I was feeling from this perfect moonlit garden. I came here with a purpose. Here we go.

I take a deep breath and grab the front of his shirt to pull him close enough to kiss.

My first kiss.

This will be fine.

My stomach is doing backflips in a bad way that would normally signal my last meal to repeat on me.

But this will be fine. It's time.

But then my hand is empty, and the male body in front of me is gone, and the peace of the garden is shredded by shouting and movement.

"What the fuck?" My almost hookup is shouting.

At the same time, Taylor—with his arms wrapped tightly around the poor guy like a boa constrictor—is shouting something about being sorry. He doesn't sound very sorry at all.

And then there's Gabe, standing in the still-open doorway with his hand over his mouth in what looks suspiciously like an attempt at not laughing.

"Let him go!" I shout, tugging ineffectually at Taylor's forearm.

He glares down at me for a beat before seeming to realize what he's doing. He steps away with a jerk.

I try to form an apology, but none of these men are able to listen to reason right now. Gabe is the most clearheaded, and the asshole is definitely hiding a snicker behind his hand.

Gabe waves over the other guy. "Here, I'll get you something to drink, and you can complain about it to me. Those two have some things to figure out."

And what the damn hell does he mean by that?

It doesn't matter because my nameless almost hookup takes him up on the offer with barely a glance back at me.

Taylor's still standing a few feet from me, where he first stepped back and let the other guy go. Everything in his body language shouts shame and regret, which would mean a lot more if I weren't so fucking pissed right now.

"What the hell do you think you're doing?" I explode at him as soon as the door closes, leaving us alone.

CHAPTER 21

Taylor

Bee is right. What the hell do I think I'm doing? Not only do I have no right to police what Bee does, but she was doing it off my instructions. Who the hell do I think I am to push her toward the guy and then pull him off her like he wasn't doing exactly what I wanted to?

"I didn't mean to! I just . . ."

She cocks an eyebrow, probably as curious as I am to see where I'm going with this argument.

"I just couldn't stand thinking about him . . . touching you."

She adds crossed arms to her look of annoyance and disbelief. "You couldn't stand thinking about him touching me?"

It sounds even worse when she's repeating it back to me like that.

"I was worried he would hurt you."

"You were worried he would hurt me?"

No, I guess that doesn't hold up either.

"Just trying to get this all sorted out in my head," she continues. "You—a vampire who is fully twice the size of some people at this party—sent me over to introduce myself to a man who you thought I might be interested in, and then you decided I shouldn't feel safe with him after all and dove in to protect me. From someone who is half your size. And human. Anything I'm missing from this story?"

I tug at my hair, wishing for any escape from this situation. "Look, I get why you're mad. Can we please just go home now? You can rip me a new asshole when we get back to the house."

"I won't need to rip you a new asshole because you already are the biggest asshole I've ever met," she growls at me before stalking away.

At least she's heading to the front door, so I follow.

"If you think you're walking home with me, you're delusional," she tells me when I get out to the front step.

"Bee, come on. You're going home. I'm going home. You really aren't going to let me walk with you?"

Her eyes narrow. If she were a wolf, I'm sure her hackles would be up, and she'd be growling at me, but Bee is a lot more subtle than any shifter I've met.

"Just because we're walking the same direction doesn't mean I'm willing to walk with you," she finally says in a prim voice that makes me want to tear all of my hair out by the roots. "If you come within twenty feet, I'll . . ."

I don't really want her to finish that thought, but my masochistic side has to know. "You'll what?"

Bee throws her hands in the air. "I don't know! Call Grey and tell him I need his protection after all? Move to a different house and not tell you the address? Just give me some space so I don't have to think up a punishment."

I step back and put my hands up to show that she wins. With a huff, she spins on her heel and starts walking home. Without a tape measure, it's not like I can tell exactly when she's twenty feet away, but I don't want to give her any excuses. Just to be safe, I let her get to the end of the block before I start trailing behind like the pathetic lost puppy I am.

When I get inside the house, I walk in on a shitstorm in progress.

"Why won't you just tell me where you were?" Grey is shouting while Gloria puts herself physically between the two siblings.

"Grey, she's allowed to go out without your permission. Remember how we talked about the fact that Bee doesn't need a chaperone all the time?"

"She needs someone to keep her safe!" Grey sees me and rounds on me. "And where have you been? I thought the whole point of you living here was to keep an eye on Bee when I can't. That means you need to actually be with Bee. Why did she come back alone tonight?"

I'm still thinking of a response when Bee surprises me by jumping to my defense. "Taylor was keeping me safe. We were at the same place. And he's an actual person, not just my bodyguard, so quit acting like he's let you down every time I have five minutes alone!"

Gloria is still standing between Grey and Bee, but the two have stepped closer and closer to each other as they shouted, so now Gloria is sandwiched tightly between them. This situation is only going to get worse unless someone does something to diffuse it.

"Bee," I ask tentatively, terrified that I'm about to have large parts of my body torn off and used as weapons against me, "do you want to go someplace else so I can explain what I was doing earlier?"

Gloria, thankfully, leaps at that opening. "Grey, how about you and I go somewhere else to cool off."

Grey and Bee take simultaneous angry breaths before stepping apart. Gloria takes Grey by the elbow and practically drags him into her room. Bee stretches to her full height—still barely reaching my chest—and walks to her own bedroom like she's royalty and she's decided to grant me an audience. It's a vast improvement over the brawl I was about to be in the middle of, so I'll count it as a win. But thinking about brawls reminds me of the one I started at that party not long ago. I can tell by the set of her shoulders that she's nowhere near forgiving me for that. I follow her with a mounting sense of dread.

CHAPTER 22

Bee

I f I weren't still so pissed off, I would have to feel bad for Taylor, who is hunched in on himself like he hopes I'll forget he's here if he makes himself small enough. Or maybe like he's afraid of breaking something by accident.

"You're as bad as Grey," I whisper shout at him as soon as the door is latched. "What the actual fuck were you thinking?"

He flinches when I cuss, which really makes me want to do it again. That will have to wait, though.

"I wasn't thinking, okay?" he admits. "I thought I was alright with you . . . going off like that . . . but then I saw you actually walking off with someone, and my brain stopped working. Next thing I knew, I'd followed you out there and pulled the guy off of you. Not my most shining moment, I realize, but it's not like I can take it back."

I take a long moment to try and figure out what's actually going on in his head.

If Ceallach's mind-reading trick is real, though, I don't seem to have the knack. All I can "hear" of Taylor's thoughts is the regret on his face and the apology on his lips. He seems genuine, but these kinds of actions are exactly why I'm not willing to live with Grey. I don't need some big brother protector watching over me every second.

"You're going to find a way to make it up to me."

He swallows audibly. "What do you mean by 'make it up'? Make what up?"

"I was supposed to be losing my virginity tonight, but you made sure that couldn't happen. You're going to make that up to me."

He shuffles his feet and stares down at the floor. "How?" he finally asks.

The answer becomes obvious to me before he finishes asking the question.

"You're going to do it."

"What?"

"You're going to take my virginity."

"What?" he repeats with a shout.

I have to shush him so Grey won't come in here on high alert.

"I said, since you wouldn't let someone else do it, you're going to take my virginity instead."

Taylor looks absolutely panicked. "No, I can't. We can't."

"Why not? You do find me attractive, right?" At least, I'm pretty sure I didn't make that part up.

"I . . . Yes, of course I find you attractive. But you know damn well that there's more to it than that. I could hurt you. I probably would hurt you, and I couldn't live with that."

Crossing my arms in front of me, I do my best to stare him down, but he doesn't budge or lower his eyes.

"Okay, I know there's"—I make sarcastic air quotes with my fingers—"'more to it than that,' but saying you'll hurt me is a bullshit excuse."

"No, it's not bullshit," he insists. "I could bite you in the heat of the moment." He holds up a finger to start a list of points. "I could get you pregnant and turn you by accident." He holds up another finger.

I cut him off before he can add to his list. "I could stick a gag in your mouth so you couldn't bite me. And obviously, we would use protection to prevent pregnancy."

"Bee, you're not taking this seriously. I can't take that risk, even if you're willing to."

I take a slow breath to get my thoughts in order again.

"Fine. I don't want to force you into anything, even if I could. But that means I'm finding someone else to do it."

Taylor groans and scrubs at his face.

"How serious are you about gagging me? Because that is absolutely the only way I would be able to trust myself not to bite you. And condoms. Every time we do anything. No exceptions. Vampire pregnancy is serious. It literally kills the mother, and I'm not willing to take that risk with you."

I can't help the grin that takes over my face. "Let's go shopping for condoms and a gag, then."

CHAPTER 23

Taylor

I try to keep my eyes in my head, even as I take in the massive store full of wall-to-wall sex toys. I had no idea a place like this existed, and I certainly have no idea where to look now that I'm here.

Bee seems less out of her element. Only slightly, though.

"Where do we even start?" She nudges me.

"I don't know. Should we ask someone?" The mere thought makes me want to bury myself in a deep hole with no marker for anyone to find me.

Bee squares her shoulders and walks up to the man sitting behind the register, reading a comic book and blowing giant bubbles with his bubblegum.

"Excuse me. Sir? Excuse me?"

He doesn't bother taking off his headphones, but he does look away from his book long enough to give Bee a lascivious once-over that has me seeing red. Just as my fist is about to cock back and slam into his nose, he jerks his chin to the far wall.

"First-timers should start there. All your basic stuff."

Is my "first-timer" status really that obvious, even to this creep in the sex toy shop?

Not a first-timer for much longer, I remind myself. Not that I could have forgotten. My stomach has been alternately flipping in panic and excitement since Bee set her little ultimatum. If I don't sleep with her, she'll find someone else to do it.

Bee grabs me by the hand—actually grabs me, the guy who is way too big and awkward and dangerous and worthless for her—and pulls me over to the supposed first-timer section.

And I don't recognize a single thing here.

No, that's not quite true. I recognize several things that are obviously meant to look phallic, but they don't look like . . . well, they sure don't look like me. They're arrayed in a rainbow of colors and vaguely organized by size. But the thing that has me scratching my head is that all of them are smaller than I expected. Even the biggest one is smaller than me.

"We don't need those." Bee jerks me out of my speculation and back to reality. "Come look at these."

While I'd found a wall full of silicone, she's found a wall of leather in every form I'd never imagined. Harnesses and leashes and everything I would expect to find in a pet store, though these are the wrong shape and size for any dog I've seen before.

"What about something like this?" she asks, pressing something into my hands.

"Huh?"

"Will you feel safe with this in your mouth?"

I look down for the first time and almost shriek and drop what I'm holding.

Leather straps cross at multiple points, with one buckle holding the whole thing together on one side and the other side balanced out by a thick leather rectangle and a rubbery ball. I'm not sure why I'm so surprised at Bee casually handing a leather gag to me like it's nothing. What's actually surprising to me is how my dick is coming to life in my jeans just from holding the damn thing in my hands.

"Yeah." I stop and clear some of the scratch from my throat. "This should do it."

Is it because I'm attracted to Bee already, so my body responds to everything she does? Or is my response to the gag itself? For some reason, the thought of having this pressed hard against my mouth is making me desperate to get back to the house to try it out.

Bee is just as eager. She doesn't give me any chance to check the price tag or try to argue about who should pay for it. Before I realize it, she's already paid and is carrying a discreet paper bag as we walk home through the tunnels.

"So, um, when should we . . ." she starts and trails off.

Is she really asking what I think she is? Bee has been the one in charge through all of this, and I'm coming to realize that's exactly how I like it.

I've spent my whole life taking care of Mom and trying to nudge her into taking care of herself. I like having someone else nudging me for once.

"What were you thinking?" I ask, partly because I really think it should be up to her and partly because I really don't want it to be up to me.

Bee hums something quiet and tuneless while she thinks. "I think we should do it the next time Gloria stays over with Grey. Best to get it over with."

Well, isn't that just heart-meltingly romantic? But it's way more than I ever dared hope for, so I won't complain.

CHAPTER 24

Bee

Taylor is giving me serious eyes again. Taylor is always way too serious, I've decided. Last year, I didn't think too hard about it because I figured we all had plenty of reasons to be serious. But then things got back to normal, and I thought everyone would lighten up a little. I know that I relaxed a lot after I stopped worrying about powerful vampires being after me. Taylor is just as serious as I remember him from the height of the danger, though. I'm beginning to think this is his natural state.

"Are you really sure about this?" he asks again.

I hate that I probably look like a spoiled brat when I roll my eyes at him, but I can't help it.

"I've been sure about this for two weeks now." And damn Grey and Gloria for choosing the past two weeks to finally get control of their hormones. It's been agony, waiting for this after I made the decision. Well, I'm not interested in waiting any longer.

"Gag now, or should we at least kiss first?"

Taylor's eyes bug out of his head. "Did you really just ask me that? And like that?"

"Yes. I've been waiting too long for this to wait anymore. Let's get it over with so I can say I've done it."

He takes a moment to have a whole conversation with himself that I'm not privy to. He'd better not be thinking up arguments to weasel out of this, or I might just have to practice my purple nurple skills on a vampire.

"Gag now," he finally tells me. "Better safe than sorry."

I search his eyes, trying to find what he's so afraid of. "You're really that worried about being able to control yourself?"

"I mean, I wouldn't be the first vampire to accidentally hurt someone during . . ."

Pressing my hand to the center of his chest, I step in closer to him. "I know you're worried," I whisper, "but I'm not. I trust you."

A shiver runs through him, and he drops his gaze. "I wish I had your confidence. Will you put the gag on for me?"

"Yeah. I can do that."

My fingers tremble a little as I fasten, then adjust the straps around his head, but a few nerves are normal in a situation like this, right? This will be the last day I can claim to be a virgin. My stomach does a nervous-excited flip. Who knows? Maybe today will be the last day I can say I've never had an orgasm. It will be nice to know what all the fuss is about.

Taylor is sitting on the edge of my bed, where I made him sit so I could put the gag on, his spine still ramrod straight and all of his muscles tensed.

Here I go, I think, before straddling his legs.

"Is this okay?" I ask with my fingers poised over the top button of his shirt. Maybe it was a mistake to gag him before we started. It's not like he can tell me if I do something wrong. But it's not like I have the power to force him to do anything he doesn't want to do. Still, I wait until he nods before I actually start undoing the buttons.

It's hard to tell for sure. The difference is subtle, but I think I see something change in his eyes. Instead of looking worried and somber, I could almost swear he looks . . . smoldering? His dark eyes are like two hot coals on my face as I push his shirt down until his arms are free.

Or maybe all of that heat is just coming from my own cheeks, which could literally be on fire, and they wouldn't feel any hotter than this.

"You could touch me, you know," I say. "Only if you want to, though," I amend.

Heat flares in his eyes, and I'm sure I'm not imagining things now. With utmost care, he brings his hands up and strokes them up and down my back. I almost think I hear a whisper—or some kind of ripple—in the back of my mind when his finger brushes the skin of my neck, just above my collar. Like catching a glimpse of a fish after it dives back beneath the surface. Or maybe I'm just imagining things.

Each of his hands reaches almost all the way across my back from his palm to his fingertip. That reminder of his size gives me second thoughts, if I'm being completely honest. And there's another reminder of his size, giving me even more second thoughts as it juts up against me. But I've been told that my body is meant to stretch to accommodate large objects, so this should be fine.

Taylor sucks in a sharp breath through his nose when I peel my own shirt off, which makes me wonder about whether vampires actually need to breathe after all, and that thankfully distracts me from thinking too hard about the massive appendage between us.

Nope. Not thinking about that at all. It is not even slightly terrifying that he'll be able to rearrange my organs from inside my body with that thing.

It does feel good pressed against the seam of my pants, at least. I give an experimental rock of my hips and feel what could almost be an electric current zip through some deep part of my belly. Taylor's hands clench reflexively against my back, then go back to their slow stroking. Did I really think his eyes were smoldering coals before? Now they're molten lava.

I take one of his hands and slide it up to cover my breast through my bra, and his head rolls back in what I would think was agony if I hadn't seen those smoldering eyes. With a groan, he uses one hand against my ass to hold me close while he continues to palm me through my bra. I've always felt a bit self-conscious about my small breasts, but Taylor doesn't seem to mind at all, even though the palm of his hand is barely full from what I have to offer.

We both move our hips at the same time and instinctively find a rhythm that seems to suit both of us. For the first time in my life, I feel a heat and a tightening in my abdomen, like an elastic band being stretched to its limit, or maybe like a segment of bubble wrap with a thumb pressing down.

Is this . . . am I actually—finally—going to come?

Suddenly, Taylor lets out a sound like a protest and grabs my hips to hold me still. I could almost swear I hear an echo of, *No, no, no, not yet*, in my head. A spasm racks his whole body, and he meets my eyes with a look of horror. It's not until I feel the dampness seeping through his pants to mine that I realize what just happened.

"You came? Already?" I can hear the accusation, annoyance, and disbelief all jumbled together in my voice, but I can't help it.

He nods slowly. I can practically hear the apology his eyes are giving me, but that doesn't help me much, does it? That stretched-elastic feeling has snapped, the sensation gone so fast I'm not sure I'll ever get it back.

I stand up and step away from him. "I guess you'd better go get cleaned up," I tell him.

He doesn't argue. With shoulders slumped and the gag still covering his mouth, he shuffles out of my room and leaves me more frustrated than I ever thought I could be.

CHAPTER 25

Taylor

Fuck! That did not just happen. That could not have just happened to me!

The sticky mess in my pants tells me otherwise.

Motherfucking gods damned piece of shit!

I whip off the gag and throw it across my room, then immediately regret it because I want to scream, and it might have muffled the sound.

How is my self-control so bad that I come in my pants at the first chance I might lose my virginity? How did I so thoroughly cockblock myself before I even felt under her bra?

But fuck, it had felt too good, the way I could feel Bee's heat against me as she rode me. And the way I could smell her arousal. I never would have guessed how sexy that would be, to smell someone getting wet and to know it was for me.

Too bad my body decided to revert to its teenage state of constant horniness and zero control. By the time I realized I was about to come, it was too late to slow down or stop it.

I am never going to have another chance with her. No way in any reality is she going to try anything with me again after I embarrassed myself like that. I peel my soiled clothes away from my body with disgust. My come has already cooled to room temperature and started to dry, leaving me feeling itchy as well as slimy and sticky.

Oh, and humiliated. Can't forget that one. Most of what I'm feeling right now, in fact, is abject humiliation. I want so badly to crawl inside of myself and never come out again. With rough, punishing motions, I use my pants as a rag to clean the rest of my spunk from my skin and throw them in my hamper. Belatedly, I realize my shirt is still in Bee's room. I guess I'm down a shirt now because I'm going to do my best to never have to look Bee in the eye again.

Yeah. That's probably the only way I'll survive this. I have to avoid Bee at all costs until she forgets that I exist, and then, maybe, my humiliation will be over.

After getting dressed, I pack up my dirty laundry in one bag and my clean clothes in another and slip out of the house to go back to my mother's house with my tail tucked between my legs.

Bee

Me: I need girl time. Right now.

Gloria: I'll be home in ten minutes. Are you okay?

Me: I will be if I can talk to someone.

Gloria: I'll hurry.

Thank fuck, Gloria actually turns up eight minutes after I texted her. Which was five minutes after I heard Taylor leave the house. Which was twelve minutes after our ill-fated attempt at sex. Which means I've been spiraling for twenty-five minutes now.

And I'm convinced the whole house still smells like sex. Or

—more accurately—the whole house smells like his come. And wolf shifters have acute senses of smell.

"Whoa. What happened in here?" Gloria asks the instant she's through the door.

"Nothing." I probably look guilty as fuck, the way I stopped my pacing and looked at her with deer-in-headlights eyes to say that. Whatever. I need to talk to her anyway, so the story is about to come out in all of its shameful glory.

"Okay, nothing happened in here," I amend. "It happened in there." I point to my bedroom door.

Her eyes get huge. Like dinner plates stuck to her face.

"You had sex?" She practically screams it, then sobers and draws back from me, looking me over. "Was it consensual? Are you okay? With who? Was *it* okay?"

I grab a chunk of her hair and pull to shut her up.

"I can't answer any of your questions if you keep asking them."

She looks abashed. "Right. Shutting up now."

I start talking, even as I drag her over to the couch. "Yes, it was consensual. Yes, I'm fine. I'm not telling you who. And *it* . . . didn't actually happen. Not really."

"What does that mean?"

I take a deep, fortifying breath. "It means . . . right when I thought things were starting to get good, he finished."

"He came early? And he didn't offer to . . . you know . . . put in the work, even though he'd already been paid?"

I stare at her in confusion. "What do you mean?"

Gloria, who is usually embarrassingly straightforward when talking about anything related to sex, turns bright pink. "I mean . . . ugh!" She flops backward on the couch and covers her face with her hands. "You're going to know I'm talking about your brother, and I know you don't want to hear about it, but it is what it is." She sits up again and gives a decisive nod. "A guy who's worth it will always make sure you come.

Even—no, especially—if he already came. He'll finger fuck you or eat you out or use your vibrator or something to make sure you finish too. I take it your guy didn't?"

"I . . . don't think I gave him the option." It's not like he could have eaten me out with the gag in his mouth, I don't tell her. And I don't have a vibrator. "I . . . might have kicked him out as soon as it happened."

Gloria cocks her head to the side and thinks. "Do you think you want to give him another chance?"

"I don't know. Do you think he would be willing to? I mean, it's not like I'd go back for round two of getting thrown out of someone's bedroom."

She shrugs. "Maybe he wants a shot at redemption. Guys always seem to want to prove themselves or something. He might want to prove to you that he can actually get the job done."

I slump down into the couch. "What if I'm not sure anyone can get the job done?"

Gloria bolts up again in shock. "Are you saying you've never even—"

"Finished? Orgasmed? Come? Yes. I'm seriously not even sure I can. I think my body is broken in that department."

"But . . . you grew up in a shifter pack. Wouldn't someone have given you a vibrator or a dildo or . . . a sex-positive talk about masturbation at some point?"

That actually makes me giggle before reality sets in on me.

"It's not like I ever went into heat, so I never had a First Heat Party like a wolf might. Besides, being raised by the pack leader? No one in the pack would have risked even trying to kiss me. And that was before Grey grew into his overprotective brother phase. So, no. Nobody gave me a vibrator or . . . any of that stuff." I feel embarrassed just saying it out loud.

"Wow." Gloria huffs a sigh. "Sorry. That's all I've got. I guess I shouldn't have assumed anything."

I wave that off. "It's not like I've taken out an ad saying, 'I'm a virgin who's never had an orgasm!' or anything like that. I mean, it's not like it's a vital part of life and I'm going to die from lack of sex, right? I just need to accept that sex is not for me, and orgasms are not something my body can do, and move on with my life. No big deal."

At that, Gloria looks sad. Sad bordering on pitying.

"Look, it's not that big of a deal," I promise her. "I get that sex is an important part of your life, but it doesn't have to be for everyone, okay?"

"But—" She gives me a *come on, humor me for a moment* look. "—sex is not for everyone. I get that. I understand—okay, at least in an intellectual way, since it's not my experience—that not everyone has any sexual desire or appetite. But I also know that you're looking all kinds of upset when you say that it can't happen for you, which I think means that you want it to happen for you. And—" She holds up a hand to hold off any potential arguments. "—you said it yourself just a couple minutes ago. You thought something was happening with that guy. Until he came early and you lost the moment, at least. Why shouldn't you try it again? With him or with someone else. You might get closer next time."

We both pause and think for a moment before she breaks the silence again.

"And whether you want to try with another person or not, I'm going to buy you a vibrator. Just because you don't go into heat doesn't mean you should miss out on important milestones."

The snicker I try to hold in at that comes out as a snort, which sets her off, and no serious conversation comes out for a long time.

Once our laughing fit wears off, I ask, "Can I show you something? But you have to promise not to freak out on me. And not to tell Grey. And not to lecture me."

Her brows wrinkle in confusion. "Yeah, of course. You can tell me anything."

I take a bracing breath and lift my shirt up to reveal the tattoo that stretches from one hip bone to the other. Neatly arranged purple flowers that are wilting, but as the petals fall, they turn into butterflies that fly away across my abdomen.

"What the f—"

"No freaking out," I remind her.

"Is that a tattoo? Did you actually get an actual tattoo on your actual body? Your dad is going to kill you. When did you do this? How did you do this without me noticing? Have I been oblivious? Oh my fucking moon goddess, I've been so wrapped up in my relationship that my best friend got a tattoo without me noticing."

"Remember the no-freaking-out thing?"

I'm not sure if she hears me over her hyperventilating.

"You said I could tell you anything and you wouldn't freak out."

"But I thought it would be more sex stuff! Not a secret tattoo! I'm comfortable with sex stuff. In fact, maybe we can go back to talking about the sex stuff."

I jab her hard in the shoulder. "Gloria! Calm down, okay? I know that most shifters see tattoos as a form of mutilation. I grew up with those lectures too, remember? But I'm not a shifter, and it's my body. I'm allowed to do what I want. And I think I'm in the clear anyway. If my parents were checking my credit card activity, they would have already seen it a couple weeks ago. I'm still alive, so I have to assume they didn't notice it."

She half laughs, half gasps. "You put it on your credit card? You want to get caught, don't you?"

I shrug. "When I first did it, I just wasn't thinking things through, okay? I was pissed off and frustrated and just . . . desperate to do something—anything—other than being the good girl who's so fragile everyone has to protect her all the time. But now, it's grown into something else. I mean, it definitely started out as a simple rebellious thing I could do, but now? I really love it. I love the way it looks in the mirror. I love the way my skin feels where the ink is. It's this whole part of me that I wouldn't give up for anything."

"That's . . . Okay then." Gloria looks a little dazed. "I guess, as long as you don't feel like you've mutilated yourself, I should stop thinking of it like that."

"You should definitely stop thinking of it like that," I promise her. "It feels good. Like artwork that I get to be a part of."

She gives an awkward smile. "Okay then. Sorry I freaked out after I promised I wouldn't."

"You're forgiven. If you buy me ice cream."

Gloria makes a sick face. Wolves don't like sweets the way I do. "Ice cream and a vibrator?" she asks.

"If you must. Let's go get some ice cream and a vibrator."

CHAPTER 27

Taylor

"Taylor? Is that you? I didn't think it was Friday yet."

The waver in my mom's voice crashes through me, reminding me why I wanted to get away so badly in the first place.

She's afraid when I'm here, but she hates it when I'm gone. There's no way to win.

I make myself as small as I can and tiptoe through the familiar maze of clutter to her nest in the living room. "I decided to come back a little early and check on you," I whisper.

Her face twists in a flash. "Making sure I stay in my place, right?" The fearful waver has been replaced entirely by something harsh and angry, dripping with venom. "Have to make sure I don't make trouble, don't you?"

I kneel down so she won't think I'm looming over her and tentatively take one of her hands. "I'm not trying to keep you here, Mom. I just wanted to make sure you're eating."

Without warning, her other hand snakes out, lightning fast, and lashes me across the cheek. I feel the burning trails left by her fingernails, but it's the surprise that hurts more. How am I still surprised when she turns like this? How can I still be surprised when it's happened so many times?

Backing carefully out of her reach, I stand up and turn toward the fridge. "When was the last time you fed?"

"I don't need that shit. They put poison in it, you know. The men who drop it off on Wednesdays? I've seen the way they look at me. They're looking for signs that their poison is working. Well, they won't get the satisfaction. I wait until the Sunday delivery. I only feed from the Sunday deliveries. That blood is safe."

I learned a long time ago that it does no good to try and reason with her when she's like this. This part of the conspiracy theory is new, though. I had instructed the Blood Assistance people to keep an eye on her and make sure she's not throwing the blood away immediately, but I guess she interpreted their interest through her twisted lens of paranoia, and this is what came out of it. Brilliant. Does that make it two or three weeks she's been going with only half her allotted blood bank rations?

Opening the fridge, I hold up a blood bag. "How about this one? Is it safe for you to drink?"

She narrows her eyes, then shakes her head. "I don't know which ones they poisoned. It could be all of them."

I sit on the floor and stare at the perfectly good bag of blood in my hands. "What if I drink this one?" I ask.

Her eyes widen in horror. "No, baby, you can't! It's dangerous!"

There she is again. The caring mommy. The one I'd always hoped for as a kid. Eventually, I learned that she never stays. Knowing that doesn't keep me from wanting her to.

I bite down on the corner of the bag. There's a nozzle on the other side, which I would normally use, but acting civilized right now won't get me what I want.

Mom shifts forward in her chair with a gasp. "No, don't! It might be poisoned!"

I ignore her warning and take a long sip before holding the torn corner of the bag toward her. "It tastes safe to me. Let's wait and see what it does to me, just to be sure."

Her eyes follow the bag as I wave it between us. Her pupils are dilated like a predator on the prowl. She licks her lips, still locked in on the blood bag that I purposefully opened wider than necessary. My nose prickles with awareness at the scent of blood wafting from the bag. If I were hungrier, I wouldn't be able to hold myself back from finishing the bag myself. Thankfully, her hunger wins out before I have to search for another plan. With a grunt of desperation, she snatches the bag from my hands and sucks hungrily at it until it's empty. I've already got a second bag open so I can test it for her by the time she's done with the first. This time, she doesn't protest, just takes the bag as soon as I've taken the first swallow from it.

CHAPTER 28

Taylor

Fact one: I finished way too early the first time I tried to have sex and am never going to have another chance to lose my virginity and have also probably ruined things with my housemates and can't face going back there when they're home. Or at least when Bee is home.

Fact two: My mom has been spiraling without me, and I can't safely leave her alone for the time being.

Fact three: If I can't leave this house, I can't go back to school, and I'm going to have to drop out and probably end up just like my mother.

Fact four: I really, desperately, don't want to end up like my mother, so I need to get out of this house again. Somehow.

I dial the number for the government-funded blood bank that's been delivering her blood for years. Of course, I end up on hold for almost an hour after navigating what seems like an endless maze of menu options. I'm about to give up when a woman's voice picks up.

"Thank-you-for-contacting-the-Blood-Assistance-Program-we-apologize-for-the-wait-this-call-may-be-moni-tored-how-may-I-assist-you-today?" She says it without pauses or inflections, so it takes me a moment to decipher what she's asking.

"My mother is convinced her blood is being poisoned and won't drink it unless she sees me doing it first," I explain, not sure what can be done but needing to unload some of this burden.

"I assure you, your blood has not been poisoned."

I press the heel of my hand into my forehead in a hopeless attempt to soothe the zap of irritation pulsing there.

"I know the blood isn't poisoned. It's my mom who thinks the blood is poisoned. And it doesn't work to tell her it's not poisoned because she just won't believe you. I need to know what I can do so she keeps feeding, even if I can't be here."

"How old was she when she turned?"

"Eighteen." She was only eighteen when she had me.

"So she's what doctors refer to as an ETV, an Early Turned Vampire. ETVs often present with health problems that regular vampires don't have to deal with, such as blood aversion, super-sensitivity, and paranoid delusions."

I grind my teeth. "I know all of that. What I'm saying is that it's gotten bad again, and I need help to make sure she doesn't starve herself every time I leave the house."

The pulse of irritation in my head has grown into a full-blown throb.

"Sir, I'm just giving you the information that we're required to share with every inquiry of this nature, if you would just let me finish."

I clench and unclench my fist ten times to calm myself down. "Fine. Go ahead and tell me more things I learned when I was a toddler."

I can hear her breath over the line. Human, then. Human and being paid to explain vampire problems to vampires. Perfect.

"As I was saying, ETVs are prone to health issues such as blood aversion and paranoid delusions. Sometimes, when an underdeveloped brain is turned, it results in ongoing mental health concerns that can affect the vampire for the rest of their life. The Blood Assistance Program does have a mental health outreach program, but I am afraid there is currently a waitlist to access those services. I would be happy to add you to that list today, or I can give you the names of some private organizations that offer similar services. Please be aware, not all of these services are covered by insurance. What would you like me to do for you today?"

Throb. Throb. Throb.

I'm pretty sure my head is going to explode from this conversation.

"She's already on the waitlist," I grind out because I can't seem to unclench my teeth. "She's been on the waitlist for twelve years now. I was hoping, considering her worsening condition, that it might be possible to move her up on the waitlist."

"I'm afraid we can't do that, sir," the woman on the other end of my phone says immediately. I notice she doesn't bother to say how sorry she is that she can't help me. They're probably trained not to make promises or apologies to people like me. It might be a liability or something.

I don't bother with continuing the conversation or saying a polite goodbye. What difference could it make? I hang up and sink down on my bed. My old bed. The one I thought I had gotten away from. But I'll be back here a lot more for the foreseeable future. Between trying to make it to classes and make it back here often enough to check on Mom, I probably won't be seeing either of my roommates much at all. Maybe that's for the best. If I never have to see Bee again, I'll never have the experience of dying from embarrassment right where I stand. Silver linings, or something like that.

CHAPTER 29

Bee

With a wink and a grin, Gloria pushes me and my shiny new vibrator toward my bedroom.

"I think that Grey might appreciate me staying with him for the next couple of nights," she tells me in a knowing voice. I guess that translates to, "Time for you to learn how to masturbate, Bee."

My cheeks have been flaming hot since we set foot in the store. I was worried the man at the counter would recognize me from my visit with Taylor, and I did not want to explain to Gloria the who or the why of that visit. Thankfully, Gloria is way too practical to get distracted by knowing looks from a cashier. Not to mention, she took the job of choosing "baby's first vibrator" way too seriously to even notice there were other people in the store.

Well, I might as well get down to it.

It takes more work than it should to get the damn thing out of its packaging, and then it takes time to wash it and charge it, of course, which leaves me at loose ends for a while. I stand in front of my full-length mirror and admire myself. Decorated like this, in clothes that I chose carefully to suit my body, I feel pretty. Maybe even beautiful, at least by some definitions. But I can't see myself as sexy. Cute? Absolutely. Like a little kid that everyone just wants to protect. Aesthetically pleasing? Absolutely. But I know I'm not sexy. I'm not the type of attractive that would make someone's mouth dry up or have them desperate to tear my clothes off like in an old-school bodice ripper.

But now that I'm thinking about it, the hunger in Taylor's eyes when I straddled him, the way he pressed me close against him and encouraged me to ride him, his look of misery when I told him to go, all point toward the same conclusion. Maybe at least one person thinks I'm sexy, not just cute.

I watch myself in the mirror as I strip off one piece of clothing after another, trying to catch a glimpse of what Taylor saw. I trace the flowers and butterflies fluttering across my belly and wonder what it might feel like to have someone trace them with their lips and tongue, rather than a finger.

No effect.

I can't picture it clearly enough, maybe. My brain refuses to be tricked into believing it's anything other than my own finger touching me.

The only person I can picture clearly is Taylor.

Taylor and the way his eyes stayed on me like I was a meal he was desperate to catch and eat. Taylor and the way his big body felt against my small one. Taylor and the way his eyelids drooped for a moment when I first put his hand on my breast. The shadow of his long lashes stark against his bloodless skin. The press of his erection against my clit through our clothes.

My body heats, feeling like a nuclear reactor at my core.

I hope the vibrator is charged now because this is the closest I've ever come to actually feeling anything at all when I've tried to pleasure myself. I don't look away from the mirror as I pull the toy from its charger, but then I hesitate, holding it at my entrance but not sure what to do next.

It's not a big toy. Gloria had taken one look at the wall of dildos marketed for "size queens" and dismissed them all with a roll of her eyes. "Maybe another day, if you want to try it, but size really isn't everything," she'd said.

Which is how I ended up with a two-pronged device that fits easily in my hand without any of it visible.

Gloria knows what she's doing, I reason, but at the same time, how can this little thing possibly do . . . anything?

If I stall any longer, the little bit of arousal I've worked up is going to disappear, though. I can already feel the heat dissipating.

With a silent little prayer to the sex gods, I stick the toy inside of myself.

And immediately regret it.

Why does it hurt? This isn't supposed to hurt, I'm sure of it. But it does. It feels like a thousand paper cuts inside my vaginal canal. With a moan, I pull the toy out. Thankfully, there's almost instant relief.

I inspect the traitorous little toy but don't see any blood. Judging by the sheen of moisture on the tip, I only got it an inch, maybe less, inside my body. If nothing else, I'm glad I didn't try something bigger. What is wrong with me that I can't even use a sex toy—a beginner-friendly sex toy—properly? I'm done trying, though. At least for today, and probably tomorrow.

I wash and dry the toy carefully before shoving it in the back of my sock drawer, still feeling weirdly betrayed by the object.

It's not like it's the vibrator's fault that I'm fucked-up.

I pace my room a few times but can't settle. I've got too much unspent energy bottled up. With a huff, I grab my purse and head outside. Maybe walking will clear my head.

I'm not sure where I'm headed until I find myself standing in front of the same tattoo shop where I got my butterflies. Finally, calm comes over me. Forget sex and orgasms that won't happen. Forget my overprotective family and my uncooperative body and guys claiming to be fairies. This is something I can control. This is something that can be all mine.

Brigitte, the same tattoo artist from before, comes to greet me when I come in. Her face flashes from startled recognition to genuine concern when she recognizes me.

"Is everything alright? Has it not been healing properly?"

"It's fine," I assure her. "Healed perfectly. Actually, I want another one."

Her eyebrows shoot up. "I mean, they're a bit addictive, in my experience, but usually my repeat customers wait more than a few weeks before asking for their second. Are you sure?"

"Very sure. Super sure. Desperately sure."

She crosses her arms and gives me a skeptical head-to-toe perusal. "But?"

I sigh. "But I have no idea what I want."

Relaxing with a laugh, she opens the door to the back and motions me through. "That isn't really a problem," she says. "You'd be amazed how many people come in with only a vague idea or no idea at all what they're going to get. As long as you're not impaired or coerced, I can work with you to figure out what you want."

She waits until I sit before she pulls her chair close and sits facing me. "So, you want a tattoo, but you're not sure what. Is there anything you're leaning toward, or maybe an image that keeps recurring in your life?"

I shake my head. "Not really. Unless you count . . ." I lift my shirt enough to show the first tattoo she gave me. "Unless you count this. But it would naturally still be fresh in my mind, right?"

"If it's the right tattoo, it will always feel fresh." She gives her handiwork an appraising look. "Would you want to do a continuation of what you already have?"

"Is that possible? I mean, wasn't the original art meant as a finished piece? It might feel wrong to add something on if it was already finished."

She smiles her understanding. "Tattoos go on living bodies. They're not meant to stay still the way a painting should. You can always add and develop the art as you add to your own life. Sometimes you grow out of a piece, and that's okay too. Tell me the first thing that pops into your head. What do you love about your tattoo?"

Easy. "The butterflies. The way they look beautiful on my skin and I can almost see their wings beating. But . . . I can't just get more butterflies. What would be the point?"

She leans back in her chair and thinks. "How do you feel about tarot?"

"What? Like, the cards?"

"The cards, yes, but also the concept. Some people are uncomfortable with the mystic arts, and I wouldn't want to suggest something you're not comfortable with. But if it's okay, I might have an idea for something we can try."

I wonder whether "fae gifts" fall under the heading of "mystic arts." If I'm going to entertain the possibility of one being real, I probably have to entertain the possibility of the other as well. "Sure." I shrug. "It doesn't make me uncomfortable. I'm not exactly a believer, if that makes a difference."

"I guess we'll find out," she says with a mysterious smile, standing up and pulling something wrapped in a colorful silk scarf from one of the shelves. "Here. Hold this. You don't need to untie the scarf or do anything particular. Just hold it and think about the butterflies in your tattoo. Can you do that?"

"Sure. Of course."

I sit there with the silk-wrapped parcel, which feels heavier and heavier in my hands. We sit there in silence until I can feel the heat from my fingers radiating back at me through the silk.

I'm about to hand the thing back to her and say it isn't working when she breaks our silence.

"Okay. Now, untie the silk and pick a card from the deck."

"Just . . . any card?"

"Whichever card feels like the right choice," she confirms placidly.

If nothing else, this will make for a fun story someday, I tell myself before following her instructions.

I'm not expecting much but decide I should give Ceallach's suggestion a try and reach out with my mind. There's nothing at first, but right when I'm telling myself to give up and grab the first card from the top, I feel heat pulsing from somewhere in the middle of the deck. Yes, odd, but I decide to trust my gut, which is telling me, *this one, here, pick this one.*

I'm a little shakier than I'd like to admit when I pull a card a third of the way from the top of the deck. "This one," I tell her through a scratchy voice and hold the card out to her.

"Turn it over so we can both see," she says.

The first thing I notice is a grinning skull. Yikes. Not what I was hoping for, if I was hoping for something.

She must recognize the look on my face because she jumps in to explain. "It's not a bad thing. This is Death, but it doesn't necessarily mean a literal death. This card indicates change. Yes, there might be an ending, but there always follows a new beginning. See this?" She points to the bottom of the card, where a man—a dead man, I realize—is lying in the grass. "This card reminds us that death comes for all of us, even vampires, though it usually takes longer, but we can choose how to face it. Or not, as the case may be. This dead man was a king. See the crown beside him? But death came for him anyway, and now he's the same as anyone else. And look at what Death is holding. Not a sword or a weapon, but a scythe. Death is a harvester, reminding us of the changing seasons. This reminds us that there's a season for growth and a season for death. Sometimes the fields are thick with living crops, but sometimes they're fallow. Each season has its time and its place in the order of things."

I look more closely at the card with fresh eyes. The skeleton is riding a white horse and wearing a black cape that swirls around the two of them. The skull's empty eye sockets could be looking at me or at someplace far over my shoulder.

Huh. Change.

"So, this card shows something dying to make way for something new, kind of like my butterflies, right?"

"Exactly like your butterflies," she confirms, and I can practically see a new piece of art forming in her eyes.

"Okay then. I guess I'd like something like this. Something that connects the changing butterflies to the change the card represents. Can you do that?"

"I can. If you're sure you're ready."

I smile, feeling a weight lift now that a choice has been made.

"I'm ready."

CHAPTER 30

Bee

I walk out of the tattoo shop in a daze a few hours later. When I first went in at dusk, the streets had a different quality than they do now, closing in on midnight. I might have to admit to Taylor and Grey that they were right about that.

No, I decide. I can admit to myself that they were right about it, but I'm not going to feed into their overprotective male egos by telling them.

But for now, I just have to get home safe.

I do my best to walk faster while still looking like I'm just out for a casual stroll and ignoring the prickly feeling that someone is watching me.

Don't turn around. Don't turn around. If there's someone there, you don't want them to know you've noticed them.

The sidewalk is crowded with buskers and college students and vampires going about their business. It's not like I would be able to pick someone out from the crowd and know they were watching me.

It's almost definitely all in my head anyway.

Weaving through the throng, I pick up my pace a little

more. I'm not running. Just walking fast. Nothing interesting to see. No reason for anyone to notice me.

I breathe a sigh of relief when I get away from the busy strip and turn into my now familiar neighborhood. I'm almost home. My nerves were for nothing.

It's not until I reach my own street, only a few blocks from my home, that I realize I hear someone else's footsteps behind me.

Forgetting my earlier decision to keep moving forward and pretend I don't notice them, I whirl around to see who's there.

Ceallach stops walking and gives me a friendly smile and wave. "I was wondering when you would turn around. I ended up having to take heavier steps to make sure you heard me."

There's laughter in his voice and his eyes, but something feels off about this. What's he doing here? And why is he following me? My guts are twisting in fear as I calculate how far it is to my front door and how fast I'll have to run to get away from him.

"I'm not here to hurt you," he tells me.

I don't bother telling him that anyone could say that and not mean it. I inch my foot backward, all of my instincts clamoring to put as much space as possible between myself and him.

"I get it." He actually does laugh this time, the asshole. "You're smart not to trust me. But I truly intend you no harm."

"Then what do you want?"

"I want to give you a message, from your grandmother."

My foot freezes mid-step. There he goes with the grandmother thing again. None of my grandparents are still alive. My birth parents died without telling anyone where they came from, my father's parents died before I was born, and my mother left her parents behind when she changed packs. She never talks about them. Whatever grandmother Ceallach thinks he knows, there's no way this is good news.

"Who are you, really?" My voice comes out in a rasp.

"I'm your cousin." He grins at me. "Well, more or less. It's a little more complicated than that, but cousin works for our purposes."

I take another cautious step backward, praying I don't trip on any broken sidewalk. He doesn't come closer, so I take another step back. Maybe if he keeps standing there and talking, I can put enough distance between us that I'll be able to make a break for it.

Poor odds, but I've got no other hope.

"What, you're not even going to ask me about the message?"

I save my energy. I'm pretty sure he'll tell me what he wants to tell me, no matter what I say.

"You're out of time. She wants to meet you." He seems to sober up as he speaks. This part isn't a joke to him. "She thought you were gone, otherwise she would have looked for you sooner, but now she knows where you are, and she wants to finally meet you."

Too bad for her, I think.

"You don't have to give an answer," he continues. "Now that she's found you, she'll find you again."

I'm about to tell him to tell her not to bother, but he grins and disappears before I get the chance.

He actually disappeared.

No theatrics. No puff of smoke. He was there, and then the night air took his place, and he wasn't there anymore.

What. The. Fuck.

My brain feels like syrup or molasses or . . . something gooey and sticky. I shake my head to try and clear it. I'm afraid to think about how he does things like disappear or turn a coffee shop into a forest. If I think about it, I might end up believing in fae gifts and fairy grandmothers. I finally unstick myself from the sidewalk and dash into my house. It's only after I'm leaning against my front door, trying to get my racing heart under control, that the oh-so-comforting thought that someone who can disappear into thin air can probably reappear anywhere else just as easily pops into my head.

CHAPTER 31

Taylor

My plans to avoid the house and avoid Bee and avoid all of my problems are crushed less than twelve hours later.

In my desperation to get away quickly, I grabbed clothes but forgot my laptop, books, and every single item I might have needed to complete my assignments.

But it's early. Maybe because it's early, and if I'm quiet enough, I can sneak in and out without having to face Bee.

Mom is asleep in her nest chair when I leave, and I was able to convince her to feed again last night, so she should be okay on her own for a bit while I go back to school and sort out my life.

"Oh my god, thank fuck it's you!" Bee slams into me about three seconds after I cross the threshold. So much for sneaking in unnoticed.

"Er. Is there someone else you thought it might be?"

My mind is racing. Why is she scared? Why is she hugging me? Does this mean she's forgiven me for the disaster yesterday? Is it possible she's forgotten?

"There was this thing last night with this guy I know

following me home, and he said some shit, and I'd already called Gloria earlier, so I couldn't call her again so soon, and you were . . . out . . . so I couldn't call you. I swear, I didn't get even five minutes of sleep."

Okay, so she definitely hasn't forgotten, and she hasn't forgiven me enough to call me for help. But she has forgiven me enough to be happy when I come back anyway? Also, what the fuck was she doing walking home alone at night? Shouldn't Grey have been here, since I wasn't? The thought that she was in danger because of my poor self-control sends a wave of nausea through me.

"Bee, I need you to slow down. What's this about a guy following you? Did he threaten you? Hurt you? Are you okay?"

She drags me to the couch, and I follow willingly, if only just because it feels so good to have her hand touching mine.

"I'm fine. He didn't actually do anything. Just said some things that freaked me out."

"So, who was he? Just some random guy?"

Bee looks uncomfortable. "No. At least, he's in my chem class, and he claims to know me, or he says he knows my grandmother, which is even less likely because my only living family is my adoptive family—Grey and his parents. Everyone else is either dead or those ties were cut a long time ago." She looks up at me, and it breaks my heart to see a sheen of tears in her eyes. "He couldn't have been telling the truth, right? There's no way I have a grandmother I never knew about and a cousin who wants to introduce us. It's ridiculous. It has to be some kind of a con, right? I just can't figure out what the angle would be."

A few things click into place in my mind. "What does he look like?"

"Blond. Kind of small. Maybe just a few inches taller than me. He calls himself Ceallach."

Could that be the guy I saw? How many small, blond men could there be hanging out around campus?

"Could you tell if he was human or not?" Not likely, but worth asking.

She gets a shifty look I can't name.

"Bee? What aren't you saying?"

Squaring her shoulders, Bee takes a deep breath and turns to face me. "This sounds crazy, and you're not going to believe me. You don't have to tell me how impossible it sounds, okay?"

I try to cover my confused look with encouragement and wait for her to go on.

"He looks human. I mean, obviously, I can't actually tell by looking, but my gut says he's the same as me. But he says . . ." She trails off and makes me wait for her to start again. "He says that he's fae, and that I'm fae, and then, when he was done talking, he didn't just walk away. He disappeared."

"Disappeared," I repeat, still trying to process what she might mean by that.

"Yeah. Like I said, I know how it sounds, but one moment, he was there, then he wasn't. He didn't shout, 'Look behind you!' and then he was gone when I turned back. He just . . . was gone. And I know it's impossible, and that's not something shifters or vampires can do, but I saw it happen."

I think back to someone with the body temperature of a vampire and the heart rate of a hummingbird, sitting at a table full of food and not eating anything. A blond man smiling at me in the hallway and then seeming to disappear into the crowd. The smell of a person who didn't smell like a fellow vampire or like potential food.

"Actually, I believe you." I tell her about the man in the diner and how I saw him again on campus. She doesn't ask questions when I explain about how he doesn't smell quite right, for which I'm grateful, and she doesn't even seem upset when I admit I was trying to keep an eye on her to keep her safe.

At the end of my part of the story, Bee curls in on herself and hugs her knees to her chest.

"I never thought I would have to admit Grey might be right about there being dangers out there I wasn't aware of," she says in a sad, lost voice.

I put a tentative hand on her shoulder—and damn, but it feels good to touch her like this, to be the one she allows to comfort her—and rub what I hope is a soothing pattern across her shoulder blades.

Bee scoots close to me and leans the curve of her back against my chest, making something swell inside me. Her touch makes me feel like my chest expands enough to actually handle a real heartbeat.

"I'm sorry I kicked you out yesterday after . . ."

A new wave of embarrassment washes over me.

"No, I mean, I'm sorry. You don't need to be sorry when it was my . . . um . . ." Gods, save me from having to actually say it, please.

She stays tucked against my side but turns her head up to look at me.

"But it was me who kicked you out before . . . I mean . . . there were other things we could have done, even after . . ."

I try to keep my hand steady on her shoulder, even though thinking of "other things" is heating me to a boil on the inside.

"Maybe you should try and get some rest," I say in a bid to change the subject before thinking of "other things" causes me to pop an inappropriate hard-on.

Bee snuggles closer into my side. "I don't think I could rest. I've still got too much energy from earlier."

Right. Of course she's still freaked-out about being followed by someone. I hug her to me, hoping I'm coming across as comforting rather than stifling with the embrace.

"You don't have to worry about that guy. I'll be here to watch out for you, and Grey and Gloria will be here to watch out for you. We'll make sure you're safe."

She presses a hand to my chest, lighting me on fire where she's touching me, and gives me a pleading look.

"Maybe I should be worried about my safety, but I'm not. I don't know if I'm just still processing or what, but mostly, I'm just feeling the leftover adrenaline that has nowhere to go."

I slide my hand up and down her back, wishing for something more I could do to help her, and she keeps looking up at me, and my hand keeps sliding, and then she stretches up without warning and presses a kiss to my jaw.

I freeze, staring at her for a hint of what she wants, and all I see in her eyes is need.

Slower, this time, she presses her lips just below my ear and shifts in my arms so even more of her body is pressed against mine.

"Bee, are you sure—" My voice cuts out when her tongue licks a trail from my ear to my neck.

"I don't want to think about families, or fairies, or guys following me home, right now," she tells me, continuing the torture on my neck. "I want to do something to keep my mind off of all that."

My body, traitor that it is, is very much on board with this idea, so I can't seem to make myself stop her when she throws a leg over me and straddles my lap.

"We shouldn't . . ." The words die on my lips when Bee nips at my neck with her teeth.

"I want to, though," she says, and I can't argue, because fuck do I want to also.

"Maybe—" I struggle to string together a full coherent thought. "—not out here? In case Gloria comes home?"

Bee sits back and looks me in the eye. "Okay, my room. Do you still want to use the gag?"

I nod, because I can practically taste her pulse from here, and I'm too close to guarantee her safety.

"Okay. You get the gag and meet me in my room. And don't you dare chicken out."

I don't think I would be capable of that at this point. The thought of stopping what we've started right now is downright painful.

"I'll just be a minute," I promise.

CHAPTER 32

Bee

I spin around my room and take inventory before we get started.

Condoms? Check. Gag so Taylor isn't afraid of accidentally biting me? Successfully retrieved from his bedroom. Bed cleared off so there's space for his giant body as well as mine? I may have been forced to shove a pile of clean clothes haphazardly into my closet, but it's done.

The main problem right now is that all of the tension from a minute ago in the living room has snapped. I'm pretty sure I ruined the moment by letting him move us off the couch.

I take a steadying breath. "Alright, let's do this."

Taylor gives me a serious look. "We don't have to do this, you know, if you don't actually want to."

"I want to do it," I argue. "I'm just . . . not sure I'll enjoy it much."

He gives me a confused look. "Will it help to know that I really want you to enjoy it?"

"No, that just puts extra pressure on. I've never had an orgasm, and I'm not sure I can have an orgasm. I just need a distraction, you know? I want to burn off some energy, and I want to be able to say I'm not a virgin anymore."

"Bee . . . Okay. Fine. I won't pressure you into trying to have an orgasm. But that doesn't mean I can't try to make it a little pleasant for you, right? You'll let me know if there's something you want me to change or something I should try or . . ." He trails off, sounding lost and helpless.

"Are you worried about what happened last time?" I ask. "I mean, does that happen often? Would it help if we just do it fast?"

Taylor looks like he might be sick.

"No. I mean, it's never happened before, but also . . ."

"What?"

He bites at his lip and stares at the floor before answering. "That had never happened before, but the rest of it had also never happened before, so I don't really know for sure if it's something that would happen again."

I stare at him, slack-jawed, while he continues to stare at a spot on the floor.

"Are you saying that you're a virgin too?" I finally ask, then go on before he has a chance to answer. "How? I mean, you're this big, hot vampire. How could you still be a virgin?"

He glances up at me, surprise on his face. "You think I'm hot?"

I give him a look. "Of course I think you're hot. Everyone thinks you're hot. It's an empirical fact that you're hot."

He looks pleased but still surprised at that.

"Look, I probably should have told you before . . . well, you know, before we did anything, but I was embarrassed. The way I grew up . . . if you were there, you would understand how I could still be a virgin."

I step close to him and cup his face in my hand. I feel . . . almost like a weight tugging at my heart. Almost like a string, and if I follow it, I'll find him at the other end. When I touch that weight, that invisible string, I feel a tangle of shame and guilt and a sick mother and fearful classmates.

I pull my hand back with a jerk.

It takes a few swallows and a deep breath to regain my equilibrium. "I guess we'll both lose our virginity today, then," I say. "If something feels good, I'll let you know, and you should do the same. Now, take off my clothes."

It's impossible to miss the smolder in his eyes when I say that. For all of his hesitance and worry, this is something he wants.

With surgical care, he unbuttons my jacket and slides it down my arms. Before he has a chance to try and hang it up in my disaster of a closet, I toss it in the direction of my desk.

"Can I . . ." He leans down until our lips are maybe an inch apart. He can probably taste my breath, which I try not to feel self-conscious about.

"Yeah." I nod. "You can kiss me."

He dips the last inch and brushes my lips with his, the gentlest butterfly brush I could have ever imagined, before pressing close again so our lips meet and explore each other.

And it feels good.

No, not just good.

Delicious. Electric. Delightful.

With a hungry moan, I thread my fingers through his hair and pull him closer to me so we can properly devour each other. My world narrows down to a pinprick. Nothing outside of this moment, this kiss, matters. When I finally pull back, I'm gasping for air, and maybe it's just my imagination, but I swear I see his chest heaving as if he needs to catch his breath. Never mind that vampires don't need air the way humans do. Never mind that his lungs don't even function the way mine do. Taylor looks absolutely overcome by this moment.

"I guess I should take off your dress now?"

I nod and turn so he can reach the zipper.

It's nothing special, just a pastel sundress with flowers embroidered on the bodice and around the hem, and I'm nothing special in it, but Taylor looks at me like I'm the most beautiful woman he's ever seen. He leans down and nuzzles a sensitive spot behind my ear and inhales like my scent will give him eternal life, and my knees feel strangely wobbly from that.

He tugs the zipper down at an agonizingly slow pace. A spark of heat ignites in my spine every time his fingers brush my skin, and he follows the same slow path with his lips and tongue all the way down until he's kneeling behind me with my dress gaping open to my tailbone.

"Holy shit," he gasps and pulls the right side of my dress away to reveal my new artwork. "When did you add this?"

I don't answer, just spin to face him and shimmy the rest of the way out of my dress with a grin. "You don't like it?"

His eyes take me in like a starving man at a banquet. "You're so beautiful," he whispers, then traces one of my butterflies with his tongue.

I guess that's sort of an answer.

He escalates from tracing each butterfly to placing open-mouthed kisses on them, grabbing me by my hips and pulling me close to burrow his nose and mouth into my skin. With a growl, he tears himself away from me and looks up in desperation.

"Where's the gag? I can't trust myself not to . . ."

He's worried about biting me right now? Is that the hunger I saw in his eyes before?

I brush the thought away and grab the gag from my bedside table. He stays perfectly still, kneeling on the floor as I fit the ball into his mouth and adjust the straps around his head. A look of relief and, I'm not sure, maybe tenderness, washes over his face once the gag is in place.

He takes a moment to react when I hold out my hand for him, but then he understands and stands up to follow me to the bed. I let out a squeak of surprise when he lifts me up and lays me down gently on top of the covers, but he doesn't give me time to process what he's doing. Still in his jeans and a button-up shirt, he lies down on top of me, his elbows and knees taking most of his weight so he doesn't crush me. It's nice, though, the way I feel the pressure of his body along the entire length of mine. Like every inch of him wants to explore every inch of me.

He looks a question into my eyes, and I answer by brushing his hair back from his forehead. "Yes. This is good." The words are inadequate to describe the way my skin burns at his touch or the flip-flops my organs do when he gives me the earnest look he's currently giving me. I feel cared for. Protected, but not in the condescending way my family always wants to protect me because I'm helpless. Protected in a simpler, sturdier way. Protected because this man was built like a shelter from the elements. Come what may, he'll be there.

Experimentally, I lift my hips and press my core, still covered by the lace of my panties, against his hip bone.

Fuck, that feels good.

I do it again, and Taylor drops his forehead to mine with a moan and a look of absolute concentration. What's he concentrating so hard on? I can't exactly ask him, with the gag in his mouth. If I could just take a peek inside his thoughts, that would be ideal. Is this actually doing anything for him, or is he going over his math homework in his head so that it looks like he's engaged in what we're doing?

I feel that thread connecting us, wonder what might happen if I pluck at it. I'm on the verge of reaching out and trying to trace it back to its source, but fear stops me.

Taylor breaks me out of my thoughts with a nudge of his own hips, managing to hit that same spot that felt so good before.

Right. Maybe instead of worrying about whether he's engaged or distracted right now, I should try to be a little less distracted myself.

Another press of his hip bone against me makes my muscles tighten in a promising way. He presses against me again, and the heat inside of me coils tighter still.

It feels almost like my body isn't broken after all. It feels almost like maybe I'm building up to something that I've never been able to feel before.

Our hips sync into a steady rhythm that has the spring inside of me coiling tighter and tighter with each movement until I start to wonder if I'll die from this tension before I find any release. And then, Taylor looks into my eyes with such a combination of need and care and hope, and I shatter beneath him. The tension that was pulled so tight inside of me releases with enough force that my limbs jerk uncontrollably. My skin buzzes, too tight on my body. There's a distant sound that I finally realize is my own voice, but I have no control over it.

Maybe it lasts a second, or maybe ten hours, but Taylor helps me ride through it until I return to my body, shaking and wrung out with my knuckles white from clasping reflexively around his shirt collar.

"I guess you were right," I manage to say once I've finally found my voice again. "I guess I can come after all." And Taylor looks incredibly pleased about that.

CHAPTER 33

Taylor

Bee is looking up at me like I'm water in the desert. Or maybe land after being lost at sea. The way she spasmed and cried out beneath me a moment ago was hands down the hottest thing I've ever seen, and now she's giving me *this look* that has me coming apart at the seams.

"Taylor."

I nod so she knows I'm with her.

"I want you to fuck me now."

I nod again. How could I possibly argue? Getting up as gently as I can so I don't jostle her, I strip off my shirt and pants and lay them over the desk chair, where she tossed her other clothes.

Her eyes zero in on my erection, which is making itself known even though my underwear is still on. She isn't looking at me with excitement or anything positive at all, though. She looks worried. No, terrified, actually. She looks like she's finally done the math and realized how much bigger I am than she is.

I pluck at my waistband and give a questioning look. *We*

don't have to do this, I try to communicate telepathically. *You shouldn't feel scared.*

Maybe I reach her, because her shoulders relax incrementally.

"Yes. I'm ready. I want this," she tells me in a breathy voice.

And I want this too. I'm desperate to have more of what we just had, and anything she'll let me have, and everything I never thought someone would want to give to me.

I slide off my last scrap of clothing and stand there for a moment, letting her look over me, drinking in the way she looks, propped up on her elbows and wearing only her lacy bra and panties. My dick gives a little twitch at the sight of her, reminding me that we were good this time and held off on coming because we knew there was something worth waiting for.

She set a box of condoms on her bedside table before we even started, so I don't have to ask where they are, thankfully. Actually getting the rubber rolled down my shaft is a little trickier, and I have a moment of panic when I can't easily tell which direction it's supposed to go. I figure it out and manage to get myself properly suited up for what's supposed to happen next.

With another questioning look, I kneel between Bee's legs.

"I'm sure," she says, and I suspect she's reassuring herself as much as me. "Please, just do it."

Is it the most romantic thing a woman has ever said to a man? Probably not. Is it the sexiest thing someone could say to me at this moment? Possibly. I can't think of anything hotter than having Bee asking for me, maybe even wanting me. Needing me? Maybe that's too much to ask.

I carefully fit my rubber-sheathed cock to her entrance and try to ease myself in slowly.

Bee bites her lip and whimpers like she's in pain, so I pull back.

"No, it's fine," she says. "It's supposed to hurt the first time, right?"

Maybe a little bit, I guess, but I don't think it's supposed to hurt that much. Is she just not ready? I've heard it can help if she's more turned on. I thought her orgasm would count as being turned on enough for this, but maybe the effects have already worn off.

I slip a finger between us and dip it into her pussy, needing to take a moment to calm my own desire, which flares at the feel of heat and wet dripping from her. My finger slides easily between her folds before finding a raised nub that has to be her clit. Based on the way she groans and arches into my hand, I'm right. I set to work, taking my cues from the sounds she makes and the way she moves in response to my fingers, learning to play her body the way someone else might teach themself to play a guitar. I strum, and if I like what I hear, I strum the same way again.

Bee's fingers tangle in my hair, sending shivers of desire shooting down my spine to gather in my balls. If I weren't so determined to get her to come again, I could come right now, just from having her writhe beneath me and pull my hair.

I feel the moment she snaps and crumbles, every muscle in her body tensing so hard that her whole body ripples with the effort, then releasing with a gasp and a moan.

"Now, Taylor," she begs. "Fuck me now."

Thank fuck for whatever instinct has kicked into gear in my mind, because my conscious brain has no idea what she's talking about. I fit myself at her entrance again and try my absolute best to be gentle as I thrust inside.

Her scream of pain has me off the bed and across the room in an instant.

I fumble at the straps on my gag, desperate to get it off so I can ask her what's wrong. Meanwhile, she's saying something that I should probably try to pay attention to.

" . . . not that big of a deal. I told you, it's supposed to hurt. At least the first time, right? That's why we need to get it over with."

I finally get the damn gag off my face.

"That wasn't a normal amount of pain," I argue. "You shouldn't be in that much pain, and I don't want to be the person who hurts you like that. And for what? Just so you can say that you had sex? It's not worth it. We don't have to do something that's going to hurt you."

I'm desperate for her to agree with me on this, but instead, I can see her jaw twitch as she clenches her teeth.

"Yes," she says after a long pause. "This *is* just so I can say I had sex, an experience that a lot of people claim is a critical rite of passage that everyone should experience."

"And what we did before, when I'm pretty sure you came twice—unless that was fake—didn't that count as sex? Can't we say we had sex and leave it at that?"

"No," she splutters. "That doesn't count. It only counts if . . . I mean . . . I'm still a virgin . . ."

"So . . . you're saying the only part that matters to you is being able to say that you had penetrative sex?" I go slowly, trying to choose my words carefully and wondering if I'm really ready for what I'm about to suggest.

She huffs and crosses her arms. "Yeah, I guess that's what I mean. I want to feel like I actually achieved the milestone, you know? It's not like I'm hiring a skywriter or anything, but if someone is looking for virgin sacrifices, I want to be able to take my name off the list."

"Okay then." My decision snaps into place, crystal clear in front of me. "Okay, hear me out. If what matters to you is the penetration part of sex, and I'm not willing to hurt you by penetrating you, you'll just have to penetrate me."

Bee gapes at me, completely lost for words.

"We'll go back to that same store and get something for

you to use. It seemed like there were plenty of options. Strap-ons and plugs and . . . well, I don't really know what all the options are, but I'm sure we can find something."

She gapes some more, her chin practically on the floor.

"I'm saying, if it's that important for you to be able to say you fucked someone, you should fuck me, because I'm not going to fuck you. Not when I can tell how much it hurts you."

Bee's mouth closes with a click, but she's still staring at me warily, like I might be rabid and she doesn't want to make any sudden moves.

"Okay, fine," she says when she finally speaks again. I don't know if she's actually on board or just trying to call my bluff, but I'm ready either way. I made my choice, and I'm not bluffing. "We'll go back to the sex toy shop, and I'm going to choose a giant, realistic-looking, strap-on dildo, and you're going to stand right beside me while I pay for it so the cashier knows exactly who I'm planning to use it on. Do I have that right?"

I have to swallow before I answer, but not because I'm having second thoughts. It's because having her spell it out like that is actually really turning me on for some reason. My cock, which had completely deflated at her scream of pain earlier, plumps up again in anticipation.

"That sounds like a good plan," I say, my voice coming out husky and low. "And while we're at it, maybe we should get some cuffs as well."

She draws back in confusion. "Cuffs?"

"If you cuff me to the bed, we won't need the gag to make sure you're safe, and I'll be able to talk to you and, you know, give consent if it's needed."

"You're . . . you're actually serious about this, aren't you?"

I sit on the edge of the bed and cup her face. "I'm really serious about this," I promise. "I want to be with you, Bee.

Believe me, I really, really want to be with you. But I can't do something that I know is going to hurt you. Are you up for doing it this way?"

She searches my face, and I'm not sure what she finds there, but she brings her hand up to stroke the hand I still have against her cheek.

"Okay. Let's try it your way. Let's go to the store."

"Let's go to the store later," I amend. "For now, are you okay with cuddling, or should I go back to my own bed to sleep?"

With a surprised laugh, she slides over in the bed and pats the empty space beside her. I take about two seconds to throw the unused condom away and slide into bed beside her. I hesitate for a moment before curling my body protectively around hers, but I'm rewarded by Bee scooting up against me and pulling my arm across her.

Her slowing breaths soothe me as I try to sleep. I barely slept before coming here, and I think she slept even less. I catalog the coming day in my mind. I'll need to go to classes, run home and check on Mom, pick out a toy for Bee to fuck me with. If I were any less tired, all of those thoughts would probably keep me awake. As it is, I drop off a few breaths after Bee and don't hear a thing until her alarm wakes us both for our morning classes.

CHAPTER 34

Bee

How is the giant wall of sex toys even more intimidating on my third time viewing it?

Oh, right. Because this time, I'm possibly going to buy one to use on someone else. In someone else.

I slide my gaze over to Taylor to try and catch a hint of whether he's still serious about this or just playing a crazy game of sex toy chicken with me. Is that a thing? Because it never occurred to me before that it might be a thing, but I'm pretty sure it's what we're doing right now.

Unless I'm mistaken, and Taylor really is willing to be—possibly even interested in being—pegged by me.

Yes, I looked it up. Yes, that's what it's called. Am I just that innocent that I didn't realize this was a thing before now? Or maybe the internet is lying to me, and everyone is laughing at me for falling for their "pegging is a real thing" practical joke.

I sneak another glance at Taylor, and he catches me looking this time. Looking away quickly isn't going to fool him into thinking it was a random glance, especially when I can feel the flames of embarrassment on my cheeks.

"Do you want something to hold or something you can wear?" he asks me like that's a completely normal, everyday, mundane question for one roommate to ask another in the middle of a sex store.

"Okay, you've made your point," I murmur, moving closer to him so no one can overhear us. "I won't try to get you to do anything you're not comfortable with again. I'm not holding you to this . . . plan."

He gives me a long, serious look. "What if I *am* comfortable with this, though? Would you still want to try?"

I open my mouth to say, "No, of course not, this was never what I had in mind," but an image pops into my head of him splayed out on my bed with his ankles and wrists cuffed to the bedposts. Why does the thought send a bolt of electricity through my center? Why does it make my mouth water to imagine him lying in front of me, basically helpless, while I do anything I want?

"So let's pick out a toy," he tells me, making me wonder whether I spoke my thoughts out loud by accident.

Fine. I can admit this is something I want to do, and he didn't back out when I gave him the chance, so maybe he really does want this too. Which means it's time for me to stop messing around and actually do it.

"I changed my mind." His face actually falls for a moment in disappointment, so I hurry to explain. "I want to surprise you. You should go so I can pick something out without ruining the surprise."

"Oh. Yeah. Sure. I can wait out front for you if you prefer that."

"Perfect." I catch him as he turns to go. "Wait! Is there anything that I definitely shouldn't get?"

He eyeballs the giant dildo that's a pretty close size match to his real-life monster of a cock before turning back to me. "Nope. I trust you."

My stomach flutters and just about flies away.

He trusts me. He wants me to cuff him to the bed and peg him with whatever toy I choose because he trusts me.

"Well, okay then," I say with a smile and a shove toward the front of the store.

Now that the choice to do this is made, the rest of the choices are easy. It's just shopping, which I've always been pretty good at. You look at the options and determine which ones serve your needs or not. In this case, more things serve my needs than Taylor is probably expecting, but since I won't be able to try any of these things out beforehand, well, I might as well get everything I might be interested in trying.

The guy at the register definitely recognizes me this time. His eyebrows shoot up when I drop my armload of items on the counter.

I refuse to be embarrassed by this. I refuse to feel shame for exploring my sexuality. Besides, who is this guy, this sex shop worker, to question my sex toy purchasing habits?

"Er. Cash or card?" he asks.

I almost open the floodgates to lecture him about how my sexuality is none of his business and he has no right to look down on me for wanting to explore all of these possibilities and . . . then I register what he actually asked me, and I deflate.

"Oh. Um. Card, please."

If my parents are tracking my purchases, I'd honestly much rather they notice the sex shop than the tattoo parlor in the receipts.

Maybe I should be offended when Taylor doesn't even blink in surprise when I walk out of the store with two large bags. Or maybe that just means he knows me.

"Do I get to ask any questions about what you got?"

He asks it with a smile and no visible worry, so I don't think I have to put his mind at ease. I probably shouldn't torture him either.

"No questions. All I'll say is that we're going to be trying out some different options so we can find the best one."

"I can liv—" He breaks off and takes my elbow as we walk. I can feel tension practically buzzing through his fingers and up my arm. "Don't be obvious about it, but I want you to look across the street and tell me who you see."

I try to look without turning my head and feel the most conspicuous I've ever felt in my life. Proof that I would make a terrible spy.

Ceallach is walking apace with us on the other side of the street. He catches my eye, smiles, and gives a jaunty half wave, half salute before jogging across the street to meet us.

"It's good to see you again, cousin," he greets me like he didn't recently stalk me down an empty street in the middle of the night. "I was so curious which of you would notice me first. On the one hand, I thought maybe our bond of kinship would alert you to my presence. On the other hand, I've heard so much about vampires and their heightened senses."

He smiles and glances back and forth between us expectantly.

"Well, which one of you noticed me first? I'm dying to know!"

Taylor growls, "Who are you? Why are you here?"

The man's grin widens, and he wags his finger at Taylor. "It was you, wasn't it? I shouldn't have underestimated you. Not after you noticed me outside of your class the other day."

"And the diner," Taylor adds. "Now, answer the question."

"You did notice me at the diner? What gave me away? I thought I'd kept my cover."

Taylor takes a menacing step toward Ceallach, who steps backward and puts his hands up defensively.

"Okay. Fine. Maybe we can talk later. I'm Bee's cousin . . . of sorts. Our family tree is too complicated to get into the details right now, but we do share a grandmother, which makes us cousins by human definitions."

I finally find my voice. "Ceallach, I am human. Both of my parents were human."

He cocks his head to the side and looks at me with one of his rare serious looks.

"You really don't know, do you? I really can't believe they never told you anything! Well, that's going to put a stick in it, but I think we can still make it work." His cheerful grin takes over again. "I'm supposed to bring you to Grandmother, but there might be an issue if you can't travel with me. I need you to keep practicing like I taught you. If you can't learn how to use your gifts . . ." He trails off with an ominous headshake. "If you can't learn to use your gifts, I think she'll still want to meet you. I'll just have to convince her to come here."

Without an explanation or a goodbye, he winks out of existence again.

Taylor and I both startle back away from where he was standing, then look around to see how everyone around us responds to the disappearing man.

The answer is not at all. Everyone continues whatever they were doing before.

"What the fuck just happened?" I ask Taylor.

He rubs a soothing hand across my shoulders. "I'm not sure, but I really think we have to tell your brother about this. Maybe he knows something about your birth parents that you don't. And if he doesn't know, he probably should. He's your closest family, right?"

I dig my heels in.

"No. We're not telling Grey." I shake a bag of sex toys at him. "Have you already forgotten that we have plans for tonight? Besides, you heard Ceallach. He's not trying to hurt me. Don't you think he could and would have already hurt me if that was his goal? And *if* I believe him about wanting to introduce me to my grandmother, what's the harm there? Grey doesn't need to know about this."

Taylor looks pained but puts his hands up in defeat.

"Fine. Grey is *your* brother, so you get to decide when to tell him, but I think it's a bad idea to take that guy at his word that he's not planning to hurt you. Maybe he isn't, or maybe he's lying to you. You have no idea what his actual plans are."

Deep breaths. Don't get mad at Taylor just because he sounds a lot like Grey right now. Don't get mad at someone just because he's trying to protect you. After you've told him numerous times that protection is the last thing you want. Deep breaths.

"I'll be careful," I promise him. "Now, are we going home to try these things out or what?"

CHAPTER 35

Taylor

Okay. Confession time.

I might have scoured the internet for everything there is to know about pegging as soon as I got a minute alone after Bee and I talked about it. Knowledge is power, right? For some reason, all of my newly gained knowledge isn't making me feel any more prepared for what we're about to do. I thought about asking Devon or Marcus for advice but dismissed the idea because I'm pretty sure they have better things to do than walk me through my first experience with anal. Also, it would have been embarrassing.

Bee looks even more nervous than me, though, so I move into comforting mode.

"If you want to wait, that's fine," I tell her.

She smooths her skirt and looks at the restraints she's laid out on her bed instead of at me.

"Bee? What are you thinking right now?"

It takes a while for her to answer.

"I still want to do this," she says. "I guess I'm just . . . well, I'm worried I'll be bad at it," she admits.

I turn her to look at me so she can stop obsessing over the

cuffs on the bed. "Bee, I'm pretty sure I'm going to enjoy anything you do to me." Which is the absolute truth. I can't think of anything she could do that would turn me off from her. "And even if you *are* bad at this, you'll probably get better with practice. I, personally, wouldn't mind having a chance to practice with you, at least if that's something you're interested in?"

Her shoulders relax under my hands as I talk, and she actually steps in closer to me at the end of my little speech so she can rest her hands on my chest. Taking my cues from her, I slide my hands down her back and draw her even closer. Using me for balance, she lifts up on her toes and tilts her face up to me. I take the hint—the invitation—and meet her halfway for a kiss. It starts gentle and tentative, almost like it's our first time, but hunger and instinct quickly take over when I lick at the seam of her lips, and she opens for me, then nibbles at my lower lip in a way that sends blood straight to my cock. Then, it's a contest. Who can devour, who can conquer, the other's mouth more thoroughly.

Bee moans into my mouth and tugs at my neck. By instinct, I lift her up so she can wrap her legs around my waist, her ass sitting perfectly in my hands while her pussy presses against my hard cock. Even through the fabric of her panties, I can smell her getting wet, practically taste her arousal in the air.

She rocks her hips to rub herself against my erection, and I almost lose my mind from it. The softness of her ass against my palms and the hardness of my need as she seeks friction against me. The sweet smell of her skin mixed with the sharper smell as she drips with desire. For me. That's what really gets me going. She's this turned on, and it's for me. She's in my arms right now, making sexy, needy sounds against my mouth. I almost can't believe this is real.

My body doesn't care if it's real.

Bee plucks at the buttons on my shirt, then gives a frustrated grunt and pulls back from our kisses when she can't unbutton me without looking.

"I could do that," I offer, but that would mean letting go of her glorious ass, which I don't think I'm ready to do yet.

She ignores me and continues to struggle with the button. After a moment, she drops it with a huff of annoyance that makes me smile.

Setting her down with a chuckle, I make quick work of my shirt buttons and stand there with my shirt open but still on.

Bee licks her lips as she eyes me up and down.

"Should I take the rest off?" I ask.

She considers the offer, then refuses it. "No. I want to do it."

A trail of sparks lights under my skin as she touches me to peel away the shirt. I actually gasp when she reaches my belt. I swear I feel her pulling part of my soul away as she tugs the belt through each loop, then tosses it away. I'm surprised that my pants are still intact, considering how they're stretched over my swollen dick. The zipper vibrates through to my core as she tugs it down.

"Bee, what if—" I have to stop and concentrate because she's palming me through the fabric of my underwear. I close my eyes and swallow and focus on not coming just from the heat of her hand against my cock. "What if I come too fast again?"

She gives me an assessing look. Her nerves from earlier have disappeared completely, replaced by something predatory behind her eyes. "You won't," she says, self-assured and in control now. "Because if you do, I'll have to find a way to make you pay for your lack of control."

I have to swallow again as my imagination goes wild with ways that she might make me pay. Why is the mere thought of her punishing me such a turn-on? It probably wouldn't take a psychoanalyst to trace that one back to my mother.

"Okay, I'll control myself," I promise, desperate to please but also weirdly hopeful for the attention I might get from her if I mess up.

No. No messing up. I'll be good for her, at least this first time, I tell myself.

It's a good thing that resolution is fresh in my mind when she hooks her fingers in the waistband of my briefs and pulls them down below my throbbing cock, otherwise, that probably could have been enough to tip me over the edge. As it is, with her kneeling down in front of me and giving my length a long, appraising look, I do have to close my eyes and think through some algebra so I don't make a fool of myself again.

Just when I'm proud of myself for getting everything under control, she leans forward and licks a tentative stripe up the center of my ballsack.

I put my hand on her head for balance and do my best to dig my toes into the floor.

"Bee, maybe it would be best to tie me up now," I say.

She smiles evilly up at me and licks another stripe from the bottom of my shaft to the head of my cock. A wholly undignified steam whistle sound escapes my throat, and she giggles—actually giggles—before wrapping her lips around the head and sucking in earnest.

Stars erupt behind my eyes, and just in time, I grab myself at the base to stop myself from spilling too early.

"Bee," I choke out. "I can't—"

She lets me go with a pornographic-sounding "pop" and smiles up at me again. Sliding my pants down the rest of the way, she orders me to step out, one leg at a time, then lie down on my back.

I almost tell her that she can be rougher with me as she gently guides one arm above my head and secures the cuff around my wrist, clicking the other end closed around a slat in her headboard.

"Test that out?" she says.

I tug tentatively, then a little harder, and don't feel any give, so I nod for her to do the other one.

She hooks a leg over my hips and straddles me to cuff my second wrist, giving me the most glorious view I could hope for down the front of her dress. I lick my suddenly dry lips. Bee seems to know exactly what's going through my head, because she stays there longer than she needs to, her perfect curves so close to within tasting distance, but I can't actually reach her.

I let out a desperate moan as she dismounts me like a horse and walks away, disappearing into her closet.

"I'll be back. Don't worry," she promises.

It's not that I'm worried. Desperate. That's what I am. Starving for her. Dying for her.

I jerk both hands in a bid to get free of the bed and reach her, but the bed frame I'm handcuffed to is too sturdy for that.

"Fuck, Bee. I need you." I need her heat, her skin, her scent to be on me. I need to feel her giving me life as we touch. "Please."

She's all business, though, and can't be swayed so easily by my pleas.

"Bend your knees so your feet are up by your ass," she instructs.

Relief floods me. She really isn't just going to leave me here, desperate and chained to her headboard.

Her hands are hidden behind her back when she reemerges, and she keeps them behind her even when she climbs onto the bed and kneels between my knees.

"Do you want to see what I have?" she asks.

I consider it carefully. Am I curious? Yes. I've been dying

of curiosity since we left the store and I saw that she had two whole bags' worth of purchases. I mean, how many variants on a butt plug are there?

But also, I trust her, and I want her to know that I trust her. She's not going to do something that she thinks will hurt me, so why spoil the surprise?

"No. Only if you want to show me."

A genuine smile blooms on her face. "Maybe later," she says. Then, she lowers herself between my legs so her face is just inches from my straining erection.

I let out a string of barely coherent curses as she mouths along the side of my shaft, flicking her tongue around to lap at the underside as she works her way all the way up to the tip, tonguing at my slit to capture every escaped drip of precome, then back down to my balls again.

Maybe there's a warning mixed in with my curses that if she keeps doing that, I'll come too fast again, but she ignores it, and I use what little brainpower I have left to keep myself from coming. It's an exquisite kind of torture, balancing just on this side of an orgasm but knowing I can't, under any circumstances, let myself tumble over. It becomes even more impossible when she tells me to lift up, then spreads my ass cheeks apart so she can slide her tongue between them and swirl it around my hole. It's an experience completely, wildly different from any other I've had or imagined. It's slick and intimate and feels dirty enough to make all of my muscles shake with tension, but she doesn't say anything about it seeming wrong or dirty or nasty in any way. She just dives in deeper, lighting up nerve endings that I never even realized I had.

I give a bereft moan when she draws back, taking away the source of a pleasure so profound, I almost think it must be illegal. Before I can start begging for her to keep going, I hear the click of a cap opening, followed by a wet sound.

Even knowing what we're doing here, I'm still caught by surprise at the feeling of something warm and slick being pressed to my entrance. One of her fingers, I'm pretty sure.

"Do you want me to stop?" she asks, all serious and businesslike again. "You can still say no."

"No," I hurry to answer. "I mean, no, don't stop. I want you to."

"If it hurts, though . . ."

It won't hurt, I think. Even if it hurts, I'm a vampire. There's nothing she can do that will actually harm me.

"If it hurts, I'll tell you. Promise."

"Or even if you change your mind."

"I swear, I'll tell you, but I'm pretty sure I'm going to die just from the waiting. Please, Bee. I'm begging you to fuck me."

The finger at my entrance gives a little jerk, but that's the only reaction she gives before sliding it inside.

Bee is a small woman, from her head to her toes. So, how does her finger—only in up to the first knuckle, if I had to guess—feel absolutely massive inside of me?

I gasp and lift off the bed at least a few inches, drawing a worried look from her.

"Should I stop?"

"No. Don't stop." *Don't you dare stop, for the love of everything holy in this world.* "It's just . . . more intense than I imagined," I admit. "Just . . . maybe go slow?"

She nods. "Got it. Slow. Nice and easy."

Her finger might as well be a burning coal, the way it lights me up as she burrows slowly, inexorably, deeper inside of me. If I die today, doctors are going to find that I was burned from the inside out.

Bee dips her head and wraps her lips around the head of my cock again, and my head swims. I'm not sure if I'm underwater or floating in space right now, but direction, gravity, all the regular laws of the universe have ceased to exist for me. All I know is the heat and suction from her mouth. All I feel is the heat and pressure from her finger. Anything else is a different reality entirely.

"Bee, I'm—"

"Yes," she pulls off my dick to encourage me. "Come for me."

And then her mouth is back on me, and it feels like she's sucking my release from the very center of my soul.

CHAPTER 36

Bee

I've learned a lot of surprising things today.

First, I'm not even slightly put off by putting my tongue inside someone's ass. Or maybe it's just Taylor's ass, but I really expected to have to grit my teeth to just get through it, and it wasn't like that at all.

Second, I like the taste of come. Again, maybe it's just Taylor's come, but I never would have guessed I could swallow every drop of a man's come and genuinely want more after it was done.

Third, and maybe this is the biggest revelation for the day, having an enormous, strong man wriggle beneath me from desire and desperation . . . makes me feel powerful. I have no other words for it, other than power. I feel absolutely drunk and delirious from having him come apart for me. Just from what I did with my mouth and my finger and a bottle of lube.

I never even got a chance to try the small plug I brought over. Hell, I didn't even get a chance to try a second finger. Taylor looks absolutely wrecked at the moment, though. That will be a conversation for another day. Hopefully. Assuming he recovers from this experience.

It takes a few moments of gasping to catch my breath and smiling down at him in satisfaction like a drunken idiot before I realize he's speaking.

"Sorry . . . tried to hold on . . . do better next time . . ." come through the haze of my thoughts, and I realize that he's acting at least as delirious as I am.

Carefully, I slip my finger out of his ass and climb up to lie on top of him. His rambling, incoherent apologies cut off suddenly when he realizes I'm stretched out on top of him and looking him straight in the eyes.

"You did fine," I whisper in reassurance, then lean down to claim his mouth.

He doesn't complain about the taste or flinch away when he realizes where the mouth that's kissing his was earlier. He lets me deepen the kiss and responds like there's nothing he would rather be doing.

It's just the two of us, tongues entangled, my fingers in his hair, his arms still stretched above his head, handcuffs giving an occasional soft clank, and the whole world drops away around us.

"That was incredible," he eventually murmurs into my mouth, and I pull away to look at him.

He still looks a little dazed and starry-eyed, but less like he's actually high from sex now.

"It was incredible," I agree. "We should get these handcuffs off of you."

His brow wrinkles. "But you didn't come yet," he says.

I give him another soft kiss on the lips before looking him in the eyes again. "I should let you recover."

"But—" A frown joins the wrinkled brow. "—I want you to come, Bee. Otherwise, I'll just feel guilty."

That surprises a laugh out of me. I went from being convinced I couldn't come to letting Taylor talk me into trying, even though he is obviously finished in every sense of the word.

"We can just try another day," I argue and get a stern look in return.

Huh. Stern looks from Taylor when he's handcuffed to my bed and pretty much at my mercy are apparently panty-melting. Another interesting discovery today.

I think hard about what we can do. As much as I hate to admit it when other people are right, Taylor was right to not fuck me. Whatever else we do, I don't think I'm interested in having something penetrate me. But the look he's giving me now says that he'll do just about anything to make sure I come tonight.

"Are you still worried about biting me by accident?" I ask.

He nods, then adds, "But you could gag me, and we wouldn't have to worry about it."

I pull out the gag from the drawer where it got shoved last time and hold it up questioningly.

"Yeah, put it on for me," he says.

It's trickier to get everything properly buckled in place when he's cuffed to the headboard, but I manage it in the end. I think about undoing the handcuffs, but seeing him stretched out and held in place like this has my blood heating beyond reason. In the end, I leave them on, and Taylor doesn't seem surprised or upset at all when I make no move to take them off. There is a flash of fear in his eyes when I climb off the bed with him still lying there, but then he sees that I'm reaching behind myself to unzip my dress.

I let the dress fall to the floor, then take my time and let him watch as I unsnap my bra and slide it off to land on top of my discarded dress. The sheer hunger smoldering in his eyes is enough to make my pussy drip and my clit pulse.

This man—this giant of a vampire—wants me more than

he wants anything else right now, and I'm in complete control of how much I let him have and how I let him have it.

His eyes widen with desire when I bend down to slide my panties off and step daintily out of them.

I feel like an absolute seductress as I stalk toward him in nothing but my bare skin.

He actually whimpers when I set one knee beside his head and toss the other over so I'm straddling his face.

"Can you smell that?" I ask.

Whimper. A shift in his shoulders tells me his hips just gave a jerk upward. Oh, yes. This is a good position for me to be in. There's nothing he can do to control this situation. He just has to trust that I'll do what he wants—no, needs—me to do. Because it's obvious from the look in his eyes that Taylor needs me to come.

I drag my wet pussy up the center of the gag until my clit is resting just below his nose. He groans and tries to raise his head to press into me, but I hold his hair tight and lift away from him so he can't reach. Another groan, and his eyes beg me to lower myself on his face.

"You like that scent, don't you?"

He nods, still only able to move his head an inch because of my tight grip in his hair.

"You're going to dream about that scent," I promise him. "And you're going to dream about this."

I steady myself with one hand on the headboard and use the other to pull his head up and grind his face into my pussy. His nostrils flare as I rub his nose up and down between my pussy lips, covering the gag in slick from my body. He inhales deeply, like I'm a drug he's trying to snort, and the look of combined pleasure and desperation on his face ignites me from my clit to my toes. I work myself hard against his face, riding the gag and his chin and the bridge of his nose ruthlessly. Glad he's a vampire and a lot harder to injure than a human would be, because I'm pretty sure a human wouldn't be able to let me use him like this, even if he wanted to.

Taylor's grunts and moans of pleasure are almost as loud as mine, and I wonder if I might be able to get him to come a second time, but at the moment, all of my focus is on chasing my own pleasure.

I find a rhythm to rock my hips while pulling his head forward that has me climbing high into the stratosphere, every single muscle in my core tightening beyond capacity, until everything snaps apart at once.

I'm not sure if I'm crying or shouting, shaking or shivering. I just know that my whole world shatters and crumbles, and I'm falling forever and forever and forever as my orgasm washes over me.

Who knows how long it lasts before I come back to myself. Who knows how long he has to lie there with his hands still restrained and my fingers tangled and pulling in his hair. Good thing he can't suffocate because I'm pretty sure I've had his nose pressed inside of me this whole time while I quaked and twitched through the aftershocks. A human would have been dead.

With the last scrap of energy I have, I undo the cuffs and drop into a deathlike sleep beside him.

I hold her all night and feel the crackle of electricity between us with each breath she takes. And what she said about dreaming about her scent? Gods, but nothing has ever been more true. Maybe because I keep the gag on and my face is still covered in her when the sun rises. Waking up with my worst-ever case of morning wood is a small price to pay for getting to sleep like this.

What's the proper etiquette, I wonder, for when you wake up desperate and the person in bed with you is still asleep?

Not ready to leave Bee's bed, I squeeze my erection and will it to go down.

Obviously, the situation isn't helped by Bee being naked and pressed against me.

I give my dick a rough tug, hoping to beat it into submission. Bee sighs and stretches, sending lightning through my veins.

"Hey," she murmurs, blinking sleepily up at me and smiling.

I desperately want to kiss her. Maybe to fuck her. Anything that has me close to her. But I've still got the gag on, and one arm is trapped under her, making it hard to take the gag off, so I can't very well ask her what she wants.

She slides a hand down my chest, scraping her fingernails along my stomach and making me shiver, then down lower until she wraps her fist around me and pumps me once, making me gasp.

"I guess you woke up ready this morning," she says through a giggle.

I'm sure she can see the desperation in my eyes. Not only did I wake up ready, but I woke up needy.

Thankfully, she catches on, throwing a leg over me so the base of my dick is notched between her labia. Just the heat of her there has me seeing stars.

I groan, splaying my hands over her hips and loving the way her skin gives slightly under my fingers.

She slides herself slowly, experimentally, up and down my shaft. Now I can smell and feel her getting wet, and it drives me a little mad. Looking down, I see the head of my cock, barely peeking out from between her pussy lips, then reemerging as she slides back down it.

If I could trust myself not to lose myself in a haze of blood-lust and drink her dry by accident, I would tear off this gag and eat her pussy until she was screaming on my tongue.

I can't trust myself, though, so I enjoy what I can get as she slides herself, a little faster now, up and down my cock. It's enough. Her motions are getting increasingly frantic, and the sounds she's making . . . I'll never have to watch porn again because I'll have this moment to look back on.

"Fuck!" She groans, sending a new hum of vibrations shooting through my cock and to the base of my spine. "Taylor . . . so close . . ."

I am too. Giving her an encouraging nod, I use my hands on her hips to work her up and down, just like we're trying to start a fire with the friction between our two bodies. I'm surprised there isn't any smoke, considering how hot she feels against me. I wouldn't be surprised if I burst into flames before coming.

With a long, loud moan, she closes her eyes, and her hips still. A wave of spasms runs visibly through her muscles before she collapses, panting and gasping, on my chest.

I squeeze her hips and wonder what to do now, with my own release hanging so close but still out of reach.

Wait until I can get in the shower and take care of it myself, I suppose.

Bee sways slightly as she sits up again. Her face is dazed and delirious and beautiful as she smiles down at me.

"Your turn," she says.

I give her a questioning look.

"It's your turn to come," she explains patiently, like I'm the slow kid in class.

Oh. I guess that means I don't have to take care of myself in the shower after all. My first instinct is to flip us over and fuck her, but I don't want to take the lead and do something to hurt her. Instead, I slide my hands tentatively up, over her hip bones and waist and rib cage, until I'm cupping her breasts in my hands. I try to ask with my eyes if it's okay, and she answers by covering my hands with hers and giving a sensuous roll of her hips. Just like that, I'm rock hard again and desperate to come. Bee seems to sense exactly what I need, the way she rides me, leaning forward just enough so the full weight of her breasts fills my palms, rolling her hips in a circular motion that has the sparks from before igniting from the tip of my dick to my balls to my spine.

She lets go of one of my hands to reach down and tease my slit, which has a thick drop of precome pearled and waiting. I groan my pleasure and desire as she spreads it around the head, slowing to pay special attention to the underside, where it's extra sensitive.

Suddenly unable to wait any longer, I flip her onto her back, eliciting a surprised squeak from her. She doesn't look scared, though, so I keep going. Remembering her scream of pain when I tried penetrating her the first time, I'm not even going to try that again, but this position gives me a better angle to get the friction I need.

I dip my head and breathe in the scent at her neck. It's different from the scent of arousal drifting up from her pussy, but just as delicious in its own way. My mouth waters around the gag, making me relieved that I kept it on. With a main artery right there, it would be hard to control my hunger for her.

With one hand, I hitch her ankle up over my shoulder while I wrap my other hand around her shoulder to hold her in place.

The look of trust in her eyes almost undoes me.

She's not worried about me fucking her when she doesn't want me to. She's not worried about me taking this gag off and drinking from her. She's not worried about me turning her into a vampire against her wishes or harming her in any way.

I may never believe I'm worthy of that trust, but she's giving it to me anyway. Freely and without strings.

With her opened up beneath me, I thrust against her, feeling pressure from her pubic bone against my dick as I move.

My hips find a natural rhythm that starts Bee moaning and gasping with each thrust, so now I'm chasing her orgasm as well as my own. I manage to wait until she cries out and tenses her fingers in my hair before I let loose and spill a thick stream of come across her belly.

"We should . . . probably get ourselves cleaned up?" she says, still working to catch her breath. "You might need to hold me up in the shower, though. I'm not sure I can stand on my own."

I huff out a laugh around the gag and drop my forehead to hers.

It hurts to think about it, even just admitting it to myself, but I'm never going to get over it when Bee decides she's done with me. I knew last year that I was head over heels for her, but I also knew that nothing would ever happen between us, and that made things easier. I could compartmentalize my feelings for her and hide them away where they would never be an issue. Things are so much messier now. Now, I know what it's like to make her come and to have her inside of me. And my feelings are never going to be put neatly away again.

I'm so busy wallowing in that realization that I miss whatever she just said. I hum a questioning sound at her, and she rolls her eyes before repeating herself.

"Can I take this off of you now?"

Oh, right. The gag.

I nod, then hold still so she can undo the buckles and pull it away from my mouth.

With my mouth free, I should try to tell her everything that's racing through my head, but I'm too scared to say the words and possibly have them ruin everything between us. Instead, I capture her mouth in a long, sensual kiss before carrying her to the shower.

CHAPTER 38

Bee

I'm naked, covered in come, and so weak after my orgasm that I need Taylor to carry me to the bathroom so I can get cleaned up.

And I've never felt so good in my life.

"New plan," I giggle into Taylor's shoulder. "I say we just do that every day from now on."

"And what would 'that' include exactly?" someone says with a snicker from the living room.

Taylor sets me down and stands in front of me like he's going to protect me. Never mind him being just as naked and covered in come as I am.

Jeff's grinning face appears at the end of the hall, followed by Gabe's. They take less than a second to figure out what they walked in on and burst out laughing.

Gabe leans nonchalantly against the wall and holds a hand out to Jeff, who pulls out his wallet and puts some bills in his palm with an annoyed look.

"You two couldn't have waited another month?" Jeff asks.

Taylor puffs up in anger. "Were you betting on this?"

I've got more important things to worry about. "Where's

Grey right now?" Obviously, if he were in the house, I would know about it already because he would already be attempting to kill Taylor. If he's on his way home now, though, I need to know about it.

"Relax." Gabe waves off my anxiety like it's nothing. "Gloria went into heat, so she's staying at our house until she's through it, and Jeff and I are giving the wolves some privacy by coming here for the time being."

I sway so hard with relief I have to grab the wall to stay standing.

Taylor doesn't look much steadier than me.

Jeff draws our attention back with a hand clap. "Okay. You two obviously need to get cleaned up, so Gabe and I will make some breakfast, and we can talk sleeping arrangements for tonight after you both have clothes on. Sound good?"

All Taylor or I can manage in response is a confused grunt, but that seems to be enough for Jeff, who heads toward the kitchen, whistling something tuneless.

"Don't take too long," Gabe warns with a chuckle before following Jeff and leaving us alone in the hallway.

"Shit," Taylor mutters. "I'm so sorry about that. I don't know what I was thinking, just walking out in the open like that. If it had been Gloria coming home, or Grey who walked in on us—"

I silence him with a hand on his face.

"Don't be sorry. Neither of us was thinking clearly. Obviously. But it turned out fine this time. We'll be more careful in the future, though."

"Yeah," he agrees. "We definitely have to be more careful if . . ."

"If what?"

He looks uncomfortable. "If we do this again. I understand if you don't want to. After getting caught like that, I mean."

I pull his head down enough so I can stand on my tiptoes to kiss him. "We're doing this again," I promise him. "But for now, let's get cleaned up and deal with our friends."

Sitting down to breakfast is like something from a TV show about human high school students getting into trouble with their parents.

Except both of the parents are doing a piss-poor job of hiding grins and snickers behind their hands as they pretend to deliver a serious lecture.

"Well, I hope you're both being safe," Jeff says seriously, then lets out a high-pitched giggle before getting himself under control again.

Gabe refills the coffee in his "Bulldogs do it best" tacky friend mug. It's obvious he's struggling to keep the stern father look on his face. "Now, Taylor, I think it's time you explained yourself. What are your intentions with our Bethany? She's got a lot of potential, you know."

I throw a piece of toast at his face and hit him right between the eyes.

Jeff cracks up laughing while Gabe blinks at me, looking shocked and affronted.

"Young lady, I thought we raised you better than to waste food like that," he growls in a parody of his earlier stern father voice.

"Would you all cut it out?" Taylor slams his hand on the table for emphasis, and we all sit staring at him in silent shock. He glares and points at Jeff and Gabe. "You know how serious it is that you don't tell Grey about this, right?"

Gabe raises his hands in acquiescence. "Yeah, we get it. He would be weird and overprotective about it."

"But," Jeff jumps in, "you know that we're happy for you, right? We knew it was only a matter of time."

Taylor shifts in his seat. "What are you talking about?"

Jeff waves a finger back and forth between Taylor and me.

"You two." He looks confused at our confusion. "I mean, anyone with eyes could see that Taylor has been lusting after you since last year, and when you told us you were moving in with him, we all figured it was inevitable."

I choke on some air. "He has not been 'lusting after' me," I say with my most sarcastic finger quotes. "That's ridiculous."

Taylor ducks his head and stares into the mug of coffee sitting in front of him.

Oh.

Somehow, Jeff still manages to make light of the situation. "Okay, so you didn't know. Now you do. Gabe and I are still happy for you two crazy kids finally figuring it out."

Gabe interjects. "Wait. Just for the record, I'm not voicing my approval for any serious monogamous relationships. But I'm very happy you two have stopped dancing around each other. The sexual tension was enough to choke a guy. So . . . how long has this been going on, would you say?"

Something about the way he asks it has my weird-behavior antenna twitching. "Why would you . . ."

"Oh my god," Taylor bursts out. "You have another bet on it, don't you?"

Gabe and Jeff at least both have enough decency to look ashamed of themselves.

"Come on," Jeff whines. "My love life is hopeless. Gabe's love life is loveless. You gotta give us something."

Taylor glowers at our two friends.

Deciding I'm just desperate enough that I'll do anything to change the subject, I set my fork down and clear my throat. "If I tell you my parents have been lying to me my whole life and that fairies might exist, will that get you to shut up about our sex life?"

Jaws drop and eyes bulge from all around the table, even from Taylor, though he recovers first.

"Bee, are you sure you want—"

"Yes. As long as they stop asking about personal things that they have no business knowing."

Taylor nods and sits back, waiting to see who speaks first.

Gabe and Jeff both start talking at once.

"What type of lies are you talking about?" Gabe asks at the same time Jeff blurts, "Did you just tell me fairies are real?"

"I said that fairies *might* exist. There's a guy in my chem lecture who claims to be one. And he's either really good at producing spontaneous hallucinations, or he actually has some kind of magical . . . something. I don't know. He calls them 'fae gifts.' I call them pretty fucking freaky, if I'm being completely honest."

"And did you also see these hallucinations?" Jeff asks Taylor.

Taylor looks like he'd rather go back to the sex talk, but then he nods. "I didn't see everything, but I saw him pop out of existence while I was watching, and . . . please don't freak out when I describe this in vampire terms, okay?"

Our friends agree and motion for him to continue.

"This guy . . . doesn't smell like potential food. It's like, he might as well have lizard blood, or insect blood, even. I've been pretty close to him, and my instincts never told me I could try drinking from him."

Gabe frowns. "Do *I* usually smell like food?"

Taylor cringes a little. "You said you wouldn't freak out, remember?"

"Fair enough," Gabe concedes. "So, you're entertaining the possibility of fairies. How does that tie into your parents lying to you?"

I give up completely on trying to pick at my breakfast and set my fork down. "My adoptive parents, also known as Grey's birth parents, always told me my birth parents were human. Both of them. But this guy, Ceallach, who says he's a fairy? He also says we're cousins and that my fairy grandmother wants to meet me, which I realize is absolute insanity, but now I've got this niggling thought in the back of my head, like, if one part of this is true, maybe the other parts are true too, and I'm kind of freaking out about it now that I'm saying it all out loud like this."

I finally stop my runaway voice and look around the table to see how my words landed.

Jeff is squinting at me speculatively, like maybe he'll be able to tell if I'm actually fae if he looks hard enough. Taylor looks like he wants to pick me up and comfort me with kisses or something. I wouldn't argue with that. Gabe has the oddest expression on his face. If I had to identify it on some kind of emotion recognition chart, I might guess . . . apologetic? He saves me from wondering about it for too long.

"Shit, Bee. I'm really sorry. I assumed you knew, and I guess it wouldn't have been my place to bring it up if you didn't know, but if I'd realized what you were going through . . . maybe I should have asked. I don't know." He frowns out the window, obviously thinking hard, though he's fallen silent.

"What the fuck are you talking about?" I blurt.

Startled, Gabe jerks his gaze back to me, then looks sheepishly around the table.

"I recognized you as fae the first time we met," he says. "Like calls to like and all that, you know?"

"No. I don't know."

He sighs. "Blood calls to blood, and like calls to like. Vampires recognize each other as vampires without having to check. Same with shifters. Humans aren't quite as good at it, but most humans will feel whether they're with their own kind or not. The same goes for fae. I knew that you and I were the same from the first time I saw you."

"You . . . and I . . ."

"Are both fae. Or half fae. It's not something we're supposed to advertise, which is why I assumed you also knew, even though you never brought it up. I figured, if you wanted to, I don't know, bond over it or something, you would talk to me about it. But you never brought it up, so I never brought it up, and now I find out that you never even knew at all."

I blink at him, trying desperately to get my new reality back into focus.

Shaking my head doesn't work any better to clear it. Fortunately, Taylor comes to my rescue.

"But that doesn't make any sense. You smell human, Bee smells human. That guy smells noticeably 'other.' I can believe that he's something different because my senses tell me he is, but you and Bee are human. All of my senses say you, Bee, and Jeff are the exact same species."

Gabe shrugs. "That's why I was surprised when you said I smell like food. I had never really thought about that aspect of it, but if I'd been asked to guess, I would have thought fae and half fae smell different from humans. Maybe this is one of those instinctive camouflage things . . . or something."

Jeff leans forward when Gabe doesn't explain. "I think I speak for the table when I say I'm going to need more information here."

"Yeah," I agree with a voice that croaks out of me. There are so many things that I need someone to explain to me right fucking now.

Standing up, Gabe paces the room like a trapped animal before facing me. "The fae are dangerous, and they have very particular ideas about purity in breeding. Sometimes, one of them will rebel, travel to our world, and . . ." He waves his hand in a "you get the gist" sort of motion. "My father was one of those, so here I am, half fae and half human, and I've spent my whole life trying to avoid notice from the fae. I don't know which of your parents was fae, but I'm guessing your story is similar to mine, except my father bowed to the queen's wishes and went home, while I'm guessing your parents refused and died for it."

"And the smell thing? The instinct thing? If we really are half fae, why doesn't everyone know about it?"

"Because we're born with the instinctual need to camouflage ourselves, to hide from anyone dangerous. I suspect full fae are as well, since one of the fae gifts is the glamor. They can make people see, and sometimes even feel, exactly what they want them to. I've been wearing a human costume since before I can remember. It wasn't something my father taught me. I was just born into this human-dominated world and automatically pretended to be human from birth."

Now that I've found my voice again, I can't seem to stop. I stand up and start my own pattern of pacing around the room.

"Okay, and this 'fae gifts' thing. Ceallach said something about that too, but he didn't, like, give me a list or anything."

Gabe lets me pace, turning to watch me as I go but making no moves to stop me. Taylor and Jeff seem to have decided this is a conversation for Gabe and me and are both sitting still, as if they've been glued to their chairs.

"I can teach you some things about the fae gifts," Gabe explains, "but they can be hit-or-miss for half fae. A lot of it is instinct, like I said. Like how I've made myself appear as human my whole life. That wasn't a skill someone taught me; it's just something I've always done as easily as breathing."

"But . . . that can't be right, because if I was instinctively camouflaging myself to fit in with the people around me, wouldn't I have tricked everyone into believing I'm a shifter, since everyone I grew up around is a shifter?" I keep working through the train of thought out loud. "Unless there's a limit to how different you can appear from your basic nature, I guess. Maybe if one of my parents was human and the other was fae, appearing human was within my reach, but appearing shifter was too far from my natural state?"

Gabe gives a helpless shrug. "I don't know all the answers. All I have is my own experience and the things my father has taught me."

"So, your father," I follow the tangent my mind takes. "You said he went back? But he taught you about all of this before he left?"

"He went back there, but he comes to visit me when he can. Usually, once every few years. More often would draw unwanted attention."

"Right. So, because neither of my parents have come to visit me, it probably means they really are dead."

He looks apologetic as he takes me by the elbow and leads me back to my seat.

"That's my guess," he says.

"And you think it was fae who killed them?"

He nods. "Fae are difficult to kill, so it's not likely to have been something else. A vampire or a shifter probably couldn't do it, and definitely not a human."

Which means we've circled back to the first lie again. "I was always told that my birth parents were humans who got on the bad side of some vampires, and that's who killed them. I wonder how much my adoptive parents actually know. Probably all of it, right? They probably know the full truth and have been lying to me about all of it this whole time."

Taylor kneels beside me and rubs a hand up and down my back. "Maybe," he says gently. "Maybe they've been lying to you, or maybe they've been trying to protect you, or maybe they really didn't know. I don't think we should make assumptions."

I look around at my friends. All of them have matching worried looks on their faces, and I hate that I'm the cause of all that worry.

I stand up and put a bright smile on my face.

"Well, I don't know about everyone else, but I've got a class I need to get to. How quickly can we get these dishes washed?"

"Bee," Jeff says cautiously.

"Not interested," I cut him off before he can launch the lecture about how I need to be protected. "Everyone, grab a plate, and let's get this breakfast cleaned up."

I don't have to look behind me to know all three of the guys are sharing a look as I take my dirty dishes to the kitchen. Whatever else has been turned upside down in my life recently, the overprotective males around me remain a constant.

"Bee, just hang on a moment," Taylor says, trailing behind me. I'm pleased to see he at least grabbed the carafe of coffee from the table so I won't have an extra trip to clean up breakfast. "We need to talk about how we're going to keep you safe."

"No, we don't," I say.

"Yes, we do. Gabe says the fae are dangerous, and we know that at least one of them knows how to find you."

"Exactly," I agree, getting started on scraping my barely touched breakfast into the trash. "They already know how to find me, and they almost definitely killed my parents, and they possibly want to kill me for unknown fae reasons, so it seems like my best option right now is to go about my life until I figure out a better solution."

"Come on, Bee. We aren't just going to sit back and let you die without trying to do something."

I narrow my eyes at him. "Fine. You try to do something. I'm going to try to live my life. We'll see what happens."

CHAPTER 39

Taylor

So, fairies exist. Okay. I can wrap my head around this. And Bee is half fairy. That makes a lot of sense, actually. But her attitude of ignoring the dangers of this new situation? Over my dead body.

Before I was born, my mom's life ended when someone more powerful than her decided to use his advantages against her, bringing me into the world and turning her into a vampire. I've been dealing with the repercussions of that ever since. Now, someone more powerful than Bee—in this case, a dangerous fairy—is trying to control her for some purpose that I don't know but can't imagine is good. I'm not going to just let them get to her.

"Really, Taylor, I'm fine," she tells me for the fifth or sixth, or possibly seventh, time since we left the house.

"Maybe, but it can't hurt to have me watching your back, can it?"

She huffs out an annoyed breath. "I take it you're planning on sitting in on my chem lecture to protect me?"

"Absolutely."

"And what about my chem lab? That's a lot smaller, and someone will notice a random extra person in the room."

"I didn't say I had a perfect solution figured out," I retort. "If you would talk about this with me, maybe we could figure out a better plan."

"I already did talk about it with you. Ceallach knows how to find me, which means my options are: one, I stay hidden in the house and hope he can't find me there and basically wait to die, two, go back to the pack and hide there and basically wait to die, or three, do my best to live a normal life as I've been doing. It seems obvious to me. The first two aren't really options."

I grab her arm to pull her to a stop, and she rounds on me with an expectant look.

"Bee, can't you see that this isn't just about you? Everyone else in your life would feel it if these fae took you from us, so it's not a question of you choosing what to do in a vacuum that only affects your life. Everyone around you wants to help. Everyone around you wants to come up with a better solution than 'wait to die,' but you have to work with us."

"My parents had a whole wolf pack trying to keep them safe, and it didn't work!"

Her voice is anger, but her face is fear and sadness. I step close to her and wrap my arms as tightly around her as I can while still letting her breathe. She sinks into my chest, and my heart gives a heavy *thunk* as she rests her face against it. Like a puzzle piece slotting into place. Like the right key catching in its lock and turning for the first time. I don't deserve her, I'm sure of it, but I belong to her anyway, and I will fight tooth and nail to keep her safe.

"Maybe a pack of wolves wasn't enough to save them," I say into the crown of her head, "but you've got wolves and vampires and at least one half fae on your side. Please, Bee.

Don't just give up and pretend there's nothing you can do. The rest of us aren't giving up."

Looking up at me, she blinks away what might be tears, though I can't be sure. "You really think there's something you could do?"

If I can't save her, I'll die trying.

"I think there's nothing I wouldn't be willing to try."

My heart gives another *thub-thunk* when she wraps her arms around my waist and holds me tight.

"You're going to say I have to tell Grey, aren't you?" she whispers into my chest so I feel the vibration of her voice more than I actually hear it.

"Don't you think we have to?"

She pulls back enough to give me a worried look. "What if he's known about all of this the whole time and he's been lying to me?" she asks.

"Only one way to find out," I say.

Taylor

Bee isn't happy about bringing her brother in, but it's the only logical solution I can see. That doesn't make it any more comfortable to deal with Grey taking up all of the energy in the living room right now.

"Let's go over this again," he grumbles, pacing the floor in front of the TV. "You've had someone following you and watching you for *weeks*, and you're just telling me about it now because . . . what? You didn't want the inconvenience of someone protecting you?"

"Taylor was protecting me," Bee argues, which I don't think actually helps our case much.

"I'm supposed to be the one protecting you!" Grey explodes. "That's the whole reason I'm at Berring in the first place, because our parents wanted me here protecting you!"

"No, *your* parents wanted that. Apparently, *my* parents weren't at all who I thought they were—what everyone *told me* they were. What do you know about that?"

Grey deflates at that. "Bee, I swear, all I ever knew is they were human friends of my father that he took in to protect them, but whoever was after them killed them anyway. I don't know anything about fae, or this guy claiming to be your cousin, or your grandmother wanting to meet you, or any of it. If I'd known, I would have . . ."

"Sided with your parents and argued against me ever going to college in the first place?"

"No! Well, maybe. But can't you see why? This world is dangerous. If you'd stayed with the pack, you would have a lot more protection than I can give you."

Bee crosses her arms and glares him down. "Grey, someone still got to my birth parents, even though they had the protection of the pack. Unless your father has been lying about that all along."

Grey deflates the rest of the way and sinks down on the couch beside Gloria. "I wouldn't even know how to ask him. I mean, I was one at the time. It's not like I have any memories of what happened. And if the rest of the pack knows something, that's a pretty big conspiracy for them to cover up for nineteen years, don't you think?"

Bee sits down beside me. I freeze, wondering if Grey will notice the new intimacy between us, but he doesn't say anything if he does.

"What about Mom?" Bee asks.

Grey shrugs. "She's never given any hint there's something going on, but she's also the best secret keeper in the pack, so who knows? She might tell you the truth if you ask her directly."

Bee sighs and leans against me. Grey might be too wrapped up in our current predicament to notice, but Gloria raises an eyebrow and looks between us. Turning bright pink, Bee stands up again and takes over Grey's previous job of pacing the living room.

Jeff and Gabe have stayed blissfully silent from their places wedged onto the other couch beside Devon and Marcus, who haven't commented on any of this beyond sharing a surprised look at the revelation about fairies being real.

"You know, we aren't even sure about any of this," she says. "I mean, we have Gabe's word that fae are real and that they're dangerous. I'm not saying I don't believe you," she cuts him off before he can argue the point, "I'm just saying that our only knowledge about these fae consists of what Gabe has said and what Ceallach has said. That's not much to go on."

Grey leans forward in his seat. "Which brings us back around to, you should probably tell Mom about this."

That stops Bee's pacing in an instant. "And that brings us back to, if she's been keeping this from me all this time, why would she tell me now?"

I want to put my arm around her. I want to pull her close to me and cuddle her against my chest and tell her this is going to be okay and I'll keep her safe and she doesn't have to worry about anything. But none of that can happen. None of that is true. No matter what I do to keep her safe, I can't give her any guarantees, and my heart aches because of that.

Gloria gives Bee an assessing look. "I agree with Grey, as much as it pains me to admit it. Your mom might know more than she's told you before, but maybe she was waiting to tell you until you were old enough to understand, or she wasn't sure how to bring it up. We can speculate all we want about how much she knows or why she's kept it hidden, but if there's someone who might actually know the truth, we should ask them."

Bee glares at Gloria like she killed her puppy. "I'll think about it," she grumbles.

"Um, speaking of mothers," I say hesitantly, "while there's backup here to watch you, I need to go home and check on my own mom."

They all turn to me with the same surprised and expectant

face, which I suppose is fair since I haven't said anything about her in the past, but it's nobody's business. Until it is. Like now.

I try to explain. "She's on her own, and she's got some health issues. I try to check in on her a couple times a week." No need for them to know details like how her health issues are mental health issues that make her too paranoid to feed unless I can talk her into it. I can't see how that would be relevant information for them.

Grey looks like he might argue that I need to stay, but Bee sits back down beside me and puts a hand on my knee.

"You should go. Take care of what you need to. I'm not going anywhere."

The promise in her voice makes my heart give another unnecessary *thump* in my chest before stilling again.

Bee will be right here, waiting for me. Bee's not going anywhere.

CHAPTER 41

Bee

Even though I rehearsed what to say for an hour before actually hitting the Call button, I still have no idea how to respond when Mom answers with a breathless "Bee? Are you okay? What's wrong?"

I stare at my phone, frozen and tongue-tied and guilt-ridden, for a long moment.

"Bee? Are you there?"

There's a lot more sadness in her voice than I expected, and I wasn't prepared to be hit so hard by her worry.

I finally unstick my tongue to answer her.

"I'm fine. I'm really fine. There's nothing wrong."

A shuddering sigh comes through my speaker, and I can almost see her drooping, closing her eyes in relief, maybe letting herself collapse onto the nearest chair.

"Okay. Good. That's so good to hear. And it's good to hear your voice again."

There's the guilt again. Maybe I shouldn't have cut her out so thoroughly in my quest to figure out who I am away from the pack.

"It's good to hear your voice too," I admit. I can't believe it's been over a year since I spoke to her directly. I'm sure Grey has been sending home updates, but this is the first time I've reached out to talk to her since I moved to Berring last fall.

"We've missed you. It's been so quiet in the house with you gone." Her tone isn't accusatory, but it feels like an accusation all the same.

"I'm sorry, Mom. I know you don't understand, but I really needed to do this. I really needed to learn how to live on my own, without the pack, without you." Without feeling helpless and inadequate all the time. But I can't explain that to her, not when I know perfectly well that it was never her intention that I feel that way.

"Sweetheart, I left my own pack for a reason, you know. I might understand better than you realize."

I think about asking. It's not something she talks about much. The widely known story is that she left her pack and then met Dad and found herself mated to him. Grey was born sometime later, and they've all been living—more or less—happily ever after since. What's not widely known is that Dad can be a difficult person to get along with, and the two of them have always had a complicated relationship. I think, when it comes down to it, they really do love each other, but he's so busy keeping up the facade of being the pack leader, in control of everything—and everyone—in his pack, that his personal relationships tend to have a lower priority.

But I'm not calling to ask about her and Dad. I need to know about my birth parents. And I need to know what she's been keeping from me.

"Maybe . . . another time . . ." I struggle to find the right words again.

"I take it you called for a reason other than to tell me you're dropping out of school and coming home because you've found what you were looking for?"

I pick at the hem of my skirt. "Yeah. I guess you could put it that way."

"Bee, you know you can tell me anything, right?"

Can I really, though? I could never tell her how helpless I felt, needing Grey to watch over me like a bodyguard, even when we were kids. And I never told her about how I felt when all of the girls in the pack started going into heat for the first time and I was left out. Left behind. Then there's the fact that I've always been the beautiful, breakable thing to be kept on the shelf, away from danger but also away from life.

"Who were my birth parents?" I blurt out. "Who were they really, and don't lie to me about it this time."

She sucks in a shocked breath. "Bee, what's happened?"

Okay, I was expecting immediate denial. I made this call thinking she would feed me the old story about two humans that Dad wanted to protect from vampires. I wasn't expecting her to basically confirm my accusation that she's been lying to me.

"What's happened is that there's this man who says he's my cousin and that my grandmother wants to meet me. And this man is not human, which means, if he really is my cousin, my parents probably weren't human either, so now I'm wondering what the fuck I am, if I'm not human like I thought I was—like you *told me* I was—my whole life." And if she knows about the fae, now is her chance to tell me about them.

The briefest moment of silence in which I wonder if she'll lecture me about cursing or try to deny everything, but she does neither.

"Bee, I need you to come home. Today. Right now. Don't bother packing, just get your brother and get in the car. Can you do that for me? Where's Grey right now?"

"No, Mom, I need answers, not demands, right now. Who were my parents?"

I hear her breathing like she's trying to calm herself. "Sweetheart, there's no time right now. I can explain everything once you're safe, but you're not safe right now."

I plant my feet. She can't see it, but she knows me well enough to know she's activated my stubbornness.

"If you can't answer my questions, then I guess there's nothing to talk about," I tell her, then add, "I'm not going back to the pack, though," and hang up before she can argue.

My phone immediately starts ringing again, and I hit Ignore without a second thought.

I should have known that her first response would be to try and drag me home for my supposed safety. I should have known she wouldn't actually tell me anything useful.

I stomp out of my room and see that Grey is already on his phone.

"Yeah, she's fine. She's right—"

"I'm not going," I cut him off before he can try and hand the phone off to me.

"But Mom just—"

"You can tell her I'm not going back. I'm fine here."

His face drops as he listens to whatever our mother is saying.

"Okay. I'll see what I can do."

He listens again.

"Yeah, Mom, I'll call you back and let you know," he says and ends the call.

"What the fuck was that?" He rounds on me. "I thought you were talking to her, then she calls me, completely panicking, saying it's not safe for you here and I need to convince you to come home."

I stand my ground. I don't need yet another lecture about this today. "She's never going to believe it's safe away from the pack," I argue. "In her mind, I need to be bundled up carefully and kept away from anything that might ever possibly happen, but let me remind you, again, my parents were with the pack when they died. The pack wasn't an obstacle for whoever killed them. So, no, I'm not going back, and I'm not letting her scare me into staying home for the rest of my life."

A muscle in his jaw ticks as he glares at me.

Gloria comes up behind him and puts a hand on his shoulder. "Don't you think Bee is old enough to make her own choice here?" she asks gently. "We were planning on doing whatever it took to protect her here, and that doesn't have to change. Besides, Bee has a point about the pack not being able to protect her parents. Why would it help to go back to them now?"

Grey heaves a put-upon sigh and hits Call. "Yeah . . ." He pauses and listens. "No, Mom . . ." Another long pause, and all I can hear is a murmur that might be our mother lecturing him. "Yeah. No. Mom, I tried, but she's not budging. I can't convince her to come home." There's another long pause, and then Grey pulls the phone from his ear and frowns at it.

"What?" I ask.

"She hung up on me," he says in disbelief. "I don't think she's ever hung up on me."

Gloria gives his shoulder a comforting pat. "And what did she say before she hung up on you?"

Grey suddenly looks like he might be sick. "Um. She said she's coming here? She might have said something about carrying you over her shoulder if that's what it takes to get you safely home."

Great. Just what I needed.

CHAPTER 42

Taylor

When I get to the house, I'm relieved to see my mother already drinking from a blood bag. Her eyes don't have the fevered sheen of paranoia in them either. Always a comforting sign.

"Taylor! What has you home so early in the week?"

I give her the hug she's asking for and sit on the couch beside her.

"I just thought I'd stop by and see how you're doing," I say. It never does any good to remind her of the bad times when she's in the midst of the good. "Have the blood deliveries been coming as scheduled?"

She waves her current bag at me. "Right on time. With new drivers this time. They looked much more trustworthy."

"That's great. I'm glad to hear it." Though I'm already doing the math for how long she'll tolerate the new delivery guys before it becomes an issue. "Anything else going on this week?"

"Nothing interesting happens here, you know that," she tells me with a laugh, and I have a pang of wondering, or maybe wishing, if this could be her all the time, what would our lives be like?

"Nothing interesting doesn't actually sound that bad."

"I used to wish for something interesting," she confesses, and I freeze in my seat, waiting to see where she goes with this. "I used to wish that something exciting would happen in my life, and then your father came along and taught me the error of my ways."

Shit. I guess we're going there tonight.

"And what did he do, Mom?"

She narrows her eyes at me and takes a long, ominous pull from her blood bag.

"He got me pregnant, that's what. He ended my life and left me with a little monster to take care of. Fucking oldest story ever told, right?"

I brace myself for the rest, and sure enough, here it comes.

"You know, I was happy before him. Before you came along. I could have done anything with my life, but instead, I ended up here."

Pinching the bridge of my nose, I search for calm and balance and the correct way to respond when I'm being verbally attacked by my mother.

"Yep," I end up agreeing with her. "We both ended up here."

"That's right." She emphasizes her point by jabbing the blood bag in my direction. "We both ended up here, and your father went off on his merry way and left us both behind. He made me all sorts of promises, but when it came down to it, he didn't keep even one of them."

"Yeah, I know, Mom." I sit, curling in on myself. Even knowing the story, it still hurts to have her throw it at me like this.

"He broke every promise he made, and he ruined my life, and now, you have the nerve to sit there and act like you're any different? You'll do the exact same fucking thing. Don't act like you won't."

"But Mom—"

"I know you, because I know him. I bet you've already ruined someone the same way he ruined me, haven't you?"

It doesn't matter that I know it's not true. The shame of it still lances through me like a physical wound, along with the fear that I may have tainted Bee just through her association with me.

"No, don't bother denying it. I know the truth. You're his son, and I know how he was."

"How about—" But she cuts me off. She's not interested in letting me argue.

"How about you go back where you came from," she sneers. "How about you go back and play pretend for a little longer, and then you can come back home and tell me how you're nothing like your father."

Some days, it's easier to take. Today, when I know that Bee is waiting for me, when I know what I have is different and better than what my parents had? Today, I need to get out of here to be with people who might be able to care about me. I hate it that my mom will never truly be able to care about me, but it's a reality. I need to accept it.

"Fine." I stand and stride all the way across the room before I turn back. "I'll go back, but you know—we both know—that I'm not like him, so stop saying I am."

I hear her skeptical "hmph" at that as I'm leaving the house, but I don't turn back. I can't turn back, or else she'll suck me right back into her vortex. Whatever my mom thinks, I can help Bee. I can be good for her, if she'll let me. And I will never become my father, turning vampires and fathering unwanted children without any thought for the consequences.

CHAPTER 43

Taylor

I don't really sleep. I lie in bed, trying to fend off my mother's attacks. Sometimes, it's the repetition of her words and accusations.

You're just like him.

You've probably already ruined someone the way he ruined me.

I turn over and press a pillow over my ear to keep her voice out, but of course, you can't keep something out that's already gotten in.

And then, other times, it's her face, which I see every time I close my eyes. Her eyes fevered with anger and fear and a dangerous kind of nervous energy. Hands that are just as likely to slap as they are to comfort.

You'll see. You're your father's child.

You ruined everything when you came along.

All you can do is break things. You'll never add anything good to the world.

I turn over again with the exact same results.

Deciding to give up, I tiptoe out of my room, thinking I can at least waste some time by drinking tea and attempting to study. Not that I think I'll be able to focus on any of my schoolwork, but I can try. It'll be better than seeing Mom's angry face every time I close my eyes.

The house was dark and quiet when I got home, the lumpy shapes of most of my friends sleeping on the couches visible only to my vampire eyes, but someone is up now.

I stand in the kitchen doorway for a minute, just watching as Bee putters around with food that I'm only vaguely familiar with.

"You couldn't sleep either, I guess," I say quietly so I don't startle her.

It doesn't work. She lets out a yelp and jumps about three feet in the air, then lands facing me with a dull knife pointed at my chest.

All of the tension sloughs out of her when she realizes who I am. "Shit, Taylor, I didn't know you were back."

"Yeah. Things with my mom didn't go . . . great . . . so I decided to come back here. I'll try checking on her again in a few days."

Worried eyes look me up and down. "She's not well? Is everything okay?"

I let out a tense laugh. "Everything is . . . fine. It is what it is. Everything is complicated," I admit.

Wanting an escape, I turn toward the kettle and start heating water for tea.

"How about with you? Did you call your mom or decide to wait?"

Bee growls—actually growls, like a snarling puppy sound —and turns back to what she was doing. "I called her, and she freaked out even worse than I expected. She refused to talk to me about what's going on, but she definitely knows more than she's telling me. Oh, and she's coming here to try and convince me to go back home with her."

Bee's movements become increasingly jerky and violent as

she speaks, slapping one, then two, then three thick dollops of peanut butter on a slice of bread.

Before she has a chance to break the plate she's using, I come up behind her and still her hands with mine.

"Why don't you tell me about it while I make this for you?"

She leans her back into me and takes a long breath in.

Something about feeling her lungs fill against me, the way her eyes close and her face turns up, the heat of her wrists where my fingers are touching them . . . I feel myself melt against her.

"Have you ever made a sandwich?" she asks, and I hear it from a distance because all I can think about is her in my arms and the sound of her heartbeat and the rushing of blood through her veins. Faster than any other human's heartbeat, I notice for the first time, or maybe she's just as affected by this moment as I am.

"A sandwich?" I ask from a million miles away, my voice dazed.

"Yeah, that's what I'm making. You offered to make it for me, so I asked if you had ever done it before."

"No," I admit, "but I'm sure you could teach me."

She stays pressed against me and allows my hands to keep their place on her wrists as she resumes her sandwich making. Her movements are calm again as she spreads what looks to me like a ridiculous amount of peanut butter over the bread, then an even more ridiculous amount of red jelly.

"Do you want to taste it?" she asks and holds the sandwich up as an offering.

"No. All for you." It would probably make me sick to try and eat that much solid food.

As she takes a bite from the corner of her sandwich, my hands drift down her forearms, past her elbows, and land on her hips.

She doesn't jerk away or even acknowledge that I'm still touching her. The rhythm of bite, chew, swallow stays the same as I slide my fingers around her front to cup her belly, then up to cradle her breasts, one in each hand. She's wearing a satiny sleeveless top, so I can feel the slide of every curve against my palms. I can feel her nipples hardening against my fingers.

Maybe I should be worried about someone walking in, about Grey and Gloria in the other room, about the guys asleep on the couch, but all I can do is stay in this moment, and Bee is right here with me. She lets out a shuddery moan when I lower my head so I can bury my nose in her hair and catch every drop of her scent. When I lick the skin behind her ear and nip at her earlobe, she sets down the half-eaten sandwich and turns in my arms.

Our lips meet in a desperate, hungry slide of tongues and small noises as I steal each breath she gives me.

In one easy motion, I lift her up and set her on the counter, careful not to set her down on her plate, and grind against her.

Her shorts are made from the same satin material as her shirt, and it's easy to slide my hand down the front and reach her already drenched pussy.

"Is this okay?" I check before going on. My voice might be strained from holding myself back, but it's important to ask.

"Yes," she half whispers, half whines. "Touch me."

I slide my finger lower, between her petal-like labia, to find the hard nub of her clit. She gasps, so I roll my finger over it again, letting her responses guide me into a rhythm that seems to have her climbing closer and closer to her release until she bites hard on my shoulder to muffle her cries and wraps her legs tight around my hips to ride out her orgasm.

She gasps for breath and clings to me like the last piece of dry land in a flood, and I can't say I'm faring much better. I slip my hand from her shorts and suck at the finger that's covered in her arousal.

"Oh," I hear from behind me and spin to put Bee at my back while I face whatever new threat just arrived.

A sleepy Gloria stands blinking at us for a moment.

Any hope that she doesn't know what she just walked in on disintegrates when she claps a hand over her mouth to cover the laugh that bursts out of her and whispers, "I knew it! I knew it had to be Taylor!"

Bee rushes out from behind me and clamps her own hand over Gloria's mouth. Belatedly, I realize I'm still sucking on my finger and try to inconspicuously pull it out of my mouth and wipe it dry on my pajama pants. With my other hand, I'm trying to casually cover my erection without drawing any attention to it.

"Gloria," Bee whispers, "you can't say anything. Please don't say anything."

Hearing her say it stings, even though I know all of the reasons it's best to keep this secret. I want to shout from the rooftops that I, Taylor, the worthless monster who nobody in their right mind would trust, just made Bee come on my finger.

"Yeah, of course," Gloria agrees. "Grey and the rest of them were asleep when I got up, so they probably didn't hear anything, and I really don't want to be the one who breaks this news to him." She gives Bee a significant look.

Bee rakes her fingers through her hair and pulls hard, pacing the room like she's desperate to find an exit.

"Shit, shit, shit. What was I thinking?"

I still her with a hand on her shoulder. It hurts, but this is what she needs from me right now. Calming down distressed women seems to be what I was put on this planet to do. "It's going to be fine. Gloria won't say anything. I won't say anything. I'll go back to my room now, you'll finish eating, and any evidence this happened will be gone by the morning. Nothing to stress about."

She looks up at me with . . . it's probably wishful thinking to believe she's looking at me with longing in her eyes. More likely, it's gratitude that I'm willing to keep this secret. The longing, the needing, the unhinged desire? Those are all my own emotions that I'm projecting onto her.

"I'd better get to bed, then," I mutter and duck out of the kitchen before it can all be too much.

CHAPTER 44

Bee

Gloria gives me a lascivious eyebrow waggle as soon as Taylor is out of the room. "Well, based on what I was hearing from you a minute ago, it was worth it to give him another chance."

Is my face on fire? I'm pretty sure my face is on fire. And my ears. And my neck. I turn to the sink and splash some cold water on my cheeks.

I can't believe I just did that. I can't believe I just did that *here*, and when the house is full of people, and that Gloria walked in on us.

I round on her and point a finger at her like a weapon. Not a very intimidating weapon, but hopefully, she gets the idea.

"Whatever you're about to say, don't. I can't have this conversation now."

"Oh, come on, Bee. After the number of times you've walked in on me and Gr—"

"No. No. Two horny wolves not being able to control themselves is different from me not being able to control myself. And if Grey finds out . . ." I feel dizzy when I think it could just have easily been my brother who walked into the kitchen and saw what was happening.

Gloria's smile drops, and she takes me by the shoulders. "Hey. It's okay to have whatever feelings. It's okay to let someone make you feel good, and it sounded to me like he makes you feel good. Am I right about that part?"

I let the tension in my shoulders go with a sigh. "Yes. You're right about that part. But Grey absolutely cannot find out."

She cocks an eyebrow at me. "You know I would never tell him, but maybe you want to be a little more careful about where you do these things?"

She gives a meaningful look around the kitchen, and I drop my face to my hands with a groan.

"I can't believe I was that careless," I confess.

"Oh, sweetie." She rubs my back. "We all have our moments."

She comforts me for a moment before turning on me again. "Now, as I was saying before, I take it you gave him another chance? And? How was it? Has his . . . little issue . . . cleared up?"

"Gloria!" I glare at her. "I'm not talking about this."

"Fine," she huffs. "Eat your sandwich and go back to bed. But don't think we won't revisit this discussion when we've both had more sleep," she whispers in a cheerful singsong over her shoulder before disappearing back into her own bedroom.

I lean against the counter, my whole body like jelly after the roller coaster of the last few minutes.

I mean, I went from the most sensual sandwich-making experience of my life, to coming on Taylor's finger, to Gloria walking in on me coming on Taylor's finger, all in less than a fifteen-minute time span. I feel wrung out.

My stomach growling reminds me of why I couldn't sleep to begin with. I finish my sandwich in a few bites but still feel like there's a black hole eating me from the inside. My eating habits have always been another thing that held me apart from my adoptive family. Wolves are carnivores, and wolf shifters—even in their human forms—have trouble digesting food other than meat. On the other end of the spectrum, I've never been able to eat much meat at all. Even a few bites can make me sick for days afterward. Waking up and needing food in the middle of the night is unusual for me, as is needing more than a few bites of anything.

I give in to my hunger and make a second sandwich for myself. I feel less like an empty cavern after I finish eating it, but I'm still hungry. It's only after a third sandwich that I feel sated and put everything away.

What is going on with me?

The insatiable hunger and sudden horniness honestly remind me of Gloria when she goes into heat.

But I'm a nineteen-year-old human who's . . . I catch myself in the lie I've been told my whole life. Apparently, I'm not human. Apparently, I have a fae cousin who can disappear into thin air and a grandmother who terrifies my adoptive mother, a fact which brings me back around to the bitter realization that my adoptive mother—probably my adoptive father as well—has known about my birth parents and been lying about them all along.

Who were they?

Who does that make me?

And those questions have me circling back on even more upsetting questions.

If my adoptive parents have been hiding the truth for all these years, what else are they hiding? Are my birth parents actually dead, like I've been told? Or is that a lie too? Gabe thinks so, but what does he actually know?

I want to punch something or break something. Just to have some sort of release. I want to walk out of this house right now and . . . I'm not even sure what. Walk away and search for my parents? Or maybe just walk to the tattoo shop to see if another tattoo would numb my feelings for a while.

Remembering what happened the last time I went out on my own, I slink back to my bed to fail at sleeping until my mother gets here.

CHAPTER 45

Bee

It's not even 6:30 when I hear a car pull up outside. She must have gotten an early start to be here before the sun is up.

My stomach clenches, thinking about the confrontation we're about to have. Gods, I hope Dad isn't with her. This will be bad enough without the potential of being literally carried out of the house, kicking and screaming.

Dread rises in me as I feel my chance at freedom slipping away.

This is it. This is going to be the end of my time at Berring. The end of my time away from the pack. No way am I going to get a chance to explore what's been happening with Taylor. It's stupid, but I feel a pang of grief over the sex toys I bought that I'll never get to try out.

I wonder if the cloud hanging over me as I come out of my bedroom to answer the door is visible to anyone else. Before I reach the door, though, Gloria grabs me by the elbow, hustles me into her bedroom, and closes the door.

Her normal practical calm has vanished without a trace.

"What do I wear?" she hisses in a panicked whisper.

"Wear?"

"To meet your and Grey's mom for the first time. I thought I was fine and it would be no big deal, but I've been losing my mind all morning, freaking out about what I should wear so she doesn't hate me."

I stop the laughter that automatically wants to bubble over at this and guide her to her bed, where it looks like she's pulled out every single item of clothing she owns, tried it on, then discarded it in a rumpled heap.

Is it bad that I find some comfort in the fact that I'm not alone in freaking out right now?

But a good friend doesn't let her friends panic spiral, so I put on a soothing facade for Gloria.

"You could go out there naked to meet her, and she would still fall instantly in love with you. You're everything she ever dreamed of for Grey. There is nothing you could do that would stop you from being her ideal daughter. I promise."

She gives me a sad look. "Even if I've put her actual daughter in danger by being absent and distracted all summer? What about if I'm the reason her actual daughter is hooking up with a vampire?"

My laugh sounds bitter in my own ears.

"First of all, I'm not her actual daughter, am I? I always thought I was her adopted daughter, but I don't even know about that anymore, if she's been lying to me about it all along. Second of all, you haven't put me in any danger. You know our friendship would have been over if you'd tried being overbearing and protective like Grey. Getting away from over-protective wolves is the whole reason I left the pack to go to school. Third of all, she's not going to find out about that other thing, and I don't see how it's going to continue after this anyway. If she drags me home today, I'll probably never see Taylor again."

I do my best to shrug off my own doom and plaster a bright smile on my face.

"But if you're asking for help picking out an outfit to wear right now, that's something I can do."

It takes about three minutes of rummaging through the mess of clothes on Gloria's bed to pick out a cute blouse and fitted jeans that say "I want to look good for you without looking like I tried too hard," and then the two of us are facing the door and holding hands like we're about to face down a monster.

"Me first," Gloria says. "I want to get it over with, and maybe meeting me will distract her from trying to pack you into the car and leave."

I give her hand a grateful squeeze before letting go so she can walk ahead of me.

"Oh, good, you're up!" Grey says as if Gloria didn't send him out here to greet Mom and buy us time to get ready. "Mom, I'd like to officially introduce you to someone. Mom, this is Gloria, my mate. Gloria, this is my mom, Astrid."

Mom's eyes mist up a little at that, and I hang back to let them have a proper meeting. Not to put off speaking to my mom. That has nothing to do with it.

Okay, fine. It might have something to do with it.

"I have heard so much about you," she says, then, in true wolf fashion, grabs Gloria by the biceps and drags her closer for a long sniff. She's smiling when she pulls away. "I can't believe it's taken this long, but I know you've had your reasons for not coming to visit the pack, and I wanted to give you space. No one wants their mate's mother looking over their shoulder all the time. But it's good to meet you now."

Gloria lets out a little squeak when Mom grabs her again, this time for a hug tight enough that even I can hear Gloria's bones creaking under the strain.

"And now that that's out of the way . . ." Mom turns to me with narrowed eyes. "Let's see it."

"See it? See what?" Of everything I imagined, those aren't the first words I was expecting from her when I saw her again.

She glances upward like she's begging the gods for strength in dealing with me, then comes to me and spins me around in a circle.

"The tattoo. Let's see it."

"The *what*?" Grey shouts from his place across the room.

Mom rolls her eyes at him. "I guess that means you didn't know about it?" Then she turns back to me. "Well?"

With a sigh, I lift my shirt up to reveal the flowers and butterflies on my stomach.

She doesn't react with the shock and horror I'm expecting. While Grey continues to splutter a "What the fuck, Bee?" Mom just turns me around again, slower this time, so she can see the full tattoo as the butterflies continue onto my back and swirl around the skeleton.

"It's beautiful," she finally murmurs, tracing the place where Death's horse's skeletal head tosses.

"I thought if you'd seen it on the credit card statement, I would have heard about it right away."

"You thought you'd gotten away with it," she corrects me in a matter-of-fact voice. "And you did, after a fashion. I've been the one keeping track of the money for a few years now, so it was pretty easy to do some creative accounting so your father didn't see it."

I'm not sure what I expected. Maybe I wanted both of my parents to come here and rip me apart for doing something they don't approve of, but now it's just Mom here, and she's not angry, at least not about the tattoo.

"He didn't come with you?" I ask tentatively.

She gives my cheek a reassuring pat. "We decided it would do more damage if he came and tried to force you to come home. Why don't we make some breakfast, then we can all sit down together and strategize? Maybe all of the boys hiding in that other bedroom can even come out and join the conversation too."

Who is this woman? My mother is the woman I spoke to on the phone last night, whose immediate, knee-jerk reaction to the situation was to come here and bring me home. This woman is talking about breakfast and accounting as if she weren't convinced of my immediate danger less than twelve hours ago.

"I don't get it," I say.

"Get what?"

"You." I plant my hands on my hips. "I don't get you, or this change of plans, or the fact that you're not mad about the tattoo, or any of it. What's going on?"

She matches my stance with a firm look of her own. "The plans have changed because your father and I talked about it, and you're right about the pack not being the safest place. Your birth mother's family was able to get to her, even with the pack's protection, but I'm also not willing to just hand you over to them without a fight, so I'm here, ready to fight for you. And I'm not mad about the tattoo because, in the grand scheme of things, I care more about you than any of these little rebellions!"

Her voice rises with each word until she's shouting, and I match her in volume.

"They aren't just 'little rebellions'! I'm living my life! You've never understood that I'm just trying to live a normal life!"

"And you've never understood that we're just trying to keep you safe!"

"Well, maybe I'd rather have a little danger in my life, just so I can say I experienced *something*!"

We're about three seconds from actually throwing things

when I realize there are several sets of wide eyes staring at us in a mixture of fascination and horror. Mom has the same realization at the same time, and we both make a visible effort to step back from the argument.

After a moment of awkward silence, Mom turns to Taylor, who must have run out of his room when he heard shouting, because he's still wearing the flannel pants and threadbare white T-shirt from last night.

"You must be Bethany's other roommate. I've heard so much about you. From my son."

Of course she has to add that last part. A spiteful part of me feels compelled to mutter, "My name is Bee, not Bethany," even though she's known my preference for years and only honors it half the time.

Taylor looks like he's trying to collapse in on himself, with his shoulders hunched and his head turtled down. He's probably a full four inches shorter than usual.

"Er . . . hi." He stretches out his hand tentatively. "I'm Taylor."

"I know you're a vampire, have known, so you can stop worrying about how I'm going to react to that revelation," she says, taking his hand for a firmer than absolutely necessary handshake. "And everyone else?"

The rest of the guys file out and introduce themselves with varying degrees of confidence. Jeff, of course, is practically buzzing with the excitement of meeting new people, whereas Gabe keeps a guarded look on his face the whole time. Devon is his usual friendly self, while Marcus is just as stiff and withdrawn as ever.

After the introductions, Mom gives a sharp hand clap to draw everyone's attention. "I was serious when I suggested breakfast and strategizing. We're not leaving this house without a plan, so I hope your fridge is stocked."

CHAPTER 46

Bee

Most. Uncomfortable. Breakfast. Ever.

Taylor tried to get out of it by sneaking back to his room during the bustle of Mom and Marcus cooking for everyone—and who was betting on my mother cooking a meal with a vampire, because I know I wasn't—but I gave him a death glare that convinced him to help set the table instead.

Then there's this thing between Taylor and me, which has me worried Jeff is going to open his mouth and tell everyone about how he caught us, naked in the hallway and covered in come, fairly recently. I don't want to think about how Mom would respond to that. Anyway, she probably wouldn't get a chance to respond because Grey would immediately do something stupid.

And in case the whole secret vampire boyfriend thing wasn't enough, there's still the fae elephant in the room. I think Gabe is just as anxious as I am to know exactly what my mom knows about the situation. He keeps sneaking wary glances at her, then hurriedly looking away and pretending to be interested in the eggs on his plate. All I can manage is to vaguely push a bit of egg around in circles while I wait for the wolves to finish eating.

Mom, Grey, and Gloria all have heaping piles of meat on their plates and are eating, well, exactly how wolves eat. Devon looks a little more green each time someone makes an audible chewing noise. Which is constantly. He's had a hand clamped on his boyfriend's wrist since the beginning of breakfast, and his only movement has been a steady clench and unclench of his jaw. I don't know the details, but I remember he had some sort of health problem last year that kept him from feeding the way vampires are supposed to. I wonder if this is a continuation of that. None of the vampires has anything other than coffee in front of them.

"So," Mom announces from her end of the dining table, "now that we have some food in our stomachs, are we ready to start planning?"

Finally. I drop my fork on my plate with a clink.

"Are you ever going to tell me the truth about my parents, or are you going to keep on pretending that you don't know anything?" I ask, trying to exude calm and maturity, even though I'm screaming and raging on the inside.

Mom sets down her own fork. Multiple expressions play across her face as she marshals her thoughts.

"We had good reason to keep the full truth from you," she starts. Seats creak as everyone around the table leans forward. "Bee, your mother's family . . . they're dangerous. More dangerous than you can imagine."

I slam my palm down on the table hard enough to make everyone jump. So much for calm and maturity.

"This again? This stupid excuse about how you've just been protecting me? You lied to me!"

The rest of them flick glances at each other, probably debating whether to get involved in this conversation or to try to sneak out of the room so Mom and I can argue in private.

No one moves to stand, though. Taylor looks like he's trying to freeze and take up the least amount of space possible so we won't notice him there.

"We protected you from a truth that would have destroyed you!"

"You can't be serious." I rake my fingers through my hair and pull so hard it hurts. "What could be more dangerous than not having the information?"

"What could be more dangerous?" Mom repeats. "Your grandmother could be more dangerous. Your mother warned us how dangerous, and we did all we could to protect you, but we couldn't save them. We told your grandmother's people that you were dead, and that's the only reason they didn't kill you when they killed your parents."

Everyone sits gaping at the revelation. Somehow, I'm the first one to find my voice again.

"Are you saying it was my mother's own family that killed her? Her own mother?" I try to rearrange the puzzle pieces in my mind. Ceallach, claiming to be helpful. But also, Ceallach, freaking me out with his supposed fae gifts. Ceallach, saying he won't hurt me. At the same time, Ceallach, wanting to introduce me to my grandmother . . . who maybe killed my mother? None of the pieces fit together.

Mom stares out the window for the longest minute ever before answering.

"Yes, it was your mother's family that killed her."

"So, my mother's family . . . aren't human? What about my father?"

"No," Mom admits with a shake of her head. "They weren't human. Neither of your parents were human."

Everyone in the room holds their breath. I'm the first one to break.

"Well? What were they? Who were they?"

"Bee, there's no taking it back once I tell you. You have to be certain that you're ready. Everyone here has to be certain that they're ready, because there's no way to keep any of you from danger once I tell you." She gives a pleading look around the room, but I'm not budging. I need to know the truth. *Finally*, I'll know the truth. And everyone else already made their choice to stay.

"It's too late to try and keep any of us in the dark. We know part of it already. Now we need to know the rest of it."

The tension of holding on to a secret for almost two decades leaves Mom with a whoosh.

"Fae," she says. "Your mother and all of her family are fae, and now none of you are safe because you know." She gives an apologetic look around the table. "I'm sorry to bring you all in on this. If I could have thought of any other way to keep Bee safe while keeping you all out of it, I would have."

Gabe sits up straighter. "Bee's father. He wasn't fae, was he? Otherwise, they simply would have brought them both home instead of killing them."

Mom shows a moment of surprise before she gets herself back under control.

"No," she says, then looks back and forth between Grey and me like she's still undecided about telling the full story. After a long pause, she takes a deep breath and squares her shoulders. "Bee, your birth father was Greyson's older brother."

"What?" Grey and I shout at the same time.

"Dad doesn't have any siblings," Grey goes on, looking disgruntled.

I'm not sure if I'm more shocked or confused. Dad is a shifter. His brother would be a shifter. "That's not possible, though. How could I be half shifter when I've only ever seemed human? I don't have an animal form. I don't have a shifter's strength or ability to heal or anything. This makes no fucking sense."

Mom grimaces at my cursing but doesn't say anything about it. "None of us knew what to expect with you," she explains. "It might have been easier if you'd appeared as a wolf."

Ha. Understatement.

"We'd already kept your mother a secret from the rest of the pack. It would have been easy to claim you were my own baby. Aliya knew better, though. She said a mixed child might come out in any number of forms, and she had already cut off her own wings to stay hidden, so the first form you saw when you were born appeared human. I think that you saw your mother for the first time, and you made yourself exactly like her. That's just my theory, though." She pauses to blink back some tears while the rest of us sit in horrified silence.

It's all I can do to keep breathing, and even that is rasping and strained.

In. Slow.

Cut off her own wings.

Out. Slow.

She'd already cut off her wings.

Those words, and their implied horror, won't stop echoing in my mind. I must have misheard. Or misunderstood. That can't be what happened.

"Did you . . ." I lick my lips, swallow, and try again. "Did you say she cut her wings off?"

With a deep breath, Mom visibly readies herself to tell us more.

"I'd better tell the whole thing," she says, almost to herself, then looks at us again. "It's not a nice story, but it's important. If you're going to understand all of this, you need to hear the full thing, so don't interrupt."

We all nod some kind of agreement, afraid that speaking now might count as an interruption and cause her to stop.

"Owen was Greyson's—my husband's—older brother. He

was the favorite in just about every way. Presumptive heir to the pack leader, popular among his peers, he had a magnetic personality that drew people into his orbit whether they liked it or not. Greyson was always more serious and withdrawn. He was always happy that Owen was there to shoulder the responsibilities of leadership. We thought Owen was perfectly made to fill that place in society. Right up until Owen ran away."

Mom's eyes flick up to me, then down to her hands, which she's been twisting nervously together, before she goes on. Is she thinking about when I ran away?

"Owen wanted to leave the pack and experience life before coming home and taking on the duties of pack leader. But then he called Greyson from the road and told him he had fallen in love and was never coming back. It was the last thing Greyson wanted to hear, so he refused to accept Owen's abdication and insisted on meeting him in person. Owen gave us a meeting place that was far from the pack, in case we were planning to force him to come home. Greyson and I went to meet the two of them."

She gets a faraway look and blinks away more tears.

"Aliya was so beautiful. And smart and kind. It was obvious why he was so in love with her. Unfortunately, it was also obvious why he couldn't bring her back to live with the pack. She could never be mistaken for a human, unless she held her glamor constantly, at least, and even then, there could be slipups. There was no way to pretend she was a shifter either. Owen couldn't love her and also do his duty for the pack, so he chose her. We couldn't hold that against him. By then, they were mated. It would have been horribly cruel to separate them, if not impossible to do it safely. Greyson and I went back to the pack to take on the responsibilities that Owen and Aliya couldn't. We never told anyone why Owen had left or why he would never come back. We just helped to have his name removed from existence and memory wherever possible and mourned him as if he had died."

"Unbelievable" escapes my lips before I can reel it back in. Mom gives me a warning look, but I might as well go on, now that I've started. "I mean it. You just . . . pretended he was dead and hoped everyone would forget about him? That's a load of bullshit."

"It was what he wanted," Mom counters. "It was the plan they talked us into."

"But," Taylor speaks up before the whole conversation can dissolve into another argument between Mom and me, "obviously, something happened after that?"

"Yes," Mom sighs. "As Gabe pointed out, if Owen had been fae, the two of them would have simply traveled back to that dimension and maybe had a happier ending together, but non-fae aren't welcome there, and the fae wanted Aliya back. Aliya and Owen called us, begging for help because she was pregnant, and they knew they couldn't guarantee their child's —" She looks at me again. "They couldn't be sure you could travel with her and survive it. Owen and Aliya knew that if they were separated like that, they would never see each other again. Aliya's mother was coming closer to finding her every day. You have to understand just how desperate they were at that point."

I clench my hands together on top of the table, trying to stop them from shaking, trying to stop my voice from shaking, trying to stop any of this from being real. "You're trying to say that they were so desperate, my mother was willing to cut off her own wings, aren't you?" It barely comes out above a whisper.

With a sad nod, Mom keeps going. "I think, at first, she believed it would be easier to hide if she didn't need the glamor to keep her wings hidden. She realized quickly the fae could still find her, though. She hoped they wouldn't want her anymore with her wings gone. I suppose she was right, in a way. Her mother didn't want her after the mutilation, but she also couldn't let her go. Aliya managed to hide from the fae just long enough to give birth, then she gave you to us and begged us to keep you safe because she couldn't. They found them soon after and killed them both. Maybe your grandmother was punishing her daughter or making an example of her. We'll probably never know. But when the fae came asking about you, we told them you were stillborn, and they left us alone. It seemed the only way to keep you safe, and it worked, until now."

I once again try to put this puzzle together in my mind and instead find my whole world listing to the side.

My mother had a name. Aliya. And wings. My father was a shifter. My mother cut her own wings off. My father left his family behind. My grandmother murdered them.

I can't make sense of any of this.

My feet feel clumsy and heavy as I make my way to my room.

If I can just get to the other side of my door. If I can just close that door with me on one side and everyone else on the other side. Maybe then I can shut out all of this fae and grandmother and dead parents and wings and lies and . . .

I get my door closed and lean against it, struggling to get any air in my lungs. And nothing changes. My world is still so off-kilter I might slip off into space.

CHAPTER 47

Taylor

We clear up from breakfast in silence, still without a plan, still without strategizing as Astrid had suggested. Bee disappeared into her room after the revelation of what happened to her parents, and all of us agreed without saying a word that we should give her some space and time to process. Marcus and Devon disappeared into my room for a bit to feed, but the rest of us have been sitting in uncomfortable silence around the living room while we wait for Bee to be ready to come out.

I almost jump out of my skin when my phone buzzes with a message from her.

Bee: I need you but don't let any of them know where you're going.

Does she even know who I am? She must realize that I'm the largest body in this room, and every single person is going to notice the instant I stand up.

But she needs me. If there's something I can do to help, I'm going to do it.

I do my best casual act as I stand up. "I'm . . . uh . . . be back in a minute," I mumble as I shuffle toward the hallway.

Based on the way Jeff is covering his mouth and the way Astrid is giving me a calculating look up and down, everyone has seen straight through my attempt at sneakiness.

"See if you can convince her to come out?" Astrid says.

I shrug. "I'll see what I can do." I think Bee is going to come out when she's good and ready, not before, and it won't matter what I say to her. But I can see what I can do. That's a small enough promise.

"Did they notice you coming in here?" Bee asks as soon as I close the door behind myself.

I give her a speaking look.

"I wasn't able to turn invisible or teleport, so yes, of course they noticed."

She crosses her arms with a *humph* and a scowl that actually makes me smile until I remember why she's been hiding in here. I kneel beside her bed, where she's sitting with her knees drawn up to her chest.

"You said you need me?" And if my voice sounds a little too hopeful about that? Oh well.

"I don't want to go back out there," she mumbles to her knees.

She barely responds when I scoop her up so I can sit on the bed with her on top of me, but she does relax slightly against my chest once I've got us both arranged. It feels like a win.

"Would it help to talk about it?" I ask.

Bee shrugs against me, then burrows a little closer.

"What is there to talk about? I'm not who I thought I was. I'm not *what* I thought I was. I've put everyone I care about in danger by being too stubborn to listen to my parents' warnings. My birth parents are dead, and it's partly my fault. Maybe it's all my fa—"

I stop her doom spiral with a kiss.

She gives a surprised little "mmph" but then lets herself kiss me back. It's not a sexual kiss in any way. Her mother—who I'm sure can smell arousal through the walls and would barge in to stop it if she sensed something sexual happening between us—is just down the hall. Along with all of our friends. So I'm not kissing Bee to try and open her up for me. I'm kissing her to try and stop her whirling thoughts from derailing and crashing horribly.

She's still a little breathless by the time I pull away.

"It sounds like your parents had a choice to make. Not a choice with good options, but still, they had a choice, and they chose the option that led to their deaths. That's not your fault. And everyone out in the living room right now made a choice to be here. They might not have known exactly how dangerous your grandmother could be, but they knew there was danger, and they chose to be here anyway. We all get to make our own choices, Bee."

She gives me a grateful look, then threads her fingers through the hair at my nape and pulls me closer for another kiss.

This one is sweet. Less of a desperate distraction and more of a delicate tasting. She teases at my lips with her lips, her tongue, her teeth, and I let her, following her lead and letting her perfect lips explore me.

My heart tries to beat each time I swallow one of her breaths, and with each aborted heartbeat, the words almost break out of me.

I love you. Breath. Beat. *I love you.*

But I can't put that on her. Not when she's going through something so much bigger than me.

Once we're through this. Once she's figured out who she

is and how she's different from what she thought. Once we've dealt with her scary grandmother and she's not burrowing into my chest because she's so afraid of the outside world. Maybe then, my feelings for her won't come across as a burden or an obligation. Right now, she doesn't need me putting that on her.

"If we keep this up much longer," I mumble against her lips, "we're going to have some awkward questions to answer."

She gives me one more kiss, then sits back with a sigh. "Okay. Let's go out there and face the others." She climbs off me and takes a moment to straighten her clothes in her full-length mirror.

My heart gives one more clumsy beat as I watch her. I can't help myself. I sneak one last kiss behind her ear before she leaves the room, and she rewards me with a tiny smile in the mirror.

There's a caveman version of me, resting at the base of my skull, who wants to drag her back to the bed right now, and who gives a fuck about who's on the other side of the door? Thankfully, Bee steps out into the hall before caveman me can take over.

Astrid stands up the moment she sees us, then stands awkwardly with her hands half-raised to embrace her daughter while her feet stay planted in their spot.

Bee takes pity on her and steps gingerly into the embrace.

There are too many wolf and vampire ears in the room for any of us to miss Astrid's whispered "You know I love you so much that it hurts sometimes?"

A wet chuckle bubbles out of Bee, and she hugs her mom back in earnest. "I know, Mom," she whispers back.

Then Jeff, like the overexcited puppy he secretly is, joins in the hug, and Grey jumps in on the other side.

The rest of us pass looks around the room, wondering the most graceful way to stay out of the group hug. At least, that's what I'm doing. Staying out of it, because there's no way any of the living want us vampires involved.

It's a relief when everyone in the hug lets go and steps away from each other. It's less obvious now how out of place I am with that group.

"Now," Astrid says in a practical tone, "we need to set up a guard duty rotation with the people here until we can figure out a safe way to get you home. Vampires on night watch, naturally, so they can guard the outside of the house without worrying about the sunlight. Gabe, how much do you know about the fae? What can you do to help? Us wolves can take turns patrolling outside. We should be able to pick up a fae's scent if we know what we're looking for."

"And I'm, once again, here for the entertainment," Jeff tacks on the end, which earns him a few eye rolls, but nobody argues.

Bee sits on the couch and tucks her knees under her chin. "I hate that I've disrupted everyone's lives like this, and it's not like this is a permanent solution. Ceallach can disappear into thin air. What's to stop him from appearing in this room without warning?"

We all look suspiciously around the room like we're expecting him to appear in the next few seconds.

He doesn't, though, and the warm-blooded among us give a sigh of relief in unison.

Gabe tentatively raises his hand, and we turn to him with questioning looks.

"So, some of the legends come from a bit of truth. There are ways to put up barriers against the fae. I don't have a long-term solution, but you can keep fae from crossing a threshold using iron above the doorframe. But . . . well, no one with fae blood would be able to cross the threshold either. Bee and I would be trapped inside as much as Ceallach would be stuck outside."

Astrid wraps her arms around Bee and hugs her tightly. "It's better than nothing. Who's going to go out and get some horseshoes?"

Gabe shrugs. "I'll need someone else to come with me because I wouldn't be able to carry them, but I should go to make sure it's real iron."

"And I can go to do the carrying," Jeff says. "It's not like I'll be useful on guard duty."

CHAPTER 48

Bee

All I want in the world is to curl up in someone's arms and have them tell me it's all going to be okay. At the same time, I hate feeling so helpless and useless. I shake off my mom's embrace and start pacing again. I'm not sure it helps, but at least it feels like I'm doing *something* other than sitting and waiting for something to happen to me.

I feel Taylor's eyes following me as I pace and desperately wish I could read his thoughts. Ceallach seemed to be saying that was a fae gift. Maybe it's a fae gift that *I* have. A gift passed to me from my mother. If I believe all the rest of this fae stuff, I probably have to believe this part as well, right?

Determined to do something useful, I pause in the center of the room and close my eyes. Ceallach said something about reaching out with my mind, so that's exactly what I imagine myself doing.

I reach out, trying to stretch my mind to the corners of the room.

And all I get is silence and darkness.

"Bee?" Gloria's voice cuts into my concentration. "Are you okay?"

I open my eyes so I can glare at her. "I was trying to access these fae gifts I supposedly have. Gabe and Ceallach both said I should have inherited something. This glamor ability, or mind reading, or something, but I still just feel . . . human."

Worthless is the word in my mind, but my friends and family don't need another reason to worry about me.

Taylor leans toward me, inspecting me like a scientist with an interesting specimen. "What about the ability to shift? Is it possible you inherited that and just never tried because you didn't believe it was possible?"

My laugh is bitter in my own ears. "Believe me. I've tried."

"You have?" Grey sounds surprised and confused. "When did you try to shift?"

"I don't know." I shrug. "Every morning of third grade before school? Every Friday night when there was a full moon? Every time my friends shifted and left me behind so they could play as wolves? Knowing I was human didn't stop me from wanting . . . something else. I always had this hope that . . . I don't know . . . there had been a mistake, or an oversight, or something, and I would suddenly wake up and have a wolf form just like everyone else around me."

If I expected surprise from my mother, I was wrong, and the pitying understanding from her is so much worse.

"It's fine," I rush to reassure everyone. "Everyone has their lonely moments growing up. I'm no different. I just thought, since I'm apparently not human after all, I should try experimenting with whatever supernatural powers I might have. But it turns out I don't have any at all. Whatever. It's no big deal."

"I'm not sure about that," Taylor says.

"About what?"

He stands in front of me and ducks his head to look me in

the eye. "I'm just learning about these things, the same as you, but I think it's too early to write off any possible fae gifts or shifter abilities." He holds up a hand to stop me from interrupting. "Hear me out. Maybe you don't have a second form to shift into. That's not unheard of for shifters, right? I've heard that it's unusual but not impossible for shifters to be born without a second form. But that doesn't mean you didn't inherit any shifter abilities."

"Okay. What hidden abilities am I overlooking?"

"Healing, for one."

I narrow my eyes at him. "What are you talking about?"

"Think about it," Taylor says, warming to his topic enough to start gesticulating to everyone around the room, though he's still talking to me. "How long did it take for your tattoo to heal?"

My fingers drift up to where I know a butterfly is flitting beside my belly button. "I don't know. How long do they usually take to heal?"

"I don't know either," he counters. "More than a day, though, and I'm almost certain yours was healed within a few hours."

The memory of him kissing and licking flowers and butterflies across perfectly healed skin crashes into me. I have no idea how long a human would take to heal after a tattoo, but I do remember Brigitte giving me detailed care instructions that were implied to last days rather than hours.

"Okay," I admit. "So I healed quickly from something one time. That doesn't prove anything."

"You've also never been sick," Mom says in a slightly dazed voice. "I can't believe I never thought about it until now. A human child gets sick, but you never did." She rubs at her forehead. "I should have realized you were showing subtle signs of what you were. I kept watching for big signs, like wings or glamors. I should have paid attention to small signs."

"But—" I sputter, unable to put together a coherent argument when what they're saying goes against all of my past experiences. "What good would small signs have been anyway? If I'm supposed to have superhuman strength and shifting abilities, what good does it do for me to have skin that heals quickly and . . . apparently an iron sensitivity that I never knew about? What's the point of being half fae if that's all I get from it?"

Taylor makes a placating gesture. "We shouldn't get ahead of ourselves. Maybe the only fae traits you inherited are small, like this thing with iron. But now that we know you're not human, it will be easier to figure out what—if any—fae gifts or shifter abilities you have. And you have people willing to help you learn your capabilities, now. I bet Gabe would be happy to help you. And you've got shifters around who know about your parents. Don't you think they might help?"

I want to throw my arms around him and kiss him with everything I've got, and Mom and Grey can just . . . Well, okay, maybe I'm still not quite ready to deal with what they're going to say about me and Taylor being together. If we weren't surrounded by people, some of whom are my blood relatives, I would have already climbed Taylor and ordered him to carry me to bed. That's how grateful I am for his practical approach to all of this.

Instead of climbing him so I can claim him publicly with an epic kiss, I brush my fingers down his arm, a simple, subtle acknowledgment that I appreciate him.

Sparks seem to snap between my fingers and his skin where they touch. He jerks and stares at me in stunned silence, so I know it wasn't just in my head. Tentatively, I bring my hand up and press the tip of my finger to his cheek and am almost overwhelmed by the torrent of jumbled thoughts and emotions that wash over me.

Sad . . . so beautiful . . . don't deserve . . . looks lonely . . . all crash together as Taylor and I stand, trapped in each other's thoughts, oblivious to everything around us.

With a hiss, I jerk my finger away, and Taylor sways in place for a moment before sitting abruptly on the nearest couch.

"What was that?" Gloria asks. "What just happened between you two?"

Taylor and I stare at each other with matching shocked expressions.

"I think," Taylor says, "that was more of Bee's fae gifts coming to the surface."

Grey doesn't look happy as he stomps around the room. I wonder if he's looking for physical evidence of what I just did, the way he seems to be sniffing the air around us. "And? What happened?"

I don't want to tell him what happened. It feels too personal to share. And it will also feel extra embarrassing if I try it again and can't make it happen a second time.

Surprisingly, it's Mom who saves me from having to explain myself.

"You don't have to tell us about it if you're not ready, sweetheart. Maybe we should do something to take our minds off of things until the boys come back with some horseshoes."

I give a relieved nod and sit back down beside Taylor. He doesn't exactly scoot away from me, but I notice a tension in his body that wasn't there before. Whatever he experienced just now, he's even more freaked-out by it than I am. I can't blame him, though. As far as I can tell, I just dug into his brain and read his mind. The fact that it was accidental doesn't make it any less intrusive. I just saw and felt things that I shouldn't have been privy to.

I'm careful not to touch him as we sit beside each other and everyone settles in to watch something on TV. I have no idea what they end up putting on, or if they're having a conversation around me, or even if they're asking me questions and expecting me to answer. My brain is completely wrapped up in the feeling of Taylor's emotions surging through my mind until I can't be sure where my thoughts end and his begin.

CHAPTER 49

Taylor

Bee was in my head. Not only was Bee in my head, but I'm pretty sure she was hearing my thoughts and feeling my feelings.

I thought having her finger in my ass was personal, but this is on an entirely new level.

She was in my head. Moving around in my thoughts like a fish swimming through water.

No.

Like a worm crawling through dirt. She was moving through my thoughts and consuming my thoughts and digesting my thoughts all at once.

If it had been anyone else, anyone in the world other than Bee, I would probably feel violated right now. But it *was* Bee, and hadn't I already decided that I want her to have everything I can give her? This feels almost like an extension of the intimacy we'd already built between us. On some crazy, utterly bizarro level, it feels like the right next step.

At the same time, that level of intimacy takes some adjustment. I'm only vaguely aware of something being put on the TV and everyone else getting comfortable and watching it together. I barely notice when Gabe and Jeff come back and Gabe instructs everyone on how to nail horseshoes to doorframes and windowsills so no one with fae blood can get in or out. Mostly, I'm too busy with my own swirling thoughts, trying to process the experience of Bee being as deep inside of me as she could ever possibly go. The only reason I remember to feed is that Marcus and Devon each take me by an elbow and lead me back to my room.

"Do you have enough blood for me too?" Marcus asks. "I wasn't expecting to be here so long, and I don't feel comfortable leaving you all here while I go back to the house to stock up."

"Yeah, there's plenty." I grab a couple of bags from my fridge and offer one to Devon, but he refuses, so I drink it instead. If I weren't so wrapped up in my own revelations, I would have remembered that Devon can only drink from Marcus, or he gets horribly ill. One of the side effects of being turned too young, like my mother.

"So." Devon draws the word out for about an hour. "Are you ever going to talk about what's going on between you and Bee?"

Marcus punches his arm and gives a warning headshake, but Devon keeps giving me an expectant look.

"I don't know what you're talking about," I try.

Devon and Marcus give me matching "bullshit" looks.

"Her mom is just down the hall from us right now, okay? And her brother. And whatever's going on, it's not like she's agreed to us telling anyone about it. It's not like we've even agreed on a definition of what 'it' is."

Devon gives a pleading look skyward. "If you think that you've kept your feelings for her hidden from anyone in this house, I hate to break it to you, but you haven't. Everyone can see your cartoon heart eyes."

"No," I argue, "because if Grey could see them, he would have killed me already."

"Bee can see them. And her mom. Trust me, it will be better for you when you get it all out in the open."

Marcus puts an arm around his waist. "Maybe you're forgetting that things aren't always that simple?"

Devon rolls his eyes, then turns back to me. "Marcus is forgetting that even when there are complications, it's better to have the truth out in the open."

"Right," I say, failing to keep the bitter note out of my voice. "And in this case, the complications you're referring to are the fact that I'm a vampire who could ruin her life and definitely doesn't deserve her, the fact that she's half fae and apparently has a murderous grandmother who's out to get her, and the fact that her brother is a wolf shifter who will tear me to shreds if he catches any hint of what we've been up to. Forgive me if I struggle to see your rose-tinted view of the situation."

My friends lean toward me as one.

"So you have been up to something?" Devon whispers with a grin.

I scrub my hands over my face, wondering what to tell them. Wanting to tell them everything, but feeling like that might be a betrayal of what Bee and I have. And Bee and I haven't remotely defined what we have, anyway. I'm pretty sure I'm the toy she happens to enjoy using for the moment. I'm also the guy who's completely in love with her and therefore completely fucked when she decides to move on.

"I can't talk about this right now," I finally say after debating with myself for way too long. "I should let you feed in peace."

They both look disappointed as I leave the room, but at least they don't pull me back to pry answers out of me.

I'm so lost in my thoughts as I close the door behind me

that I'm caught by surprise by Bee standing in the hallway. We freeze, staring awkwardly at each other for a long moment before both rushing to talk over each other.

"I was just making sure the vampires are fed," I explain.

At the same time, she rushes to say, "I'm really sorry about earlier. I had no idea it would be that . . ."

"Intimate?"

"Yeah," she breathes. "It was really fucking intimate. I swear, I wouldn't have done that without consent. I just . . . didn't realize what I was doing, I guess. That seems like a shitty excuse."

She looks away, shame dripping off her.

I almost pull her to me to comfort and kiss and reassure her, but remember where we are in time to stop myself.

Nodding toward her room, I ask, "Maybe we should talk about it somewhere more private?"

She's careful not to touch me as she leads me down the hallway and holds her door open for me, and all I want to do is hold her close so I can show her it's okay.

"Should we sit?" I ask, because she's still standing by the door and staring at her toes.

"I won't do it again," she blurts out in response.

I pause in the middle of the room, torn between giving her all the space she seems to want and taking all the touch that I'm still craving.

"It was stupid to just reach out like that without thinking. I should have realized how intrusive it would be, but I just didn't think. I promise, I won't do it again."

I sit down in her chair. Maybe the problem is that I'm looming too much for her. Maybe if I'm smaller, she won't worry so much about things.

"I won't lie," I start. "That was . . . having you in my thoughts like that was . . . more intimate than I thought it was possible to be with someone. But you shouldn't feel bad or guilty or any of the things you seem to be feeling right now. I was caught off guard by it, but it wasn't terrible, at least, not from my side of it. Was it terrible for you?"

Bee gives me an assessing look, and it occurs to me that it might actually be a good thing if we can communicate without having to guess at what the other is thinking.

"Bee," I say, careful not to startle her, worried I'm about to scare her off. "Was it a bad experience for you?"

She shakes her head. "No. Of course it wasn't bad for me. You were the one being violated."

"But I don't feel violated. I told you, I was surprised. It was really intimate, yes, but I want to be intimate with you. If you're willing to try it again, I wouldn't be as surprised this time."

"You . . ." She furrows her brow, licks her lips, thinks about it long enough that the wait feels like torture to me, then finally goes on. "You would be willing to try it again?"

"I want you to be able to figure out how to use this . . . ability, or power, or fae gift, whatever we're calling it. You'll need to practice if you're going to learn how to control it, right?"

She nods reluctantly.

"So practice on me. I trust you."

Bee steps toward me. "I think . . . I can't be sure, but it seems to require physical contact. Is it okay if I touch you?"

I've only been dying for her to touch me since the moment we met. I feel like begging her to touch me now.

"You can always touch me," I promise. "Just let me know ahead of time if you're going to do the mind-meld thing?"

She smiles. "How about we start with regular touch and then see if we're ready to go on."

I smile and hold my arms open for her to sit on my lap. "Ready when you are."

I'm surprised when she straddles me and immediately

tangles her fingers in my hair to pull me in for a kiss. Surprised, but not upset.

She breathes in with a quiet moan as she devours my mouth.

"Fuck," she groans into my mouth. "I don't know why, but I've needed this the way I need food." Another deep kiss. "No. Air." She gasps for breath, and my hands find their way under her shirt, just so I can feel the heat of her skin against my palms, the movement of her ribs as she breathes against me. "I've needed this like I need to breathe," she continues.

I press myself against her, trying to show her how badly I need her. Trying to show her how desperately I want to give her everything I have, everything I am.

"Do you want to try the other thing now?" I ask. "Do you want to try touching my mind?"

She pulls back to search my eyes. "Are you really sure you're okay with that?"

"Yes. I want you to. I'm ready this time."

"I'm scared I'll hurt you. Or, I don't know, not be able to stop when you want me to. What if I'm hurting you and I don't even realize it?"

"I'm a vampire. You can't hurt me that bad. Bee, I want to do this for you. I want to give this to you."

She takes in a shaky breath.

Her fingers, tangling in my hair and stroking my scalp, and her heartbeat, racing faster now, I realize, than any human heart, are doing something to me, so I'm worried about my own control.

"Bee." I say her name like a prayer, a plea, and nuzzle into her neck to kiss and lick where I can feel her pulse the strongest. I tear myself away a split second before instinct takes over and makes me bite down and drink from her.

She looks puzzled. "What is it?"

"I'm more afraid of hurting you than being hurt by you,"

I admit. "Even just now, I almost lost control and drank from you."

Cocking her head from one side to the other, she examines me thoroughly before speaking.

"I don't think we have to worry about you hurting me," she says. I raise an eyebrow, so she goes on. "I think, if fae are really that hard to kill, and I'm half fae, and I apparently have a latent healing ability that I never knew about, it makes sense to think I might be a little hardier than I realized. Definitely hardier than a regular human. So I don't think you're as dangerous to me as we thought."

That takes a moment for me to process.

"That's a theory," I concede, "but forgive me if I'm not willing to test it out by drinking straight from your veins."

"So you understand how I feel about possibly hurting you by touching your mind again. Taylor, we don't know the actual risks involved with that."

I kiss her gently on the lips. "Fair enough. But you didn't hurt me the first time, and you were able to pull away the first time. I really think this is something we have to explore. You need to know what you can do."

"Okay," she says. Taking a deep breath, I can see her stealing herself, so I get ready to let her into my mind again. "Okay, if you're sure."

"I'm sure," I tell her. "I want you to do this."

She takes another deep breath, closes her eyes, and nuzzles her face into the crook of my neck.

It happens more slowly this time. Just wisps of a fog floating through my mind at first. I do my best to stay calm as her presence in my thoughts thickens and solidifies until I can practically feel her footsteps inside of me. The feeling of a tendril of her consciousness reaching out to touch mine makes me jerk reflexively, and I feel her pull back.

No, keep going, I think, and the tendril returns. Could she actually hear my thought? Or maybe it was just a general sense of what I was thinking. I'll have to ask her afterward what this feels like for her.

Then, my conscious thoughts end as her mind fills mine up. It feels like liquid being poured into my brain and filling every nook and cranny inside my skull.

Maybe I hear myself moan, but it's from such a distance, completely detached from the me that's being filled and simultaneously consumed by her.

CHAPTER 50

Bee

It's like I'm floating. No, that's not right. Flying? Swimming. It's like I'm swimming through Taylor's consciousness. Every part of me can feel his thoughts rushing past, brushing against my skin, pouring through my veins. A jumble of memory and sensation and thought flows around me, and all it takes is a wish for me to capture a bit in my hand and look closer.

I see a cluttered room with the windows permanently blacked out and what almost looks like the nest of a feral animal in the corner. I feel the sting of unexpected slaps from someone who should be offering comfort instead of pain. I hear the wicked snickers of children as they wait for a prank to play out and bring some fresh humiliation for the victim.

Every thought or feeling Taylor has ever had is right there, within easy reach. And I drink his thoughts the same way a vampire drinks blood, sucking each memory into me and feeling my hunger grow instead of diminishing the more I drink.

Our physical bodies aren't close enough to accommodate the way our metaphysical bodies intertwine. I need him closer.

He needs the same. I can feel it through his mind and the way he slides his hands up under my shirt and presses me against his chest. Our mouths find each other by instinct, and then we're devouring each other like this is our last meal, and the only way we'll die sated is by each of us consuming the other whole.

A whimper escapes one of us. Maybe both of us. At this point, it doesn't matter who because we're currently one entity.

Rocking my hips into him, I chase the pressure of his hardening cock against my clit, and at the same time, I'm chasing the friction I can sense he needs as I rub myself along his length.

Then there's a sound outside the door. My brain is so caught up in Taylor and this moment between us that it takes an eternity to extricate myself from his mind and recognize what's happening in the world outside of us.

There's an angry male voice on the other side of the door —Grey? Shit, that can't be good—and a more muffled voice that I can't make out.

And that's all the time I have to react before the door is opening and my brother's furious face is glaring at us, and Taylor still has the dazed expression of a man who just had someone else digging through his brain.

Everything hangs, frozen, for a split second, and then time and sound and motion all snap back into place. While I'm climbing off Taylor's lap to stand protectively in front of him, Gabe and my mother—of all people—are grabbing Grey by the arms to hold him back.

And Grey is shouting about how he's going to kill Taylor for defiling me. As if I didn't have an equal role in what Taylor and I were doing.

Mom is murmuring something to Grey, somehow staying calm even as she strains to hold him in place.

Gabe slips around Grey to stand in front of him and block him from coming closer. "Grey noticed a blond man standing outside and came to check if it's the same guy as before," he explains to me over his shoulder. He shoves Grey angrily but ineffectually in the chest. "We tried to tell him to wait for you to come out instead of barging in, but obviously, he didn't listen."

"You knew about this?" Grey shouts at Gabe, his face a mask of hurt and betrayal.

Do I deal with the issue right in front of me and try to talk sense into my brother? Do I try to deal with Ceallach possibly being outside the house right now? I can't even get out of my bedroom with Grey taking up the entire doorway, and I can't get out of the house because of the iron on all the doors and windows. But Grey has a look in his eyes like nobody's talking sense into him anytime soon. What should I do?

Part of my mind is simply panicking, shrieking at the fact that the worst thing that could happen decided to happen at this moment.

Part of my mind is still connected to Taylor, still furiously processing all of those unfamiliar thoughts and emotions while he's still sitting in a daze that has me worried I did too much—took too much—and he won't recover.

But part of me is present and rational and telling me the only solution right now is to get some distance. I need to get away from the shouting brother in the doorway and the dangerous cousin on the sidewalk and all of the noise and conflict inside this house.

Acting on instinct again, I thread my fingers through Taylor's hair and delve down. Not reaching for his thoughts this time, but something else I can sense without being able to name it. An energy within him that I can use. For what, though? No use dwelling on the question when I don't have the answer. My instinct knows something I don't, so I follow it.

There.

Heat and light and energy inside of him that I can use as a battery to power . . . I'm not sure what, but instinct tells me that it can power anything I want it to. And right now, I want to escape.

I close my eyes and tap into Taylor's soul or life source or whatever it is and think about being somewhere far away from here.

The noise drops from around us in an instant, replaced by the trilling of some kind of bird I've never heard before.

We're surrounded by trees.

I look around myself to confirm that, yes, Taylor and I are in the middle of some kind of lush rainforest.

The trees aren't quite familiar, though. They lift high above me on thick, straight stalks. Instead of brown bark, they're varying shades of green and blue. The bright green tree trunk next to me has a white fuzz growing along it that I almost reach out and touch before realizing that, for all I know, it has some kind of poison.

Taylor is lying on the ground. I guess I brought him with me but left the chair behind. He curls in on himself with a groan that sounds like pain.

"Taylor, can you hear me?"

He nods, then groans again, as I shake his shoulder.

"It's the sun," he gasps out at me. "Too bright."

"Shit. What do I do?" I look up to see that even with a canopy of giant leaves above us, the sunlight is strong enough to filter through and heat my skin. How long does it normally take for a vampire to feel sick from the sun? I know I've seen Taylor walk the block from our house to the nearest tunnel entrance without issue. Why is this sun affecting him so harshly and so quickly? Is it because of me? Because of the energy I used from him to get us here? Shit, I should have just stayed where I was and faced the consequences of getting caught.

Taylor pats at his chest pocket. "Blood caps," he whispers.

I delve into the pocket and pull out something dark red, smooth to the touch, and about the size of a large marble. What do they call those? The shooter. Realizing I'm wasting time by thinking about marbles, I force my attention back to the emergency at hand.

"What do I do with it?" I ask.

He points weakly to his mouth, so I shove the thing between his lips and silently beg the universe for that to be the right choice.

I hear a quiet *pop* as he bites down on the marble thing.

Blood cap. A capsule of blood? Is that what I just gave him? Maybe it's strange that I just now realized that I've never seen Taylor eat. I guess the blood-drinking thing was just theoretical for me all this time. But now he's swallowing reflexively, and I can see a dark red on the inside of his lips each time they part.

He points at his pocket again, so I check deeper and find three more of the red marbles. I hold one up to his lips, and he opens for me, swallowing after another *pop* that makes me think of an insect being squished. I'm glad it's him and not me who has to take them.

With a relieved sigh, his muscles relax.

"Won't last long," he tells me in a harsh, croaky voice. "Need to get inside."

"What about these?" I hold up the last two blood caps. "Will they help?"

"Little bit," he croaks, so I give them to him one at a time and am pleased that he's able to sit up for the last one.

My mind is still racing, though, trying to think of ways to get him to shelter. Maybe I can do the same thing I did to bring him here, just in reverse, but what if the traveling is part of what depleted him so badly in the first place? I don't want to get him back to my room if I just kill him in the process. That will be a last resort if we can't find shelter here, I decide.

And just when I've given up on getting Taylor to his feet and moving him anywhere in search of shelter, I hear someone whistling through the trees, and the whistling is getting closer.

"Well," Ceallach says as he steps out from behind a giant tree trunk that's the same dark blue-green of the ocean. "This is not how I was expecting you to come to us."

He looks Taylor and me over curiously. I can't read him at all. All I know is this is his world, not mine, which puts me at every kind of disadvantage. I grab onto Taylor and prepare for a desperate trip back to my room that hopefully won't kill him.

"Wait." Ceallach actually sounds a little desperate too. I pause my attempt to bring Taylor back home, but I don't let go of him either. "Please, I need you to speak to your grandmother, and even more now that you've found your way here."

I narrow my eyes, and he rushes to go on.

"And I can help you get him some help. The sun is stronger here, so it's going to kill him faster if you don't let me help you."

Taylor and I share a long look before he turns gingerly to look at Ceallach. "I won't make it anywhere without a lot of help, in case you were expecting me to walk."

I guess that's decided, then. Ceallach steps hesitantly toward us, checks that we're not going to—who knows what he's really afraid of—puff out of existence? Then he squats down in front of us and puts a hand on each of our shoulders.

With a *whoosh*, the world spins away around us, then spins back into existence again. And it's completely different.

We're in a cavernous room that seems to be entirely made

of . . . gold? No. That's not quite right. The walls have a yellowish hue and an iridescence that reminds me of gold, but there's something off. The floor beneath us is also shining and iridescent, and not quite like anything I've seen before. Tiles in shades of gold, bronze, and silver spread out in a pattern too complex for my eyes to recognize. And not only is the room enormous, but the walls stretch so high above us that I can only barely make out the shadowy form of the ceiling as it arcs to a point above us.

"What is this place?" I whisper in awe before I remember that we're in danger and can't trust the person offering possible help.

Ceallach gives an easy smile and stands back with his arms out as if he's putting the room on display just for us.

"Welcome to the Grand Hall of the Royal Fae Court."

I blink my eyes and realize that his disguise—his glamor, I suppose—from earlier is gone. Instead of jeans and a T-shirt, he's got light green leggings and a loose, dark green tunic.

Oh, and the wings. He gives them a slow flap, just in case we missed them appearing while we watched. Yep. There's no denying it. We're dealing with a guy who has actual, literal, honest-to-god wings.

"Can you help me stand?" Taylor asks. "I'd rather face whatever's about to happen standing up instead of sitting down."

"I agree," I mutter, then do my best to get my shoulder under his armpit to help him up.

Too bad he's almost three times my size.

Ceallach watches us struggle for a moment before coming to Taylor's other side to help. Between the two of us, we get Taylor on his feet, where he stands, gasping like a goldfish out of its pond and leaning most of his weight on us. I fully regret bringing him here, but all I can do now is try to get him home safe.

"If what I know about vampires is true," Ceallach says, "you won't be out of danger until you complete a feed. Though I admit I'm not an expert."

"Yes," Taylor gasps. "Need blood to regenerate. Have blood bags?"

"Not a single one," Ceallach answers with what I think is unnecessary cheerfulness.

"So, what do we do?" I ask.

"We ask the queen."

It takes both of us to keep Taylor standing as we maneuver toward the door at the far end of the room.

"Where are we going?" I ask, having to grit my teeth to stay up under Taylor's weight. "And where is everyone? If this is the grand hall or whatever, why are we the only ones in it?"

"The fae court has been shrinking in recent years. Titania doesn't like when people compare how it used to be in the past to its current size, so she holds court in the smaller chambers to make it less obvious."

"What do you mean by shrinking?"

I can almost hear Ceallach's shrug. "Sometimes fae die. Sometimes fae leave. The human world used to offer less temptation to pull people away. There are fewer of us than there were a thousand years ago. It is what it is."

I try to process that, then decide that I need more information before I'll be able to make any sense of what he's saying, so I file it away for later. Time to ask as many questions as I can so I'm ready to face this fae queen.

"What do I need to know about the queen? What does she want from me? Who is she?"

"She's . . . the queen . . . What else do you need to know?"

I let out a frustrated growl, and he sighs in response.

"Okay. Fine. Our queen is Titania. She's been around long enough that some bits of information have slipped through the cracks to the human world over the ages. She's essentially the mother of all the high fae, and since your mother was fae, that means she's your grandmother. Though she won't necessarily see it that way." He mutters the last bit under his breath, so I can barely make it out.

"Excuse me? What are you saying?"

But before he can answer me, we come to a pair of enormous double doors made of the same not-quite-gold as the walls. Standing close, I can see that there are intricate carvings covering every inch of the doors, depicting people with wings and vine-covered trees and exotic-looking animals. The carvings are so delicate and detailed that I can almost see them coming to life under my gaze.

I look over to Ceallach, wondering if he's going to knock or drop Taylor's arm and run or what. He surprises me by giving a musical whistle.

The carvings on the door spring to life for real, animals and fairies scattering into the doorframe and vines whipping around and out of the way until there's simply an open doorway to walk through.

And a room full of expectant faces staring at us from the other side.

"Who would call upon Titania, Queen of the Fae, Mother of the Tuath Dé Danann, High Seat of the Seelie Court?" a voice calls from the far end of the room.

A pit opens in my stomach. Am I supposed to answer? Am I supposed to know what to say?

Ceallach saves me.

"I, Ceallach, pureblood child of the fair folk," he calls. "And I bring two travelers. Bethany, daughter of Aliya, and one of no name, to be tested before the court."

What the fuck did he just say about being tested? I slide a suspicious glance his way and see he's making a placating gesture. If he's actually signed me up for some kind of fairy tournament, I'm coming after him first and making sure he can't pull any shit like this again.

"Bring them forth."

The three of us step forward into the hall, and I have to stifle a gasp when I see what I'm stepping into. It's smaller than the first room, but still enormous, and packed along each side with . . . well, I guess they're fae. They look like creatures. Wings and tails and fur and horns sprout from every direction I look. Something bright blue with constantly buzzing wings grins up at me with sharp teeth. Even hovering off the floor, it's only as tall as my knee. Near the wall, something man-shaped towers above everyone else, having to bend his head so it doesn't brush the high ceiling. I've never been good at estimating heights or distances, but I'm sure he's well above twenty feet tall. Is it possibly closer to forty feet? But before I can get caught up in that thought, I notice someone with the massive head and horns of a bull on top of the unbelievably wide shoulders of a muscular man. There's an actual minotaur standing in the same room as me. What is actually happening in my life right now?

Hundreds of eyes follow us in silence as we make our way down the aisle that's been left open for us. This has to be the longest, most awkward walk I've ever taken.

At the end of the aisle, a throne rises up before us with what appears to be a giant dragon statue posed menacingly behind it. The throne is so imposing I almost miss the person sitting on it. A woman, clearly older than me, but she doesn't look particularly old, draped in filmy fabric and flowers that seem to sparkle and move, even though she's sitting stone-still, watches as we make our way toward her.

Her eyes glitter as she looks me over. I get the feeling she can see straight through me and has already assigned a worth to every molecule of my being and is currently adding them up to determine my overall worth.

If I'd had any hopes of being greeted warmly and welcomed as a granddaughter, they're gone now.

"This is her?" she asks in a voice of ice and steel and everything else that's cold and hard.

Ceallach shoots me an apologetic look before stepping out from under Taylor's arm. Taylor sags without the extra support, and it's all I can do to steady him as we both sink down to the floor. If I didn't have a scary grandmother to deal with, I would be focused on helping him. I don't like the way he's kneeling and gripping the floor with his hands like that's his only hold on life right now. But something tells me that worrying about my . . . whatever Taylor is to me . . . is not an acceptable excuse for me to ignore the fae queen in front of me.

"Your Majesty." Ceallach gives a quick, precise bow. "This is your granddaughter Bethany."

I consider, then discard the idea of correcting him. I'm not sure I want this woman calling me anything at all, so it shouldn't matter if she calls me Bethany or Bee.

"Where are your wings?" she asks, and it takes me a moment to realize she's directed the question at me.

"My . . . what?"

I can't believe it's possible, but her face becomes stonier, and I catch another predatory glint in her eyes. This must be what a rabbit feels like trying to stare down a cobra.

"Your. Wings. Show them." The command snaps out, and I almost check to see if I'm bleeding from the way they lash at me.

"I . . . don't have wings," I admit.

There's a collective gasp from the crowd, followed by a mixture of scandalized whispers and birdlike titters as everyone confirms what they just heard with the people around them.

The queen's eyes narrow, and the room falls silent again.

"Ceallach," she says quietly, her voice dripping venom, "I thought you said you had found someone who could be of use to us, but she has no wings?"

His audible *gulp* echoes around the room.

With the faintest rustle of fluttering fabric, she stands and steps down from the dais her throne sits on. I'm already kneeling to support Taylor, but my instinct tells me to get even lower when Ceallach drops to his hands and knees in front of her.

"She might be untrained, but she does have fae blood," he tells the floor in front of him. "And she doesn't have wings, but I'm certain she has other fae gifts. She was able to find Tír na nÓg and bring not only herself but someone else here with her. That must mean something."

The queen gives him a distasteful look as she steps around him to stand in front of me.

"Stand up," she snaps, and I hurry to untangle myself to obey. "What do you know of your parents?"

I get the distinct impression that a wrong answer will have her slitting my throat with her fingernails, and she won't shed a tear over it.

"Not much. My mother was a fae named Aliya, and my father was a wolf shifter named Owen. They . . ." I swallow against the churning in my stomach. "They both died when I was a baby."

"And when they died, whose idea was it to lie to us and say that you were also dead?"

I have to fight to hold back the accusation that it was she who killed them. I want to scream at her that she's the reason I never really knew who I was, she's the reason I never knew my parents, she's the reason my family had to lie to her about me being dead. But I don't want to die today, and not like that, so I swallow all of that anger and press it down deep.

"I don't know what you mean," I say. I'm sure she recognizes it as a lie, but I'm not going to give up my real family to her when she might retaliate against them.

She lets out an annoyed-sounding grunt but doesn't press me. Instead, she steps behind me. I gasp in surprise when she lifts up the back of my shirt, then trails a sharp fingernail up and down one shoulder blade, then the other. Dropping my shirt and stepping around me again, she looks down her nose at me.

"Kneel," she orders, and I do because I don't want to die, but my blood might actually be boiling in my veins. "You say your father was a shifter?"

"Yes, a wolf shifter," I answer and hope I'm not betraying someone by speaking right now.

"You must have inherited some of your mother's blood, otherwise you would be like him"—she nudges Taylor with her toe—"by now. Vampires can't withstand our sunlight, even in shade, and humans can't breathe our air. It's too thin for anyone other than a fae. But there is a difference between being high fae and being half fae. Tell me, what gifts do you have to prove you belong here among the high fae?"

I glare at the floor and grind my teeth to keep from saying what's actually on my mind, that she's just a bigoted old woman and I don't want to have a place with her.

"Well?" she snaps when I don't immediately start talking.

"I have no idea what my fae gifts might be. I didn't even know fae existed until recently. What are you expecting me to tell you?"

Glancing up, I catch the heat of her glare directed at me.

She collects herself and paces slowly around Taylor and me.

"What did you do to bring yourself here?" she asks, changing tactics.

What did I do? I have no idea. I wanted to be away, so I went away. "I just . . . sensed that I could, then I did."

"And what about him? He just happened to turn up with you?"

"No." I sort through what actually happened. "I think . . . I think he helped me to get here. It felt like touching a power source, and then we were here."

She snorts a derisive laugh at that. "So you have no control over the gifts you have and no power of your own to use them. You have to siphon off someone else's power to use your own. Is that right?" I open my mouth to answer, but she keeps talking. "I know what you are now. You're not high blood fae, with a place in our court. You're barely even half blood. We can all see it now. You're just a dirty little succubus with no useful gifts and no place in our court. Unless . . ." She taps her lips thoughtfully. "Do you at least have a wolf that you inherited from your father? Show us your wolf, little succubus."

"I can't," I say through gritted teeth. I can't believe how small this woman—who is nothing to me—can make me feel with just a few offhand words.

The bitch actually bursts out laughing, musical peals of laughter that encourage everyone else in the room to join in. The only people not laughing are Taylor, Ceallach, and me.

"Let me get this straight," the fae queen says, making a show of wiping tears from the corners of her eyes. "Your fae mother died for her freedom and left you knowing nothing about your family or yourself, and no fae gifts or magical ability to speak of, and your father didn't even pass on the only bit of magic he had to give you? Your existence is so sad that it's not even worth trying to take the revenge I would have liked on my ungrateful daughter's child."

I give Ceallach a questioning look, but he just stares at the floor like he might be sick on it any moment.

The queen turns to him.

"Ceallach, why did you bring me this useless little succubus?"

He swallows. "Your Majesty, our numbers have dwindled in the last millennium. You know my thoughts on revitalizing the court by bringing new blood in."

"New blood?" She thinks that over for a moment. "New blood might be one thing, but this is weak blood. For the fae to remain strong, we need to keep our blood strong, not dilute it like this. Because you have such a love for the low-blooded and half-blooded and weak-blooded fae, you will stay with them from here on out."

Ceallach's eyes bug out of his head. "No, Your Majesty, you don't mean—"

"You are banished. I expect not to see you again. The high fae will not look at you, nor recognize you, nor welcome you if you cross their path. I have made my decision."

He looks desperate to argue, even opens his mouth to say something, then stands and stalks out of the room with a defeated set to his shoulders.

She turns back to me. "Now, as for you." Her eyes take me apart piece by piece, and I imagine myself ripping her to shreds with my bare hands in return. Her mouth twists in disgust. "If I could make Aliya watch as I killed you, I would skin you alive in front of her, the ungrateful little blood traitor, but I've already punished her as much as I can."

Self-preservation finally loses out to anger. "Why did you kill her at all?" I blurt out. "Why did you chase her until she had to cut off her own wings trying to escape you? Why couldn't you just let her go?"

One instant, the queen is towering above me while I kneel on the floor. The next, she has me by the throat, and my toes are barely scraping against the floor as I twist in her grasp. Clawlike fingernails dig into my neck, and I go still before she can do real damage.

Stupid, stupid, stupid of me to let those thoughts out. Unbelievably stupid to try and face down someone so much more powerful than me on her own turf. Part of me recognizes that I've earned whatever she decides to do with me now. Part of me is still too damn angry to care. This woman is the reason my parents are dead. This woman stood there and mocked me for not having a wolf form to shift into. This woman wants more fae, but only if they meet her ideal of "pure breeding." This woman is a piece of shit who deserves to hear my opinions about her.

"Little succubus," she whispers venomously into my ear. "I killed your mother because she thought she could run away without repercussions. She thought I would stop wanting her back if she cut off her wings, and she was right, but I couldn't let her get away with that kind of defiance and not make an example of her, could I? So, you see, it was her choice to cut off her wings, and after she'd done that, my hands were tied. I had to kill her. She might as well have killed herself."

"And what about my father?" My voice comes out in a gurgling rasp because she's still holding me so tightly by the neck.

"Collateral damage. Though I did enjoy the pain in her eyes when she watched me kill him. She as good as killed him too, and they both knew it. Now, are you going to make me change my mind about letting you live, little succubus? With no wings and no wolf, you're truly no use to me alive, but I have no need to kill you, unless you choose to defy me again. Make your choice quickly."

I try and fail to swallow past the hand gripping my throat.

"Live. I want to live."

She drops me like a forgotten toy, and I stay where I land, gasping for breath on the floor beside Taylor. I catch his eye and realize that he's barely conscious, still panting in painful-looking goldfish breaths. I need to get both of us out of this fucking place.

Titania turns to the assembled fae and announces, "If the

worthless halfbreed can find her way home, she can leave in peace. If she is still in the Summer Lands by nightfall, or if she ever returns, we hunt her down and end her."

A bloodthirsty cheer goes up around us.

Returning to her throne, the queen dismisses us without another spoken word. The bustle of a busy room full of people—albeit these are a type of people I'd never seen before today—returns to the room around us. People step around Taylor and me without actually looking at us, making it clear that we're to be forgotten unless we give the fae a chance to hunt us.

Hoping I can get us home without killing Taylor, I thread my fingers through his hair and delve deep to try and carry us home.

CHAPTER 51

Bee

I can't find it. With my eyes closed, I can almost see multiple paths spread out around me, and I'm absolutely certain none of them will take me home. Instead, I slip sideways, thankfully taking Taylor with me. My eyes pop open the instant we land back on solid ground. The good news is that we're away from the court. The bad news is that we're back in full sunlight, possibly in the same place in the forest we first came through to fairy land. Or whatever it is they actually call this place. The even worse news is that we're surrounded by fae.

"We're leaving," I promise them. "The queen gave us until tonight to get back home, so you can't do anything to us yet."

A small androgynous person, barely tall enough to meet my eyes even though I'm kneeling, with skin the same purple as a ripe plum, steps forward and sniffs at me.

"What did the queen say would happen if you stayed until tonight?"

They ask it with open curiosity and innocence, but I have no idea if I can trust them or not, so I change tactics.

"My friend is in danger here. I need to get him out of the sunlight and back to our own world."

The fae around us lean forward as one to inspect Taylor. As if confirming my story, he whimpers and curls in tighter on himself.

The purple person must be their official delegate because they speak again.

"The blood drinker," they say with an odd reverence in their voice. "We smelled when you came through to our side. It's been a long time since we had visitors from your side."

I push down the worry and panic fighting their way up my throat. Who are these fae? Do they follow the queen's edicts, or do they have their own laws? I can't exactly ask if they plan on hunting us for sport come sundown.

The spokesperson kneels down to sniff at Taylor while I sit frozen in indecision.

"The blood drinker needs to feed to survive," they tell me, as if I didn't already know that. They look directly into my eyes like they're trying to make me understand something. "The blood drinker needs to feed, but he can't feed from any of us. Our blood would poison him further."

Are they trying to help us? I suddenly remember Taylor saying that Ceallach doesn't smell like food. Who can he feed from, then?

"Me?" I yelp when the realization hits me. "You're saying he needs to feed from me to survive?"

The purple person nods.

"But . . . that could kill me. If he takes too much blood from me, I'll die."

They shrug. Not their problem. "You'll be stuck here unless his life force is restored. You can't travel unless you siphon power from him, can you?"

"I—" I try to think of a response that doesn't involve admitting my weakness to a forest full of potentially dangerous fae, but come up empty. "No. I can't," I admit, but that doesn't mean I'm okay with letting him drink straight from me. Even if I'm okay with it, he's hardly in a position to let me know if he's comfortable with the idea. I don't know the finer points of vampire culture, but it doesn't take a huge leap to believe that drinking someone's blood is an intimate thing that not everyone wants to experience.

But what if I can save him?

I nudge my mind against his, not trying to see everything this time, just trying to find this one answer.

His thoughts are a jumbled mess. His body is shutting down, and his conscious mind is basically closed for business. There's still someone in here, though. I hope I'm not too late to save them.

That thought decides for me. I'm confident I can still make it home somehow, even without his help. But I can't live with myself if I let him die here. After he's done so much to help me find my power, my family, my place in the world? There should be nothing I won't do to save him.

I look at the spokesperson. "Can you give us some privacy?" Because I have a feeling this is going to feel really fucking intimate—like, delving into someone's thoughts for the first time intimate—even without a crowd of fae watching.

They raise their hands in a strangely formal pose, almost a bow, almost a salute, and step backward away from us.

"Goodbye, cousin. And best of luck. Maybe we'll see you again someday."

Just like that, the fae around us scatter and vanish, leaving us alone in the forest.

I lay my wrist experimentally against Taylor's lips, but he doesn't respond.

Shit. What's the right way to do this? I think back to when Marcus had to save Devon like this. I'm pretty sure he used a knife to cut himself and make it easier for Devon to drink from him.

Too bad I don't have a handy knife in my pocket.

What I do have is fingernails. Is it my imagination, or did they actually lengthen and sharpen when I thought that?

Rolling Taylor onto his back, I straddle his waist for what I hope is the best position possible.

"We only get one shot at this," I remind both of us, and then I slash at the side of my neck as hard as I can with my fingernail.

A line of fire races along my neck where I've managed to open the skin, but is it enough? I touch it with a finger and—while painful—come away without any blood. Not deep enough. This time, I deliberately dig my nail in where my skin is already burning from the scratch. I can't hold back a scream as I tear the skin deeper, but I'm rewarded with a splash of blood that lands across Taylor's face. He stirs and moans, which I take as my signal. Leaning down to him, I press my neck to his lips.

For one terrible moment, I think I'm too late because he doesn't respond, and then his arms snap up around me, trapping me against him, and his teeth sink in, latching onto my neck the same way a leech or a tick would. I thought I was ready for the pain, but this is a level of excruciating that I couldn't have imagined. Each spot where his teeth breach my skin is a fire that burns through my nervous system. My entire shoulder and arm are paralyzed from the pain radiating out from my neck.

And that's before I feel the pull as he sucks against my vein. Like being caught in a riptide within my own body, my heart struggles to push blood where it needs to go, but it's all getting sucked away in the wrong direction.

Knowing I won't be conscious for long, I fight for awareness so I can get us home. It won't help either of us if I die while Taylor is still stuck here.

I delve into him with my mind and am relieved to find that same power source at the core of his being, and it seems to get a little stronger with each pull he takes from my vein. I won't get a better chance than this, so I tap into him and siphon off the same power he just took from my blood until we make a kind of circuit, cycling energy between the two of us.

With my eyes pressed closed tight, trying to ignore my pain and fear and the world around us, I find the same path I used to bring us here and somehow slip us back home before everything muffles and blackens out of existence for me.

CHAPTER 52

Taylor

The sweetest thing I've ever tasted is on my lips, and every bit of me aches with some kind of pain, and there's shouting. Awareness comes to me slowly, and understanding is even slower. The blood I'm drinking is hot and fresh and better than any blood I've ever gotten from a bag, but I can't quite put together the puzzle pieces to figure out what's different. Then, the blood source is torn away from me.

And then someone punches me in the eye.

Strangely, that's the thing that brings the world back into focus around me. I'm lying on the floor of Bee's bedroom, and several people are working to haul Grey off me.

Grey doesn't matter, though.

Bee matters. Because it was her blood I was drinking. She probably just saved my life. Twice, actually, because she got me away from that place that was killing me, and she let me drink from her.

"Bee?" I search around me in a panic.

Before I can find her, Grey gets an arm loose from where Devon was holding it back and punches me in the eye again.

"Let go of me!" he shouts, and I realize that most of the shouting before I came to my senses was from him.

"You're not helping anything!" Marcus shouts back, yanking Grey backward.

I scramble to my feet, partly to avoid being punched a third time, but mostly so I can figure out where Bee is.

"Where's Bee? Where did you take her?" The only thing louder than Grey is the panicked voice in my head telling me I killed her. I took too much, and she's already dead because of me.

"Don't fucking say her name!" Grey pulls hard enough that he almost gets free again.

"Greyson James, that's enough!" Astrid's voice comes from down the hall. "We need everyone's help out here now!"

Grey freezes at his mom's words, and then we all move together to get out to the living room. My legs almost give out from under me again when I see Bee stretched out on the couch, looking ashen. Astrid has a blanket from the couch pressed to her neck, trying to stop the bleeding from where I bit her.

"What do we do?" Gabe asks, staring at her in horror. "Shouldn't she just heal naturally, between being half fae and half shifter? Why isn't she healing?"

"Because a fucking monster tore half her throat out," Grey spits out, taking a moment to glare at me before turning back to Bee.

Whatever he's feeling toward me, it's not possible for him to hate me as much as I hate myself right now. I've always known I was a monster. I've always been afraid of what would happen if I let that monstrous side of myself out. Now it's happened, and I have to face the consequences.

"Vampire blood can heal her." Astrid looks frantically around the room. "Quick. One of you."

Marcus starts forward, already rolling up his sleeve, but

Devon holds him back. "Wait," he explains when everyone looks at him in confusion. "Depending on how close to death she is, giving her vampire blood might save her, or it might turn her. I'm not saying don't do it, but it's not a risk we should take without thinking it through first."

Most of me wants to scream that of course there's no possible worse outcome than Bee dying. We need to do whatever it takes to save her. But at the same time, I'm the only one here who might understand the consequences as well as Devon does.

"He's right," I whisper, hating myself even more. "When someone is turned too young or without their consent, there are a lot of potential side effects. She might have to live with those side effects for centuries if we make that choice for her."

Jeff must have seen Grey's hand balling into a fist and cocking back to punch me again because he grabs onto Grey's arm and steps between us.

"Why the fuck did you do this to her?" Grey asks me. Accuses me. "She kept defending you, saying she was safe with you, and then you do this?"

I hunch in on myself, but the verbal blow still lands. There's no defense, especially when Bee might be dying.

A nagging thought breaks through my panic, and I turn to Gabe. "There was a woman there—where Bee and I were before—this fae queen. She said something about Bee being a . . . a succubus. She said . . . something about Bee not having fae gifts of her own, only being able to . . . borrow power. And then someone else said something about her siphoning power from me to bring us home. Maybe she could heal in the same way? If she can tap into my life source, she might be able to access those healing abilities?"

Gabe nods thoughtfully. "There are fae who have to feed off of someone else, similar to vampires, but with different types of energy instead of blood."

"It's worth a try," Astrid says. "Do you know how she did it before?"

"I don't know. It seems to be tied to touch. At least, the other times, she was touching me when it happened."

Astrid waves me over, and I kneel beside the couch.

Please let this work, I beg the universe. *Please let there be a way for Bee to live without becoming a monster like me. Like my mother.*

I twine our fingers together, horrified at how limp hers are in mine, and sense nothing from her. I try cupping her face in my hand, but her skin is just cold, her face unresponsive, her heartbeat so faint that I can only barely sense it at all.

Come on, Bee. You have to come back to me.

Imitating her earlier motions, I slide her hand along my cheek and up into my hair, praying for her fingers to suddenly twitch and tangle and tug in that way that feels so good. There's nothing, though. I lean down and press our foreheads together, brush my nose against hers. Out of options, my lips find hers, and I kiss her. I ignore the shuffle of feet and angry muttering from Grey behind me. The only thing that matters in my universe right now is Bee. The only thing I can think about is bringing her back.

Come on, Bee. I love you. I need you here.

I kiss her again, harder. More desperately than before.

Then I feel it. A twitch of someone moving against my mind. I send every thought of love I have in her direction, remember every good moment I've had with her, and feel the moment I suck her mind into my own. Suddenly, our awareness is tangled together, the two of us lost in a world of remembered moments and experiences flickering past. Bee, laughing at something I said while she eats alternating bites of three different pies. Bee's sly face as she tells me she's getting a tattoo. Bee, shuddering in my arms the first time I made her come.

And some of her thoughts shine through that tangle too. I see myself—cuffed and gagged and spread out for her—from her viewpoint, and it's a strangely beautiful sight. I see the mutual give-and-take of pleasure as we both experienced sex for the first time. And I also feel her anger at being coddled and protected and kept from experiencing life.

I see it now. That's not what you need from me. But take what you do *need.* And she does. I feel something being pulled away, not in the same way the fae sun sapped all of my energy straight out of me. This is more like sand on a beach that gets pulled up into the waves. Or water that sinks down into the sand. Bee and I are both part of the same thing, so whatever part of me she uses isn't lost; it's just rearranged. I feel my energy moving through her body and giving her strength along its path. Then, I feel it tap into something greater, something locked inside of her. I was expecting to simply help her neck heal. I was very deeply mistaken about the nature of her power, because power is exactly what I sense, locked away deep inside of her. I'm not here to help her heal. I'm here as a key to unlock whatever she's kept hidden her whole life.

The "us" of our combined awareness presses against that wall, and something on the other side roars to life and opens its eyes. A storm of fire and magic envelops me as the wall holding it back crumbles, and a new entity joins us. Not entirely new, actually. The fierce intelligence twining with our consciousness is recognizably part of Bee, just a part she wasn't aware of before.

Mine. Mate, it whisper-roars as it becomes part of us. *Ours. Mate.*

I don't need the connection between our minds to know the absolute truth of the words. Whatever Bee is, this combination of magic and fire and fae and shifter, I was created for her, and it's the greatest relief I've ever felt to be claimed like that, to belong so completely to someone else, to know that we'll never be truly separate again.

Yes. Mate, I confirm, and it . . . She? They? Settles around me.

With a contented sigh, her consciousness uncoils from my thoughts and drops away, releasing me back into the world around me.

Everything is still and silent in the room, in spite of all the same warm, breathing bodies with their hearts beating and their blood pulsing around us. Everyone is frozen, staring at Bee as we wake up from the trance we must have seemed to be under.

"What—" Astrid's voice croaks out beside me. "What happened?"

Bee blinks up at me, and I catch a swirl of gold and black in her eyes before they return to their normal blue, and then she sits up slowly to take in the room.

Grey is still frozen with his fist half-raised and Jeff standing in front of him, while Marcus and Devon have each taken hold of one of his shoulders as if to hold him back. As one, they realize that the immediate danger is over, give each other sheepish looks, and step apart. Gloria sits on the couch beside Bee and inspects her neck, which now has perfectly healed, unbroken skin where there was a gaping wound before.

"How did you . . ." Gloria trails off. "You both went completely still, then the whole house shook, like an earthquake, and suddenly, everything went still again, and you both woke up. And you're healed. What *was* that?"

Bee thoughtfully traces the spot on her neck where I drank from her. "I guess the short answer is that I tapped into my shifter power, and it allowed me to heal."

Astrid joins her on the couch and shares a quick, confused look with Gloria. "So, you inherited shifter powers from your father after all? We didn't see you shift, and we didn't sense your wolf at all."

A hysterical giggle fizzes out of Bee before she gets control of herself. Having just been intimately introduced to the entity in question, I have trouble holding back my own laugh. But it's Bee's story to tell, not mine, so I just rub her knee and give her an encouraging look.

"Well," she starts, "I'm not actually a wolf, as it turns out, and I don't think I'm ready to share that part of myself yet. Maybe someday. Just believe me when I say it's for the best that I was able to use my shifter healing without actually shifting in here."

I imagine the expansive creature I just met trying to fit inside this house, and a trickle of sweat beads up at my hair-line. No, it's definitely for the best that Bee didn't take on her full secondary form in the living room. Even without the heat and fire, I don't think any of us would have survived being crushed by the enormous black-and-gold dragon that lives inside of her, as part of her.

"How do you feel?" I ask her before anyone can ask any follow-up questions.

She smiles. "Expansive."

CHAPTER 53

Taylor

I thought—for one brief, sweet moment—that I would be allowed to sit with Bee, now that our secret is out. But Astrid has been glued to her side for the past three hours, continually wrapping an arm around her to bring her closer or lifting a hand to rearrange a piece of hair that wasn't out of place. I suppose it's fair. She thought she had lost her daughter, but now her daughter is back and healthy. I think all of us are still feeling the weight of that miracle. Grey has plastered himself on Bee's other side, though, and has spent the past three hours alternating between gazing at her in wonder and glaring at me in anger. I suspect it's going to take more than me helping to save her life to get back on his good side. What I'm not clear on is whether he's most upset about me drinking from her or the fact that we've been hooking up behind his back.

"Are we really, truly, absolutely certain that Bee is safe from this fae queen?" Jeff asks for at least the fifth time.

Bee has already told us what happened in the fae world with a lot more detail than I could remember, but that doesn't mean everyone fully believes her yet.

Bee just shrugs off his question. "She only wants me if I can do something for her. I don't have anything she's interested in, therefore, I'm free to live my life."

We both know that the queen would be very interested in the dragon that we recently unlocked from Bee's subconscious, but that's one of the things Bee isn't ready to talk about yet. Honestly, I'm not ready either. What Bee and I shared is just too personal to let everyone else in on it, at least for right now. I'd rather let them watch her peg me than try to explain how her dragon entity, which is also a part of her the same way a shifter's wolf would be part of them, claimed me as her mate and made me hers.

No, that isn't a conversation I'm ready for.

Astrid hugs Bee tight to her and rests her head on Bee's. "I can hardly believe it, but I want to believe it so bad. After we lost your parents, I thought for sure she would kill you out of spite."

"She wanted to," Bee admits. "The way Ceallach spoke, I don't think she can afford to lose anyone with fae blood. She can make a big show about keeping the blood pure or whatever, and she can banish people from the court, but there aren't enough fae left for her to kill them on a whim. I'll have to ask Ceallach to be certain. If he ever comes back, that is."

"Or I can ask my dad," Gabe adds, sounding reluctant. "He's taught me a bit about that world, but I've never planned to join him there, so it never seemed important. Maybe I should start asking him some questions."

"Don't do it for my sake," Bee says. "I'm pretty comfortable with the idea of leaving all of the fae and their world behind. I've lived here my whole life, and I don't have a reason to leave. Besides, you're all here. Everyone I care about is in this world, and the last person I want to see again is in that one. Let's just put the fae behind us."

"Well." Astrid looks afraid to bring up her next topic but

powers through anyway. "Speaking of people you care about, who would like to see you—"

Bee groans and buries her face in her hands. "I'm not sure I'm ready to see Dad yet. He'll have all sorts of questions I don't want to answer. And he lied to me about who I was my whole life! How am I even supposed to talk to him?"

Astrid tugs Bee's hand down so she can catch her eye.

"I also lied to you, remember? And it was for a good reason. Greyson deserves to see his daughter again."

"And what about Taylor?"

Bee's eyes flick toward me and then back to her mom. Astrid gives me a longer, assessing look.

"Taylor saved your life," she finally says, "and the two of you are obviously tied to each other now. Greyson will want to meet him."

And doesn't that just open a pit in my stomach that wasn't there before.

Bee sighs. "We will make plans to visit, but I'm not promising right away. We've got school, you know, and Taylor has his own life here to deal with. In fact, everyone has been focused on dealing with my issues lately. It's probably best if we all get back to our regular lives for a while before we think about taking any trips."

Astrid smiles like she just got exactly what she wanted and turns to Gloria. "You know," she says brightly, "I was just thinking about how it's probably time for you and Grey to come meet the pack. With all of this other excitement, my husband won't have time to think about trying to keep you there. You can meet the people who will be your new pack, and the pack can start getting used to the idea of letting new people in."

Gloria looks a little queasy but manages a weak smile. "Sure. Great. Why not?" she says, sounding like she's already thinking of ways to get out of it. At least, I hope she is, because the thought of visiting a wolf pack of shifters who probably think and act a lot like Grey is turning my insides to jelly.

Sharing some unspoken signal between them, Devon and Marcus stand up at the same time.

"Speaking of getting back to our lives," Marcus mutters, "we really should, now that Bee's out of danger."

Jeff and Gabe make their goodbyes as well, and suddenly, I'm the lone vampire in a house full of shifters, one of whom would probably love to rip my throat out.

Great.

"Is that my cue that I've outstayed my welcome?" Astrid asks with a sigh.

"No, of course not!" Bee starts, then thinks better of it. "Okay, we could use some quiet for a little bit, and having you around doesn't make things any quieter."

"Fine. I'll leave my children alone, as long as you promise to come visit soon. And call us from time to time? Now that everything is out in the open, there's no reason for you to spend all this time running away from us, right?"

Bee answers her with a tight hug of her own. "I guess you're right. I don't need to stay away from the pack to find myself anymore because I've figured that part out. But you have to accept that my life is here now." She glances at me. "And my life is with him, so if the pack can't handle that . . ."

Astrid kisses her forehead and smooths her hair. "You're mated," she says simply. "Anyone with eyes can see that, and no one in the pack would try to break a mate bond. They'll accept him because he's yours, and you're part of the pack."

I realize that I've been standing completely frozen, maybe hoping I would be forgotten, but Astrid's words shake me out of that.

Mated.

Bee's dragon had claimed me, and that had felt right, but hearing someone else say it out loud like that settles something inside my heart that I hadn't realized was out of place. I come to stand beside where Bee and her mom are still embracing and put a possessive hand on Bee's lower back. I can practically feel Grey's eyes scorching my hand, but I can't make myself care.

Mated. She's my mate. She's mine.

With a slightly teary smile, Astrid lets go of Bee and surprises me by pulling me in for a hug. At first, I don't know what to do with my arms, but eventually, they find their way around her to return the hug.

"Welcome to the family," she says, still holding me, and it's the most mothering I've had in my entire life.

A tear sneaks out, and I'm quick to wipe it away. I don't think anyone else noticed me crying about a hug, but Bee and I don't really have any secrets left. She knows what my mom is like, and about my childhood, and about the vampire charity programs that kept—and still keep—me fed because I'm too poor to buy blood. Bee knows all of that, and she still claims me.

When Astrid steps away, I'm barely holding back my tears, and Bee knows it, so she squeezes herself against my side and drapes her arm around my waist. And now I feel Grey's burning eyes on my back. We'll have to deal with him sometime. Not today, though. I hope.

Moments after her mother is gone, Bee turns to Grey. "Don't even say it. I know you were holding it back while Mom was here, and you can damn well keep holding it back. Nobody wants or needs your opinions on my relationships."

Grey looks affronted, gesturing expressively between Bee and me, but he doesn't say anything beyond making a few strangled sounds of disapproval.

"That's what I thought," says Gloria, giving him a steely

eye. "Don't forget that Taylor lives here, and you don't. We can choose to kick you out at any time, and probably should because of all the problems you caused today."

"Problems?" Grey's voice finally breaks free. "That *I* caused? What about the problems he caused?" He waves an angry hand in my direction.

"Taylor actually lives here," Gloria argues. "And any problems he caused were directly related to problems you caused first. And let's not forget how unhelpful your knee-jerk response of punching him in the face was. You're lucky if I don't send you back to your house tonight. Or maybe I should make you sleep on the front porch so you can think about your behavior."

Bee raises a hand to stop the argument before it can get too heated. "Gloria's right. This is Taylor's house more than it is yours, so if you can't get along, you're going to be the one who leaves."

With a few mutinous mutters, Grey sinks into himself.

Gloria cocks an eyebrow at him. "What was that?"

Grey straightens, takes a deep breath, and turns to face me. "I'm sorry about punching you. It . . . might not have been the most helpful response. And I'm sorry for giving you shit all year and for not trusting you. I was just worried about my sister. But you came through for her in the end, so I guess I owe you now."

I try to shrug off the prickly, uncomfortable feeling between my shoulder blades, but it doesn't work.

"I probably wouldn't have trusted someone like me if our positions were swapped," I admit. "Maybe we can just call it even?"

With a stiff nod, Grey sticks out his hand for me to shake. All four of us relax a little after we shake hands.

"It's been a long day," Gloria says. "Do you think we can

all just have a peaceful night of sleep, or do you boys need to punch each other again, just to be sure it's over?"

I bite my lips to keep from laughing, and I catch a smile tugging at the corner of Grey's mouth too.

"I think we're good," I say at the same time Grey says, "Please let's get some sleep."

"Actually," Bee says, then looks up at me. "I think Taylor and I still have something to take care of, and sooner is probably better."

I'm sure my confusion shows because she slides a comforting hand into mine before she goes on.

"I should meet your mom."

My first instinct is to back away. No, to run away. To hide and try to protect her from this. But then I remember that she's seen inside my head. She's seen just about every thought I've ever had. It's way too late to try and hide this from her.

"Sleep first," I tell her. "We've been through too much today to add my mom on top of it all."

She gives a serious nod. "Tomorrow, then. For now, let's get some sleep." And she leads me to her bed without giving me or anyone else a chance to argue.

CHAPTER 54

Taylor

B ee stills my bouncing knee with a gentle hand on top of it.

"We don't have to do this, you know," I say. Again. Because I said it before we left the house this morning and several times on the way over here. "She's not your problem. You don't have to go in there at all."

Bee's bland expression speaks volumes.

"Come on. It's time," she says, and that finally gets me moving out of the car and toward the house.

Of course, it's dark and silent inside, and all of the clutter is stacked up as high as ever. Bee doesn't even blink in surprise. She's seen it all already through my memories.

"Mom?" I whisper so I don't startle her. "Are you awake?"

An animallike snuffle sounds from her nest in the corner. "Who's that I smell? What did you bring here?"

Her voice is full of anger and suspicion, and I want to pull Bee back outside and tell her this might not be a good time. If I do that, though, I'm pretty sure I'll spend the rest of my life coming up with excuses to keep Bee and my mom apart.

"Mom, this is Bee. My . . ." I realize I have no idea what I should tell her. Girlfriend? That doesn't begin to describe what Bee is to me. Mate? That's not really a thing for vampires like it is for shifters.

"We're mated to each other," Bee supplies.

Mom's face twists at the words. "Sounds like just the kind of lie men tell to get what they want. Trust me. Get away while you still can. He's a monster just like all the rest."

Again, I'm ready to give up on this whole endeavor, but Bee carefully picks her way over to sit in my normal place.

"It's nice to meet you," she says as if my mother didn't just tell her I'm a monster.

Mom sniffs in Bee's direction, still suspicious.

"What is she?" Mom whispers to me like Bee isn't right there, listening to everything she says.

Bee answers before I can figure out how to respond.

"I'm not a human, and I'm not a vampire, and I'm in love with your son."

Warmth fills me inside and unclenches my muscles. Bee is in love with me, and she said it out loud to the only person who really matters to me.

Mom scoffs. "I thought I was in love once. A long time ago."

"But he disappointed you?"

Bee is looking earnestly into Mom's eyes, and Mom can't resist that magnetic pull.

"Yes," she says. Maybe the first time she's said it out loud. "I thought we were in love, but he disappointed me."

"But Taylor is different, isn't he," Bee coaxes. "He doesn't disappoint you, does he?"

"No," Mom admits. "He takes care of me."

Bee nods. "And now the two of us will take care of you, because I'm part of Taylor's life now."

A vision of the future stretches out in front of me, with Bee and my mother and me together through the years, and

I'm not sure if it's what I want. I'm not sure how long fae live. Centuries, like vampires? Or is it millennia? Did the queen say something about it? I know shifters tend to live a shorter time, closer to a normal human life.

Bee breaks me out of my panic spiral by turning to me with her eyebrows raised. "You know I can hear you thinking over there, right?"

"Sorry. I guess I got kind of stuck in my worries there for a bit."

She smiles at me, then at my mom, then back at me again. "It will work out. I'm not sure about the details, but I've got this feeling, this certainty. This is all going to work out."

Mom hugs herself and rocks back and forth, a self-soothing technique I've seen her use often through the years, and a sign that her mental state is about to nosedive.

"I'm too sick," she mutters. "It can't all work out because I'm too sick. I've been so sick for so long. You'll never be happy as long as you're stuck with me. I can't even take care of myself. I could never take care of my son. You'll leave me. That's how it will happen. I'll be too much, so you'll leave me behind. You see? I know how it works out. I know that I don't get the happy ending with everyone else."

When Bee puts a gentle hand on Mom's arm, a shudder passes through her. I wonder if it's pain or fear or disgust or something else entirely. I can read Bee pretty well, now that we've got the thread of the mate bond connecting us, but my mom is just as much a mystery as ever. I have no idea how she feels about Bee touching her.

"Sylvia?" Bee whispers. "I'd like to try doing something that might help you feel better, but I'm not certain. Would you like to try it?"

Mom trembles, a tree with just enough wind passing through to shake every single leaf. "What do you want to try?"

"I want you to drink from me."

I'm up in an instant. "No. Not happening. That is absolutely not an option."

Bee gives me a look that silences me before she goes on.

"I think that my blood just might have some healing properties beyond regular bagged human blood. Vampire blood has more healing potential than human, right? That's why Devon has to feed from Marcus, as far as I understand."

"But," I interject, "Devon is blood bound to Marcus. He literally can't drink from anyone else, and we don't want to risk someone developing that kind of dependence on your blood."

"We learned yesterday that I won't die from a vampire drinking from me," Bee points out. "I can give up a lot of blood and still heal myself, as long as I can feed from your energy. I don't see a downside to letting your mom feed from my vein—just to test if it makes any kind of difference—and then I feed from you to replenish myself. Maybe my blood will just act like regular blood and feed her for the day, but maybe my fae and shifter backgrounds mix to make something a little more powerful than average. Don't you want to see if I can help?"

"Not after yesterday," I say. "I almost killed you by drinking from you. How are you willing to take that risk again?"

"Because you didn't kill me," she says, like it's the most obvious thing in the world, then turns back to my mother. "I don't actually know if this will work, but I'm willing to try on the off chance I can help."

Mom searches her face for a long, silent moment. "Okay," she says at last. "We'll try."

My heart drops to the floor somewhere, and I have to remind myself that this is Bee's choice to make, not mine. I just have to be ready to save her if this takes a bad turn.

My stomach drops down to meet my heart when Bee pulls

a small knife out of her purse and moves to perch on the arm of Mom's chair. If she brought a knife with her, that means she was planning this before we left the house. But that makes perfect sense, now that I see the evidence in front of me. Bee was in my thoughts and saw everything my mom has been through, everything I've been through with her, and decided she needed to do something to help. Even through my fear over what's about to happen, love for her swells in my chest.

With a deceptively casual motion, Bee slices the knife across her wrist. Not deep, but the smell of fresh blood welling up into the wound fills the room immediately. Mom's nostrils flare as she takes in the scent, her predatory vampire instincts taking over.

Bee holds her arm in front of my mother's face, and Mom pauses for just a moment, staring hungrily at the stripe of blood on Bee's wrist before grabbing her and latching on with her teeth.

There's nothing I can do, I remind myself over and over. *This is Bee's choice.*

It feels terrible, though. I feel so helpless, watching someone feed on the woman I love. I put a hand on Bee's back to steady her, in case she gets dizzy and falls, but it's the only way I can help her right now. And I'll be here for her when she's ready to feed on me. At least I can help her then.

It's torture to stand by and watch while my mom sucks deep and hard from Bee's vein, but I force myself to stay where I am and let Bee do this. When Bee's eyes flutter shut and she slumps against me, though, that's my signal to pry her arm away from Mom's mouth.

"Come on, sweetheart," I whisper, rocking her in my lap and patting her cheek to bring her back to consciousness. "Time for you to feed, now."

She opens her eyes, and I'm terrified of the confusion I see there.

"Feed?" she asks.

"You remember. Just like yesterday. You need to feed from me so you can feel like yourself again."

For a long, terrifying moment, I think maybe I left it too long and she won't be able to remember how. Then, I see the pieces click into place, and her expression clears before she pulls my face to hers for a kiss. It starts innocent enough, but when her tongue touches the seam of my lips, I open willingly for her. At the same time her tongue explores my mouth, I feel her mind—or possibly something deeper than that, her soul, maybe—delving into me and claiming me the way she did before.

We spend either an eternity or less than a minute like that, sharing energy and touch and love, before she pulls away and looks at Mom.

For her part, Mom is staring at her hands and turning them over and over, as if she can't believe something she's seeing.

"I can feel . . . everything . . . I'd forgotten what it felt like . . ." she says in an awed whisper.

"Are you okay?" I ask.

She laughs. Actually laughs. The first genuine laugh I've ever heard from my mother in my entire life.

"Oh, baby. I've never felt better."

CHAPTER 55

Bee

I feel invincible. I know that I'm not. Not quite, at least. But I'm pretty fucking close. I'm still riding the high from helping Taylor's mom when we get back to our own house.

Are there still some things to work out? Yes. Of course. For one, I have a feeling that my blood won't be a permanent solution to Sylvia's illness. Blood is a miracle cure for vampires in many cases, but they have to keep drinking it for it to work, and Sylvia's condition is chronic and has been affecting her for almost twenty years now. But she feels better today than she has since becoming a vampire, and that's a pretty big win, if you ask me.

And then there's my grandmother. The evil fairy queen herself. Can I really trust that she'll leave me alone? What if she finds out about my dragon form, who's been locked away and out of reach until now? Not to mention my fae cousin who basically got himself exiled by standing up for me. It's not like I have his cell number and can ask how he's feeling about the whole thing. For all I know, I'll never see him again, and that thought just makes me sad.

So it's not like my life is suddenly perfect or easy, but I've got Taylor by my side, and I've found a side of myself that I'd never imagined before. And I've learned who my parents were, and maybe started rebuilding my relationship with my adoptive parents. That's a good thing.

"You're so quiet," Taylor says. "I'm not sure how much you can hear my thoughts when we're not touching, but I don't have any idea what's going on in your head right now."

I roll my head to watch him as he drives us home.

"I have to make a conscious effort to hear your thoughts, whether we're touching or not, and it's limited if we're not physically connected," I tell him. "Besides, I think it's probably best if I ask before going into your mind. We should have some boundaries, right?"

He spares me a glance and a smile. "That's probably the healthier approach, but my heart doesn't like that much separation."

"How about, once we get home, we fix that."

Taylor's smile widens. "What exactly do you have in mind?" he asks with a suggestive eyebrow wiggle.

I can't help but snicker. It's possible I'm still a bit immature when it comes to all things related to sex.

"Well," I say in the sexiest voice I can muster, "if you're willing, I was thinking of trying out another one of those toys I bought. Maybe I'll cuff you to the bed again so you won't be able to control how fast or slow I fuck you."

Taylor lets out a needy whimper that shoots straight through to my core so my muscles clench around emptiness.

I lean toward him so he'll feel my breath as I talk to him. "What about the gag? Do you want me to gag you, or just the handcuffs this time?"

With a gulp that echoes around the car and a thick drop of sweat sliding down his temple, he answers in a hoarse whisper.

"No gag. I'm desperate to eat your pussy without anything between us."

"You're not worried about hurting me?"

His grin widens to show all of his extra-sharp teeth. "After everything that's happened in the past two days, I don't think we have to worry about that anymore. I know that if I do drink from you, I can stop before I kill you. But even more importantly, I don't think I'll have that same craving again. I drank my fill."

I nod. I get what he means. I was never that worried about him drinking from me, but now I have proof that he won't harm me.

We don't waste time once we get back to the house. Our hunger for each other means we barely notice Grey and Gloria sitting on the couch as we breeze through with our lips already locked together.

Grey lets out a squawked "Hey!" before Gloria shuts him off with a peal of laughter and tells him something about it only being fair. Or maybe that it's our turn. Whatever she says, I can hear Grey groaning unhappily from the living room, but he doesn't try to interrupt Taylor and me.

Which is definitely for the best because I've managed to strip Taylor's clothes completely off him by the time we get to my room and shut the door behind us.

Taylor—in all of his naked, aroused glory—lifts me easily with one hand under my ass and cradles my head in his other hand so he can press me against the door and rut against my pussy with his massive cock.

"Taylor, wait," I gasp between kisses. "We should talk about some boundaries and hard limits before we go any further."

He pulls back to look at me through heavy lids.

"Hard limits like how you don't want to be penetrated?"

Maybe he's the one who can read my mind after all.

"Yes," I say. "Is that okay, though? I mean, I don't think I'll ever be comfortable with the idea of having something inside of me like that. Won't you feel like you're . . . I don't know, missing out on half of your sex life?"

He chuckles and kisses me again, deeply, with his tongue tasting every bit of my mouth before he pulls away again.

"Most people don't get to experience the kind of intimacy you and I have with each other. I will never feel like I'm missing out on anything as long as we have the mate bond between us." He rolls his hips, and his cock slides up between us. "Besides, I suspect you're going to keep me extremely satisfied in other ways. I'll never even notice the lack."

I stifle a moan in his neck as his length slides against my clit, sending a jolt of pleasure shooting through me. He does it again, and again, and again, ratcheting my pleasure higher and higher while still holding me with utmost tenderness.

As I reach my peak, I find his mouth with mine and devour him while I come apart in his arms. He keeps rolling his hips, letting me ride him all the way through my pleasure until my spasms and aftershocks slow and stop.

"On the bed," I order him, still breathless.

Taylor licks, then bites, then licks my lower lip. "Of course, my mate. Anything for you."

I cuff him to the bed with his arms stretched wide, like he's on display especially for me. His eyes widen, and he flicks his tongue out to wet his lips when I step away from the bed and start to strip for him. The way his toes curl against the bedspread as he watches me is every bit as sexy as the way his dick stands visibly straighter with each of my movements. When I stand completely naked in front of him and cradle my breasts in my hands, plucking at my nipples until they're stiff enough to cut gemstones, Taylor lets out a needy moan.

"If you see something you want, you'll have to tell me," I tease him.

"I want you," he moans. "I want all of you. On my skin. And in my mouth. Everywhere. I need you, Bee."

I trace his lower lip with my finger but pull it away when he tries to draw it into his mouth.

"Is that what you want in your mouth?" I ask. "You want my finger?"

He gives a pained groan and sinks back onto the mattress.

"I want anything you'll give me," he begs. "Fingers, tits, ass, pussy. Any of them. All of you. Fuck, Bee, I want to eat you out so bad. I want you to come all over my face while I lick your pussy. Please. Fuck. I need that so bad."

"Well, when you say it like that . . ."

I trail my fingernails down his throat to the patch of hair between his pecs, then further down still to the path of dark hair that points to his jutting erection. He makes a very satisfying, desperate sound when I finally reach his cock and brush my fingernails from the root to the tip.

"Fuck, Bee. Let me make you come first. I don't want to go too early again."

With a grin across my face, I give him what he wants and climb onto the bed, balancing with one knee beside each of his ears and my fingers already clenching on the headboard.

"Is this what you had in mind?"

He doesn't bother answering, just lifts his head and goes to work, teasing apart each layer and fold of my pussy with his tongue.

I can't help myself. I slide my fingers into his hair to hold him steady, then fuck hard into his mouth, grinding my clit into his face while he licks and sucks secret letters of love and pleasure into my skin.

Before I'm really ready for it, I'm coming on his mouth with a curse and a groan.

Taylor keeps licking at me as he lets me ride out my orgasm on his face. Was it really just a few days ago that I thought I couldn't come at all? Now, I can already feel a third building like a thunderstorm inside me.

It's Taylor's turn for some pleasure now, though. I slide down, tasting all of the places I scraped at earlier with my fingernails as I make my way lower. He yelps and lifts off the bed a few inches when I bite at his nipple, but the cuffs keep him from doing anything else.

"Fuck. Yes. Bee." He chants the words in a disjointed prayer, never actually finishing a sentence as I worship his body with my mouth. When I reach his cock, the words are even more disconnected. Less words and more grunts and moans of desperation.

"Tell me what you want, or I might stop altogether," I tell him, and he moans in what might actually be fear.

"I want . . . I need your mouth on me. I want to feel how hot and wet it is with my dick in your mouth. I need to feel you sucking on my cock."

The muscles inside of me clench at his words, and I feel a fresh drip of desire sliding from my pussy down my leg. I need to taste him right now as much as he needs me to. Still, I want to draw this out so I can wring every ounce of pleasure from it.

Kneeling down, I nuzzle into the joint of his leg where even vampires have major arteries and more sensitive skin. I bite down, not quite hard enough to break the skin but hard enough to make him jerk up with a broken "Fu—" on his tongue. I don't let go. With my teeth holding him in place, I suck hard to bring his blood to the surface to make a bruise the size of my mouth. Vampire blood may be thicker and slower than that of other species, but they do have it. This reminder of me will fade quickly from Taylor's skin, but we'll both know I've marked him. Claimed him as mine in every way I can.

While he's still feeling the sting of my bite, I shift so I can tongue at his balls. Much more carefully than before, I nip at the loose skin there, earning another broken curse from Taylor. My tongue slips easily over one side, then the other, before I take the whole thing in my mouth and suck. Taylor lets out a groan like I might actually be sucking his soul away. I can't help my grin as I pop off and lift up to reach the tip of his erection.

I start by swirling my tongue around the wide, smooth head, then hold him at the base while I explore the slit at the tip with my tongue. There's no way I can take all of him in my mouth without choking, so I wrap my hands around him, stacking them so there's less intimidating length to take. Taking a steadying breath through my nose, I let my throat and jaw hang loose and open as I slip him past my lips, over my tongue, and do my best to swallow him down.

Taylor holds perfectly still as I lower myself onto him, though I can feel tension vibrating through the muscles in his legs. His instinct is to thrust up into my mouth, but he's holding back to keep from choking me.

I swallow around him and try to take him just a little deeper before sliding back so I can do it again.

Taylor grunts and tugs at his cuffs but keeps his hips still. I reward him by quickening my pace. I try to move up and down his length at the speed he might naturally thrust into me, if he wasn't holding himself back.

"Fuck. Bee, I think I'm going to—"

I pull off him quickly and squeeze at the base of his dick.

"Don't you dare come yet," I order. "I'm not done here."

He whimpers but doesn't come.

"Good boy," I tell him, and he whimpers again.

Taking that as a sign that he's ready for the next step, I climb off the bed and fetch a vibrating anal plug and the bottle of lube.

"I'm trusting you to tell me if you want me to stop," I say.

Taylor licks his lips, his eyes locked on the items in my hands.

"I'll tell you if I want you to stop," he promises, "but right now, I want you to keep going. I want you to fuck me."

I can't stop smiling as I kneel between his legs and start working to open him up. The way his leg hair scratches at my cheeks, the way he gasps and twitches with each new touch, the way the skin around his hole feels ridged and different from the rest of him as I taste him . . . all of it brings a sensual haze down around us. My world narrows to this man on this bed. And me, licking and sucking and tasting and pressing, all in the name of drawing pleasure out of him.

"Are you ready?" I ask, and he moans a response. "I need you to say it in words," I reprimand him.

"Ready. Please, Bee. I'm ready. Fuck me now. Please."

He sounds more desperate with each word, and his need shoots pleasure straight through my center.

I almost stagger under the weight of his legs when I have him move them up so his ankles are resting on my shoulders, but I suck in my core and stay strong. It's strange to think about how powerful I feel in this position, with Taylor's hands still cuffed above his head and his hole opened up and on display for me.

With a satisfied groan, I press the vibrator slowly into him.

Taylor's eyes roll back, and he arches his back in response. It couldn't be any hotter if it were my actual body going into his.

"Should I keep going?"

"Fuck. Yes. Don't stop."

I slide the toy in the rest of the way, until the wide base is flat against his skin, then tug it back out just enough to push it back in a little harder. Taylor jerks at his cuffs, and his ankles twitch beside my ears.

"Do you like it when I'm in control like this?" I ask, though I can see the answer on his face.

He nods. "It feels so good. I love it when you fuck me like this."

I don't need to be in his head to know he's close to coming, but I'm not quite ready for that yet.

"Be good for me and don't let yourself come yet, okay?"

With a desperate moan, he meets my eyes and nods. He'll do what I ask, no matter how difficult it is.

Feeling about ready to come apart at the seams, I use one hand to move the plug in and out and take his cock in my other hand and pump it slowly. Sweat beads on his upper lip, and I can see his jaw muscles clenching as he fights back his orgasm.

"Just a little longer," I promise him. "Hang on a little longer for me."

Another nod is all he can manage. He doesn't have any words left.

Sensing I've pushed him as far as possible, I decide it's time. I press the button to start the toy vibrating inside him, and he cries out at the sensation. I keep pumping his cock and press myself up against the base of the vibrator. In only a few seconds, I feel myself climbing toward another climax.

"You can come now," I tell him through clenched teeth, and come practically explodes out of him at my words. My own climax follows soon after, but something else wells up at the same time that I can't control. Heat suffuses my back, and I feel the stretch of shifting skin and growing bones. Without thinking about it, two leathery wings unfold from somewhere inside me. They snap wide as my orgasm crashes through me, pulsing with tension as every muscle locks and freezes in place. Then it passes, and I slump down over him, feeling wrung out and empty. My fingers shake as I fumble to turn off the vibrator and pull it carefully out of his body.

"That was . . . How did . . ."

He can't finish a sentence, but he keeps trying to say something. I shut him up with a rough kiss before stretching out on top of him, heedless of the come cooling on his belly, ignoring the fact that he's still cuffed to the headboard, pretending that I don't have wings taking up most of the space in this room, and let myself sleep.

CHAPTER 56

Taylor

Everyone is draped over the couches, and some of us are draped over each other, with our drinks of choice in our tacky friend mugs.

There aren't quite enough spots for everyone, so Bee is perched on my lap with my arm around her waist to hold her steady.

Yep. This is entirely about the lack of seats and has nothing to do with anything else. And I definitely am not sporting a huge erection that's only hidden by Bee sitting on top of it.

Fuck, I don't know what I'll do when it's time for her to stand up.

Almost everyone is absorbed in laughing and either watching or playing the video game on the TV screen, but Gabe is staring into space and looking forlorn.

I nudge Bee and point at him with my chin, trying not to draw too much attention.

Bee doesn't care that much, I guess, because she grabs a piece of popcorn from the bowl in front of her and throws it at his head.

Startling out of his trance, Gabe scowls around the room at all of the possible culprits before spotting the bowl of popcorn and drawing the correct conclusion.

"What was that for?" he says, his glare radiating heat across the room at Bee.

"You tell us," Bee challenges. "Why do you look so sour?"

Gabe sinks lower in the couch with something between a sigh and a grunt. "It's nothing."

Bee gives him a look that says he's not fooling any of us.

Gabe holds his hands up defensively. "It's nothing. Really. Just family stuff I have to deal with."

"Oh." Bee hesitates. "Which family? I mean . . . I guess it's none of my business anyway, but if it's fae stuff . . . It's not because you helped me, is it?"

He shrugs. "They theoretically knew about me before, and I knew I'd have to deal with them someday. This just . . . moved the timeline up. Really, it's no big deal. I'll figure it out."

I can feel the suspicion and guilt radiating off Bee, so I rub a soothing hand up and down her back.

"You know we're willing to help," I tell Gabe. "However we can, whatever you need. Just say the word, and we'll be right there with you."

I've always wished I were in a position to offer someone help like that. The fact that I can now warms my insides and squeezes my heart into an extra few beats. I used to be barely able to keep my mom and myself afloat, but now I'm part of an unstoppable team. Bee and I together really can do anything.

Gabe breaks my reverie with a snort and a shake of his head.

"I appreciate the offer. I really do, but this is something I have to deal with on my own." He stands abruptly. "Actually, I should probably take off before I bring the rest of the group down."

I suppose it's a good thing that his words deflate my mood a bit, because I don't embarrass myself with an erection when everyone stands to say goodbye to him.

"I mean it, Gabe," I tell him in the doorway. "If you need anything at all, just let us know."

He smiles, a lot more subdued than I'm used to seeing him.

"I'll be fine," he promises me. "I'd just hoped I could get through college and have some life experiences before they caught me, but it doesn't look like that's going to happen now."

I narrow my eyes at him. "When you say *caught* . . . you'd tell us if you were in some sort of danger, wouldn't you?"

Gabe glances behind me at where our friends have already settled back in for an afternoon of video games.

"The only danger I'm in involves getting stuck in a monogamous relationship and having to live with the fae for the rest of my life. It's not like it's life or death."

He pastes a fake smile on his face that does nothing to comfort me. This is, after all, the guy who always rails against relationships and acts like monogamy is worse than death.

I decide to drop it for now. He'll take my help when he's ready. Still, I stay in the doorway to watch him walk away, kind of hoping he'll turn back and admit he does, actually, need our help. Instead, just before he turns the corner, I see someone step out from behind a tree and start walking with him.

They were too far away for me to tell for sure, but the slight build and blond hair makes me think, maybe . . . could it be Ceallach?

I shiver, thinking about dealing with the fae again. I hope, whatever Gabe is trapped in, we'll be able to help him out of it. For now, I go back to the coziness of the couches and my friends and my mate. I pull her onto my lap again and nuzzle behind her ear, one of my favorite places on her body. Bee chuckles at the display of affection. Grey catches us and gives a little eye roll. He's gotten better. Something about tasting his own medicine and being on the receiving end of hearing his roommates' sexcapades on a regular basis has put things into perspective for him. And our visit to the pack, when I was welcomed with surprising enthusiasm, helped too. Whether he likes it or not, Grey and I are family now.

Bee turns around to press a quick kiss on the corner of my mouth and whisper, "I love you," so only I can hear it.

"I love you too, mate," I whisper back, and I love that I know she can feel the words as well as she can hear them.

You can get an extra steamy scene where Bee releases her inner dragon and Taylor gets acquainted with a remote control toy if you sign up for my newsletter at https://kaylabrooksauthor. com/

Keep reading for a preview of Mate Bound, Berring College Book 4!

Mate Bound

I should be happy. Scratch that. I should be elated. Over the moon. Jumping for joy.

My friend Bee is alive. My friend Taylor is with her and can't stop mooning over her and bringing the rest of us down. Every fucking person in my life seems to be coupling off and traipsing into the sunset together.

It's terrible. A fucking plague on all of us happily single folks who just want to enjoy our lives without getting strapped down by someone else.

I swirl the drink in my plastic cup then throw it back like a shot. Drinking it slowly isn't going to help the taste at all, and I'd rather feel the effects fast instead of having to wait.

It's not that I need to be drunk to pick someone up. It's more like, my overly critical eye needs to be a little more hazy than normal tonight. I haven't gotten laid in seventeen days, and I'm starting to get twitchy like an addict who can't get a fix. Every time I've gone out to try and pick someone up for the past two weeks, I can't find anyone that might possibly work to take this edge off.

Hence, throwing back full cups of purple drink in a single

gulp so I stop noticing the flaws with every single possible hookup.

She's too short. He smiles too much. Her tits are too big. Hers are too small. He's wearing a T-shirt for a band I hate. The list keeps going on and on and on with each prospect I catch sight of. I'm not sure what's wrong with me, except that ever since Bee and Taylor got together, I haven't been able to hook up with anyone the way I normally would.

With a frustrated grunt, I refill the cup with more purple drink and gulp it down as quickly as the first.

This ends tonight. This slump, or dry spell, or . . . whatever this is has to end, because I'm going out of my fucking mind.

Filling the cup one more time for the road, I pick a direction at random and start walking.

There. She'll do. I do my best saunter towards the girl leaning against the wall and making come hither eyes at me. She's got dyed black hair and black eyeshadow and a skirt short enough we probably won't have to find a private room to fuck. I'll just take her out to the side of the house and fuck her against the wall and—boom, just like that—dry spell over.

Look, I get that it's not the most romantic thing in the world, but for a half-blood fae like me, romance takes a back seat to more important things. Like survival. Like feeding the part of myself that isn't fueled by human food.

"You look hungry," Short Skirt Girl says when I reach her.

"You have no idea."

I let her preen a bit as I take stock of her from head to toe. She's really not bad. Everything I normally look for on a Saturday night when I need to feed like this. Something feels off, but I shove that thought away and take a gulp of purple drink. Something always feels off, lately. Ever since Bee and Taylor got together. Something feeling off is how I've become the desperate, jittery mess I am right now. I can't let something feeling off keep me from feeding tonight. Not again.

"Would you—" I start to ask at the same time she says, "Want to—"

We both pause then laugh at our awkwardness before she holds a hand up to signal she's going to talk first.

"Look, I've seen you around at a few of these parties, so I know your deal. Not looking for a long term thing or a commitment beyond one night, right? Well, we're on the same page there. I need to get past my horrible ex. I'm not looking to replace him with someone new."

Did I think this girl was barely tolerable? No, she's officially my dream girl now. I resolve to make this as good as I can for her. I mean, part of what I feed on is making sure she has a good time, but I might take my time with her, if that helps with her ex situation.

"So, does that mean we should find someplace a little more private than the common room in the middle of a party?" I ask.

Short Skirt Girl grins. "We should definitely find someplace a little more private, and I know exactly where."

I let her pull me through the party to a patio that's less crowded and well-lit than the rooms inside the house. It's cold enough out here that only the smokers or, well, the desperately horny are out here.

It will work just fine for what I need.

Without conscious thought, I let tendrils of my power float toward her. Once we get started, I can use more, but at the beginning, I've learned a light touch is best. My dad hasn't been around enough to teach me much about using the gifts I inherited from him. It's mostly been a rough combination of instinct and trial and error. This gift in particular encountered an awful lot of errors when I was growing up. I've got it mostly figured out now, thank every god in existence.

She leads me to the darker end of the patio then turns around to give me a coy smile. I let my power brush against her —light as a feather, light as I can make it—and brush my fingertips down her arm at the same time. Her shiver lets me know I'm on the right track, so I step a little closer.

"You're okay out here? Not too cold?"

Her smile widens. "I thought the point was for you to warm me up."

I can't argue with her there. Stepping closer again, I trail my fingers back up her arm and over her shoulder. Her pupils dilate when I brush against her nape. Excellent. It's always best when I can find a sensitive spot early in this sort of game.

She brings her hands up to stroke across my chest then leans back against the brick wall of the house and tugs me toward her.

Perfectly willing, I follow her lead, resting my arm beside her head so I can easily tilt her head up with my other hand.

Slow. Easy. Making sure she can stop me if she wants to.

My power brushes harder against her this time and her breath hitches. I can smell her arousal on the air. My sense of smell is nothing compared to a vampire's or a shifter's, but I can tell when someone gets wet for me.

Instead of kissing her on the mouth, I tilt her head just a little farther so I can reach her neck. She gasps at my first taste of her, which is enough for my power to latch on and begin to feed. I still need to go slow. I haven't worked her up enough to have a lot of pleasure to feed from yet.

My first taste isn't enough to take the edge off my need, so I nibble up and down her neck, drinking in each gasp and moan and shiver she gives me. When she pushes her hips forward to grind against me, I take it as a sign she's ready for something more. With one hand beneath her thigh, I hitch her leg up around my hip so I can grind hard against her pussy. I know from my years of awkward trial and error that I'll be able to feed more the more aroused my partner is, and being fed on seems to bring them its own form of pleasure. As I use my power to connect more deeply from her—to draw more deeply from . . . whatever it is I feed off—she becomes more aroused.

I can feel the heat of her pussy through my jeans, and I'm relieved that my dick is responding appropriately. For the past seventeen days (not that anyone is counting or anything) I haven't been able to get hard enough with someone to finish a feed. But tonight, I'm sure of it now, I'll finally get what I need out of one of these exchanges.

Shifting her so both of her legs are around my waist, I slide her skirt up the last little bit so her pussy is fully exposed to me. There's a scrap of black lace covering her sex and that's it. I'm careful not to tear it as I slide it to the side.

That was one of those lessons I learned the hard way as a fumbling teenager. Girls get mad when you destroy their clothes. I know, shocking. Let's alert the press. I wasn't smart enough at fourteen to figure that out without help.

She gasps as I slide a finger down between us, between the bared lips of her pussy, and rub back and forth against her clit.

A little more of the energy I feed from seeps into me, finally feeling like relief instead of a painful tease. If I can make her come, I'll be able to feed for real. I let her noises and the movements of her hips guide me until I'm sure she's close.

Then the moment shatters with an almost audible crack.

Someone is watching us, I realize. Not some innocent smoker who happened to catch sight of us in the shadows. No. I can feel eyes boring into me from behind.

I set down short skirt girl and whirl around to see who it is.

He's short, and slight, with a mess of blonde curls falling into his eyes, and even if I didn't know him, I would know him as fae the instant I saw him.

"Don't stop on my account," he says, his voice betraying an unusual accent and his eyes unfocused.

"What the fuck are you doing here, Ceallach?" I growl.

He waves a half-empty vodka bottle at us. "I just came out to get some air."

Maybe I'm just being self-centered, but it feels like too much of a coincidence that Bee's cousin would show up at this party and on this patio at the same time as me. I've been wondering when the fae would catch up to me ever since Bee told us about her cousin finding her. I guess that time is now.

"Right." I step forward, away from Short Skirt Girl, and she doesn't waste any time in running back inside the house and away from us. "You just happened to be at this party. You just happened to have a sudden urge to get some air at this party. You just happened to come out here at the exact wrong moment and interrupt me. By, what? Sheer chance? Bad luck on my part?"

The man smirks and sways a little. "I probably found this party the same way you did, by following my senses toward what I needed. I guess it's not entirely honest to claim I came out here just for some air, though. If I'm being entirely honest, I felt what you were doing out here and thought I might be able to join in. It's been a long time since I let an incubus feed on me. But the real reason I'm at a party here, in this world, in this town, is because I've been banished from my home and this is the only place I can go to drown my sorrows."

He waves the bottle at me again for emphasis, then puts it to his lips and takes a long swig straight from the bottle.

Fuck. I thought I was bad with my purple drink.

Ceallach lets his arm drop and I can see he's made a noticeable dent in the level of fluid in it.

He sways in place, but he's not smirking any more. Now he's glaring at me like I'm the root of all his problems. Which is bullshit, because I am—at best—adjacent to his problems, whereas he was the cause of a lot of problems recently. He was the one who introduced Bee to her grandmother. He was the one who told Bee about her fae family without telling her anything at all about the fae themselves. He was the one who couldn't help save Taylor when he was near to dying in Tír na nÓg. From where I'm standing, Ceallach caused all of his own problems.

But at the same time, I'm a little worried about the way he's swaying and how he can't seem to focus his eyes, even as he keeps glaring at me, and I'm a little more worried that he's possibly been the only one to empty that vodka bottle more than half-way.

Shit.

I leap toward him just in time to catch him as he starts to topple over.

"Let go of me. I don't need your help." He tries to push against my chest, but the vodka bottle gets in the way. It's easy enough to pry it out of his fingers and let it thunk to the ground beside us. Good thing it's a plastic bottle, because I don't want to deal with a bunch of broken glass as well as the drunk and argumentative fairy in my arms.

With a grunt, I wrap one arm under his armpits and one arm under his knees and lift him up. With his small amount of leverage gone, he can't do much to stop me as I carry him through the house and out of the party.

He pushes halfheartedly against my chest, mumbling, "I can walk for myself," before deflating against me and passing out in my arms.

Shit. What am I supposed to do with a passed out, drunk fae? I can't take him to a hospital. Doctors aren't supposed to know about fae, much less know how to treat them. I don't think he'll die if I leave him under a discrete tree to sleep it off, but I'm not confident enough to risk it. The guy may have caused my friends and me a lot of trouble, but I don't want his death on my conscience. I briefly consider taking him back to my house near campus, but my roommates will recognize him immediately and . . . I don't know how they would respond, but I'm not willing to find out. Bee's brother is one of my roommates, and me bringing home her fae cousin will go over as well as . . . no, it won't fly at all, I decide.

Out of options, I maneuver Ceallach so he's draped over my shoulder and pull out my phone.

"Hey, Mom," I greet her before she can start talking or asking awkward questions. "I'm fine. You don't have to worry, I swear. It's just . . . well, you know how you're always saying I can call you anytime, with any problem, and you'll help me out?"

There's a beat of silence. "Okay, Gabriel, what do you need?"

To learn more about Gabe and Ceallach, to hear about upcoming releases, or to get an extra steamy scene between Bee and Taylor, sign up for my newsletter at https://kaylabrook sauthor.com/

Thank you so much for coming along on this journey with Bee and Taylor and me!

I knew pretty early when I was writing book 1 that I wanted Bee to have her own story eventually, but I didn't realize until late in book 2 what that story might be. Ah, the joys of figuring it out as I go along. I think the fae ended up slotting in pretty nicely in the end, though I have to admit some surprise at now being an author of fairy smut (even if I still think it's much more on the paranormal romance side than the romantasy side of things). That's nothing against romantasy! I just never imagined myself coming close to writing it. As a kid, I was very much a fantasy reader, but I wanted my romance to be secondary to the plot and *not* the other way around, thank you very much. The genre of fantasy romance, or romantasy, didn't even exist as we know it today.

Fast forward a bit, from the death of James Oliver Rigney Jr. (Robert Jordan) in 2007 to the summer of 2015. So, Robert Jordan's death sent my Wheel of Time loving ass into a multi-year reading slump. Like, I literally don't remember reading anything in those eight years except for a series I no longer engage with because of its hateful creator. But then as I was planning a trip to Italy and trying to decide how to keep myself entertained on a flight over the Atlantic, I stumbled across a $0.99 contemporary romance box set on Amazon. Not only did those books carry me through my trip, but they re-sparked my love of reading and kicked off my romance novel addiction.

About ten years after that, I published my first book, and the rest is history. Now I'm someone who writes steamy novels about fae and vampires and pegging. It's a strange old world, y'all. Please stay safe out there.

Acknowledgments

You can probably imagine, but let me confirm, it isn't possible to make a book happen without a whole helluva lot of help. There might be people who say otherwise. Those people are lying. Here are some of the many people who helped in the creation of this book, along with my apologies for whoever I inevitably forget to add. Please know, it's not an intentional snub. I am forever grateful for all of your help, even if I forget to write about it here. To all of you, thank you than you thank you a million times over. This really wouldn't have been possible without your help.

To Sean, of course, who makes me coffee and dutifully wears headphones on Saturday mornings when I've woken him up with my writing sprints. To my family, who are ever supportive, even when I say things like, "I think I'm going to write a smutty fairy book." I wouldn't be who I am and these stories wouldn't be what they are without all of the wackiness that is us. And, of course, to my friends and confidants who have developed pretty good poker faces when it comes to finding out that, yes, that bear book actually *was* written by me, and who have been very patient when I come to them with my ongoing debate over glossy vs matte covers.

Endless thank you to my sprinting buddies at PI, my NT friends who are wonderful brainstormers, and everyone at IAA who is kind enough to remind me when my blurbs make no feckin' sense. Also, Sandra at One Love Editing, for being an absolute saint in the way she handles my delicate artist's ego.

And, of course, I owe my thanks to you, the reader. What would be the point of doing this if I didn't have you? I mean, seriously, I don't think I could finish writing a book unless I thought there might be someone at the end willing to read it.

Thank you all a million times. I couldn't have finished this book without your help.

About the Author

Kayla channels her natural weirdness into writing steamy romance for weirdos like her. She believes that himbos are the hottest heroes ever, gender is a made up construct, love overcomes all obstacles, and everyone deserves a happily ever after.

She has moved on from waiting for the aliens to take her away in favor of preparing for her long awaited fae prince or princess.

You can find more information about Kayla on her website kaylabrooksauthor.com or under the social media handle @KaylaBrooksAuthor

Also by Kayla Brooks

BERRING COLLEGE

Bound

A Berring College Short Story

Wolf Bound

Berring College 1

Blood Bound

Berring College 2

Fae Bound

Berring College 3

Mate Bound

Berring College 4 (coming late in 2026!)

www.ingramcontent.com/pod-product-compliance
Lightning Source LLC
Chambersburg PA
CBHW032148050726
47591CB00001B/128